PRAISE FOR *PRISM*

"...The (quite literally) colorful landscape—animated by an intriguing cast—is complex but well-explained. Masterfully plotted, Walker builds to not one but several unexpected twists in the novel's final pages.

Readers will no doubt clamor for the next book in this series; a thrilling start from an exciting new talent."

– KIRKUS REVIEWS

PRISM

THE COLOR ALCHEMIST BOOK ONE

NINA WALKER

ADDISON & GRAY PRESS
WWW.NINAWALKERBOOKS.COM

Published by Addison & Gray Press, LLC.

The characters and events portrayed in this book are fictitious. Any similarity to real persons, living or dead, is coincidental and not intended by the author.

ISBN# 978-0-9992876-2-0

For everyone who believed in me.

ONE

JESSA

I didn't collect secrets. I only had one. One little, messy mistake I'd kept buried in the back of my mind for months. Now, I felt the danger of its existence as I stared into the eyes of the person whose job it was to dig up those secrets. She would inch around it, gentle at first, before she'd rip it out by the roots. Then the intruder would take it away, and I would go with it.

"Do you know why we're here?" the royal officer asked. Her glare locked me in. I shook my head, knowing the lie had to be seamless.

The officers had come with their questions on the worst possible morning. Every minute of this day should have been spent preparing for the most anticipated ballet performance of my life. Not this. Anything but this.

I wanted nothing to do with magic.

I glanced at my parents and little sister. The four of us sat side by side on the sleek couch. Our bodies stuck together as the summer heat pressed its way through the family room. Lately, our luxuries, like air conditioning, were faltering. We didn't ask why. We just waited, letting the sweat permeate our lives.

My sister Lacey nervously held our dad's arm with one hand and grasped mine with the other. Aged six, she couldn't know what was at stake, but she could sense the danger all the same.

"Lacey, I have some questions for you," the royal officer in charge said, showing a tight-lipped smile. She was a pale woman, with severe cheekbones and a glossy, tight blond bun.

Her subordinates lined the walls of our living room. They stood at attention, stony expressions etched into their features. They wore white uniforms, the royal family insignia was stitched on the left shoulder of each. I'd never actually seen a royal officer of the court before, and I'd hoped I never would. They were the highest level, the protectors of the monarchs and alchemists. They didn't belong in my living room.

The lead officer reached into her pocket and pulled out a small vial. It was deep crimson, filled to the brim. She held it up between her long fingers, showing us the blood inside. She reached into her other pocket and pulled out a second vial. The lifeless, gray fluid seemed unrelated, but from the way her eyes leered at Lacey, something wasn't right.

"Do you know what this is?"

But Lacey's face only registered the same confusion as before. How was a child supposed to understand what it was, especially when everyone else was clueless? Well, not everyone. Not me.

"What about you, Jessa?" She arched an eyebrow in my direction. "Any ideas?"

"I don't know." The lie burned my throat but came out smooth.

"This is a sample of Lacey's blood."

My father sprang from the couch. He grabbed Lacey. She wrapped her thin arms around him and began to cry. The room grew unimaginably hotter. Gray blood? That had to be linked to alchemy. And anywhere there was alchemy was not a place Lacey should be.

My mother shook her head, apparently refusing to understand. "What's wrong? Is Lacey sick?"

"Lacey is lucky. She'll be fine. Our mission is to find out who did this to your daughter. Of course, it's likely she did it to herself."

Mom's hand flew to her mouth. Dad tightened his grip on Lacey.

I sat still on the couch, lost as to how to fix this. I tried to keep my breathing in check, fighting the suffocation pressing down on my body. How could this be happening? I'd kept Lacey's run in with alchemy hidden for months. Never uttering a word, I protected my family. But despite all that, our life was about to unravel anyway.

"Did you see anything you didn't understand? Did anyone hurt you?"

The woman's voice drew us back to the truth. Something was happening to Lacey and this woman didn't care how that might affect the rest of us.

Everyone quickly settled back into the couch.

"No," Lacey replied. She looked at Dad as her lower lip trembled. He wiped at her tear-stained cheeks. "Am I in trouble?" she asked.

"No, you're not in trouble," the woman continued with fake tenderness in her voice. She wasn't fooling me. "But it's important you tell the truth so that you won't be in trouble later." The threat lingered.

Lacey nodded, her eyes glued to the woman.

It was finally clear that she was speaking of color alchemy. She had to be probing for something, hoping that Lacey would slip up on an important detail. Then they would take her away to some guarded place color alchemists go, to train her as their own. The problem with that? She wouldn't come back.

No matter how much I wanted to stay in denial, I knew it was true. Something *had* happened to Lacey on that cold day six months ago. I wanted to believe it was just a playground accident gone awry. But I'd known. Of course I'd known. It was color alchemy; the strange ability, that mysterious magic that allowed color to be used as a tool. Sure, it was mostly an unknown to a regular girl like me. But what else could it have been? It was the only explanation.

An explanation that I hated accepting.

Color alchemists were sent away from home as soon as they were discovered, no matter their age. And they didn't return. I'd seen it twice myself.

The first time, it happened to the neighbors, three houses down. Their boy seemed normal enough. He was the instigator, the ringleader of the boys our age. On those warm summer nights, I sometimes watched as they ran wild through the quiet streets. Even though I was also seven, they always said girls weren't allowed to play. I didn't mind so much, I wanted to be a ballerina anyway.

And then one day, that boy, his name long forgotten now, was simply gone. When I asked Mom and Dad, they'd briefly explained what a color alchemist was, then asked me to drop the issue. No one talked about it. His parents moved a few months later and that was the end of it. It wasn't until the next spring, when the same thing happened to a girl in the classroom across the hall, that I started to ask more questions.

Between the hushed whispers and rumors, I knew little, but enough. The younger the alchemist was when discovered, the better. They were trained, day in and day out, to harness the magic in color and use it to society's advantage. No one I knew really understood the details about color alchemy and those who wielded its supernatural power. They, and their strange magic, were kept out of the public eye. We did know that it kept our electricity strong, our medical facilities advanced, food on our tables, and most importantly, alchemy kept the rest of the world out of our prosperous kingdom. Our neighboring enemies hadn't maneuvered a successful attack in decades.

We also knew to keep a lookout for anything out of the ordinary, anything unexplainable. The law mandated us to report possible color alchemy immediately.

Again, I wasn't entirely sure what "possible alchemy" was, or how I'd recognize it. I guessed the idea was that I'd be a good citizen, going about my business, and if something magical happened, I'd report it.

Instead, I kept the secret hidden. When Lacey's blood had changed before my very eyes, I didn't report a thing. I couldn't risk the outcome!

One thing everyone knew about color alchemists: they became members of the most elite and secretive branch in the kingdom, the Guardians of Color. "GC" for short.

The Royals assured us that we needed the GC. They said the guardians assisted our society economically. Their magic provided us with extra power, aided industry in advancement, and even sustained crops. Otherwise, there wouldn't be enough food to go around. While most of the world suffered, the people of New Colony, our home, thrived. We had everything we needed in our kingdom. More, actually. And it was all because of alchemy and the royal family's guidance.

But having this mysterious ability ruined people's lives. Freedom wasn't a possibility for alchemists. Not really. Their mission was too important. I was grateful I wasn't one of them. I couldn't imagine having such valuable abilities discovered as a small child, being trained to forget about my family just to learn how to do a job. A job so important that there was absolutely no other choice but to do it, and do it well.

The royal officer droned on but I couldn't quiet my mind about the day that started all of this. The day, six months ago, when Lacey had injured herself on the playground and the unimaginable happened.

My heart ached to think Lacey was an alchemist, but I didn't have any other explanation. After all, it was little children who developed color alchemy. She was six. It made sense.

I wanted to protect her. Whether on the playground or in my own living room, I couldn't.

With the gray vial now gripped in this royal officer's hand, I was sure Lacey had used alchemy on her own blood. What had that done to her? The magic only lasted a moment.

I peered at the royal officer as she ordered her underlings to begin searching our home. They wanted answers. Too bad there was no way I was going to let Lacey slip away. Valuable to society or not, she was my little sister, my only sibling. She wasn't going anywhere.

I peered out the window and wondered if any of our neighbors were aware of what was happening in their seemingly safe neighborhood. Did they have any idea that we were harboring a potential color alchemist?

"Jessa Loxley." The royal officer turned her gaze on me. "We have reason to believe that either you or your sister may have performed unauthorized color alchemy. One of you, or someone you know, tampered with Lacey's blood and failed to report the incident to the proper authorities."

So it *was* true…

Lacey was a color alchemist. Her own blood betrayed her.

Lacey was still confused. I was grateful she didn't remember the accident. She had likely been so traumatized that she'd blocked the whole memory. Lacey needed to stay here, with us. Her family. The truth would only get in the way of that. I had to come up with a plausible story and cover for Lacey, to convince this woman that there wasn't an alchemist here.

"Why is her blood gray?" I prodded. "What does that mean for Lacey?"

"That information is classified."

"Okay," I said. "And who are you again?"

I had to be bold. I had to do something to get the attention away from Lacey.

"As I already told your parents, I'm Royal Officer Faulk, I preside over the Guardians of Color."

Her official-sounding title wouldn't stop me.

Dad reached out, resting his hand on my knee. "Jessa, please behave yourself." His tone didn't scold, but it was stern. Could he know I was lying? And if he did, would he want me to continue?

Mom and Dad were accustomed to me being on my best behavior around "important" people. I was walking a thin line.

"Are you an alchemist, then?" I asked.

"No. Royal officers are never alchemists. I'm here as part of our Illegal Color Alchemy Task Force," Faulk spoke slowly.

"Yes, I get that," I said. "Which is why it makes no sense that you're here."

"Jessa!" My mother's sharp elbow jutted against my arm. I caught her wide eyes, but quickly looked the other way. She might've disliked my attitude now, but she'd thank me later.

"We've been alerted about unusual properties in Lacey's blood work." Faulk narrowed her eyes. "You are aware that she recently underwent a physical examination?"

I stared at her dead on. *Bring it, lady, let's see what you've got.*

Dad was the first to respond. "Lacey had a bad accident about six months ago on the playground. She went to the hospital recently for a follow-up. But what does any of this have to do with Jessa?" His brow furrowed as he exchanged a quick look with Mom.

"You were the only one with Lacey during her accident." Faulk watched me as she spoke. "There were no other reported witnesses, except the person who heard the cry and called the police. After going to the hospital, Lacey was stitched up and sent home. If it hadn't have been for the follow-up, no one would have known that she had a small amount of gray blood flowing through her system. The doctor immediately extracted it. She's lucky there wasn't more of it…very lucky."

"I didn't see anything unusual during her accident," I said pointing to the vial still in Faulk's grip. "How was I supposed to know she had gray blood? Was I supposed to be watching out for something specific? No one told me."

Once again, Faulk ignored my question.

She held my gaze. "As you know, any unauthorized color alchemy is illegal. If you or someone you know has failed to report their abilities, now is your chance to speak up before we start a full-scale investigation. This is a very serious offense that could result in jail time and many citizen privileges revoked."

"Citizen privileges?" my mother asked.

"Surely, Mrs. Loxley, you already know what I am speaking of." Royal Officer Faulk peered closely at my mother.

I frowned. What did they know that I didn't?

The room was silent as I considered my next move. If I lied to cover for her, I risked getting caught. I didn't care about what would happen to me as much as I cared about how it would damage my family. What would this woman do to my parents if she knew I was hiding alchemy? I had heard rumors of people losing their jobs and homes, being forced to relocate to undesirable locations and work long hours in factories or other menial jobs outside the capital city. Was it true?

Surely, the consequences couldn't be that harsh? Surely, it was understandable why a sixteen-year-old girl wouldn't want her little sister to be taken away?

Surely, New Colony didn't care?

I didn't think my parents knew about Lacey, but if they did, what would they do? If I told the truth right now, then Lacey would be taken from our home. There was no way they'd be okay with that.

Her color alchemy had been an accident. No one had meant to break any laws. From the looks on the officials' faces, they wouldn't take pity on us either way. Maybe Faulk could help Lacey, but that was a risk I couldn't take.

And of course, there was ballet to think about. Ballet was my life. My passion. I'd worked so hard to become a dancer with New Colony's Royal Ballet Company. Last season I was signed as a novice, and had attended classes nonstop for months. I had pushed myself through vigorous training and worked through the pain of bruised feet and sore muscles— not to mention the mental and emotional stresses that were normal in the world of competitive dance.

I've worked too hard to let anything get in my way.

Tonight, in fact, was one of the deciding moments of my life. I had landed a solo. And, as small as it was, it was a significant step forward for my professional career. I finally had a chance to dance on the most coveted stage, in front of a truly respectable audience. The royal family, many members of the court, high-ranking citizens, and government officials, were all scheduled to attend. It would be the chance of a lifetime. My problem? The opening performance was tonight. If I told the truth now, I would certainly lose the opportunity. I'd no doubt be sent away for more questioning.

Even if that didn't happen, if word got out about Lacey, the Royal Ballet Company wouldn't want me anymore. They were incredibly cautious about their reputation— any opportunities they afforded us dancers came with the expectation that we were unblemished model citizens. I had no doubt that hiding a color alchemist would make me unsavory. I might never be allowed to put on another pointe shoe.

That thought alone terrified me far beyond Faulk's threats.

"I honestly don't know what you're talking about," I told Faulk. "I've never even seen color alchemy in person. Most people never do. And it's not like I would know what it was if I saw it."

Faulk shook her head. "I've been doing my job a long time, Jessa. I know that the most probable scenario here is that someone in this family or Lacey herself caused the abnormality in her blood. And you all also have the biggest motive to keep any involvement with color alchemy hidden. Illegally, I might add. So if you choose to keep lying to me, where do you think I will go from here?"

This can't be happening. How am I going to fix this? If I don't figure out how to get these people out of here, Faulk will take

Lacey away for sure.

The idea came quickly, like an unexpected gift.

"Didn't they give Lacey a blood transfusion? Have you questioned everyone at the hospital? Maybe there was an accident."

Faulk paused, and from the frustration lining her face, I knew I had backed her into a corner.

She stood up, barking orders at the other royal officers to get ready to head back to headquarters. From the way she took control over everyone, I figured she was a general or something. Didn't matter. A wave of triumph swept through my body. She wouldn't be gone forever, but at least I'd bought us some time.

My parents, each visibly relieved, stood to see the officers out. I smiled slightly, happy that I'd managed to save the day.

When she got to our front door, Faulk turned around and gave her final warning. "Color alchemy is an extremely rare and dangerous talent. There are reasons we've created strict laws policing it. Those who don't know how to use it properly aren't just hurting themselves. They are ticking time bombs waiting to explode."

She slowly looked us each over as she waited for someone to break. When a confession didn't come, she nodded at one of her remaining royal officers. He was the oldest man in the room, and I could tell he didn't buy my story either.

"Let's go, Thomas. I've got a busy day. I don't have time to deal with people who won't talk."

The man began rallying the final few officers out the door. They were eerily quiet for such large creatures.

"You had your chance," Faulk added as she moved out into the morning light. The door shook when she slammed it behind her.

We sat there for a moment, frozen, before Lacey broke the

silence.

"Am I in trouble?" She rubbed her red-rimmed eyes.

"Don't worry, honey," I said, reaching for her hand again. "Everything is going to be okay. Let's just get back to our day and forget about all of this."

"What's going on here, Jessa?" My mother turned to me, her voice shaking. "Did you lie to that royal officer? If something happened with alchemy, you need to tell us right now. We can help but we need to know what we are dealing with here."

Everything in me wanted to tell them the truth. But I just couldn't put them in such a terrible position.

"I told you. I have no idea what that was about. That woman is jumping to conclusions. Lacey is fine. I mean, look at her."

My parents exchanged a guarded glance. Mom held her hand to her hip, head cocked, as she studied me before taking in Lacey. There was no question that she appeared the same as always. After a tense moment, Dad let out a long sigh.

"We'd better get you something to eat," he said as he reached for Lacey.

I immediately went upstairs to my bedroom. Finally alone, I let out a deep breath, willing the stress to fall away. It didn't work. Not with what I now knew. Not with the truth burning its way into my every thought.

Lacey was an alchemist, and I'd just committed a crime.

◼

The accident flashed through my memory.

Babysitting Lacey for a few hours between ballet rehearsal and Mom and Dad getting home from work was part of my daily agenda. On that day, just like most days, I took Lacey to our neighborhood playground. On that brisk January afternoon, the cool air was refreshing on my sore dancer muscles.

Lacey immediately ran to the swings. She jumped in the seat and rocked herself higher and higher with each motion. Giggling as she swung, she leaned forward as if she were about to sprout wings.

"Slow down, Lace!" I yelled, and a twinge of worry cracked my voice.

Beyond her, the bare trees held onto the last fragments of fall.

I sat down on the bench and began running through the highlights from this afternoon's rehearsal. Ballet had been tough lately, but I smiled knowing that I'd done well. Better than yesterday, which was always my goal.

Abruptly, Lacey's hands slipped and her little body catapulted from the seat. For the brief moment, she was in flight.

Stunned, I watched my little sister crash into the waiting earth. Mounds of frozen gravel pummeled her face.

What followed was blood. A lot of blood.

It poured from her knees, her wrists, and her palms. And the worst of it streamed from her mouth.

I sprinted to her in a dizzying frenzy. I held her close, fumbling to assess the damage. The mix of confusion and anguish cut into her features as she let out a sharp cry. There was so much blood. I didn't know how to fix her. I frantically looked around for help. The area was deserted.

I looked back at Lacey, and something strange and peaceful grew inside. An overwhelming feeling of love passed through me. The world stilled as a gentle calm ran through my body. I looked at my beautiful little sister, battered and hurt, and a fierce urgency to help her took over my senses.

"It's okay. I'll take care of you. It will be as if this never even happened. You'll see."

Lacey wailed, oblivious as I tried to soothe her. Tears rolled down her face as she gasped for breath. I needed her to calm down, to hold still so I could help.

"Stop crying."

She immediately relaxed, her cries fading. We sat there, covered in her blood and stared at the stream of life pouring from her. All logical thought disintegrated as I realized what I was seeing.

The deep red of her blood had turned pale pink. And just as strange, it continued to change as it faded to ashy gray. I sat motionless.

Her red blood had actually *changed*, physically altered its color. How was that even possible?

It still poured out of her in waves, but the blood was no longer its normal color.

Even stranger was the air that wrapped around us, a cloud of luminous red energy, seemingly not of this world. I almost didn't notice when Lacey lost consciousness.

It all happened so fast. Too fast.

Later, when she came to, I questioned Lacey. She didn't understand what I was talking about. The whole incident was wiped from her vulnerable mind. How was that possible?

It took the medics a while to arrive at the scene and cart Lacey off to be stitched up. Thankfully, a neighbor had heard the cries and called an ambulance. Maybe Lacey had become so weak that her mind blocked the memory. I could only pray it was all a big mistake.

I still didn't want to admit how one second her blood could be gray, and the next, return to vibrant red. It had to be alchemy.

It all happened so fast. The next thing I knew, the medics were shaking me, calmly asking their standard questions. They took my pulse and gave me some water as they assessed Lacey and the wide pool of red blood around us. The gray was nowhere to be seen. She was small enough that the wounds on her knees, palms, face, and tongue warranted her going to the hospital for stitches and painkillers. She even ended up needing a blood transfusion.

They drove away with Lacey, actually leaving me in that empty playground. I couldn't believe it. At least someone had contacted our parents, who were already on their way to meet the ambulance.

I sat in a daze. The worn black crescent seat of the swing still swayed.

The next six months were spent in anguish over what really happened. I had nightmares about it, tortured by the idea of speaking up. Whatever had happened to us, it seemed no one knew. I doubted Lacey would understand it. When it turned out she didn't remember, I tried to push the memories away, hoping my suspicions were all wrong.

Either way, I was grateful no one else was on the playground that day. And thank goodness that a neighbor had alerted the authorities. That someone was able to find us, and help her.

Because, apparently, I couldn't.

■

I walked to the bedroom window and peered between the curtains. Outside, the flashing lights from the officers' vehicles were gone, but I was sure this wasn't over. It appeared to be a quiet, lazy morning in our typical capital city suburb.

The tall trees in our neighbor's yard cast long shadows in the early sunrise. Something shifted beyond them.

I stopped, not daring to move as I waited to see what, or who, was there. Several minutes passed before a royal officer emerged. He was dressed in the same white uniform. He stood motionless, his eyes scanning our house.

General Faulk might be gone for now, but that didn't mean we were in the clear. She'd left someone to watch us.

Why would she do that?

The answer hit me like an arrow to the heart.

To make sure we don't take Lacey and run.

TWO

LUCAS

"It's time to put that away, son." My father's dark tone failed to match his charming smile. The smile said, *There are people watching us, so you better behave.* A warning more than a piece of advice. I ignored him and continued swiping the glass surface of my state-of-the-art slatebook. It was the only thing that entertained me during these dull evenings. Well, that and the beautiful women.

If my parents were going to insist on my attendance at these ridiculous social events, they ought to be impressed that I was busying myself and not doing anything to embarrass them. Like flirting, or drinking, or flat-out leaving.

It was true that I liked to ruffle their feathers every now and again. But normally, I played along with their games. Yesterday, it was a political dinner; today, it would be the ballet.

Because where else would an eighteen-year-old guy want to spend his Friday nights?

My whole life I'd been told how lucky I was to be the only child of the New Colony royal family. I was the only heir to the throne of the world's leading nation. But the envy bothered me more than I let on. People only saw the façade, the smoke and mirrors of politics.

I knew the truth.

My mother softly touched my arm. Her pleasant smile contradicted the look in her eyes. "Please respect your father's wishes."

I sighed and slipped the thin device into my pocket. I'd give her this small victory. It was hard to see her this way, so meek and agreeable…a wisp of the woman she once was. She'd changed so dramatically over the years. I preferred to remember her as she had been during my childhood.

She never laughed anymore.

Lately, my mother had become "Natasha" to me. My father himself had always preferred being called "Richard" instead of "Dad." But being on a first-name basis with my parents didn't make me feel like an equal—it made me a stranger. At least she had been attending more functions with us in the past few months. I was accustomed to my mother spending most of her time in her darkened bedroom, fighting her chronic headaches. Headaches that even the most gifted color alchemists couldn't seem to cure. Now that she was out again, I was grateful not to be alone with Richard. He was easier to deal with, during the constant barrage of events, when she was there. My mother had a way of getting me to behave.

Tonight would be different.

I relaxed into the red padded theatre chair and stared blankly at the people in the auditorium below. They were always watching us. They wanted nothing more than to impress my father. *Well, good luck.*

On the surface, he was the perfect king. He was handsome, charming, and well-spoken. He was easy to believe in, easy to follow. Everyone trusted him. I, however, knew that he wasn't as he appeared.

But no one ever asked my opinion.

A few of our palace servants were strewn across the balcony with us tonight. Like my mother and our security team, they all carefully watched Richard. He was the sun and we were the planets, moving in sequence around him year after year. But lately, I had started to think of myself as something else: an asteroid. Cutting through the blackness. Making my own path.

My father motioned to Thomas. He was one of our top royal officers, our oldest. He'd known me my whole life.

The ruddy man scurried over, then straightened the white jacket of his uniform. He was a royal officer, not to be confused with a guardian. Alchemists didn't get to come to public venues like the ballet. Ever. And they didn't wear white. They wore black.

"Why is there someone else in a theatre box?" Richard asked, stiff in his over-sized chair.

I knew better than to trust the calmness in his voice.

Across the auditorium, a plump man sat with his two young boys. They were all dressed in matching tuxedos. The children were comically endearing in their formal attire. They bobbed up and down in their seats, obviously excited. I wondered how long they would last before they fell asleep from boredom.

"Sir, I wasn't aware you had a problem with them, but I am sure the family is no threat," Thomas replied.

Thomas had always had a kinder heart than most royal officers. That was probably because he'd been around for so long. He'd been my grandfather's number one advisor before my grandfather passed away. Richard, however, wasn't as impressed with Thomas's soft spot. The two kings, my father and late grandfather, took different approaches to leadership. Still, Thomas stayed on. He was almost part of the family by now. *Almost.*

"No civilians should be sitting up in the balconies," my father slowly responded.

My mother's face paled, before turning away.

"You're our royal officer in charge of security. Do I need to explain our safety procedures to you?"

"I understand, Your Highness. It was an oversight and I take complete responsibility. Where would you like us to relocate the family to?" He'd been with us so long, I was sure groveling was something he'd learned many years ago. I almost felt bad for the guy.

My father waved his hand to point below him. "I'm sorry I was so short with you, Thomas. But you know the rules. Seeing as there are no seats left in the auditorium, what am I supposed to do?"

Actually, there were plenty of open seats. But judging from the swarms of people mingling in the aisles, those seats wouldn't stay empty for long. Did it really matter if someone other than royalty sat up there?

"They will just have to leave," Richard said.

"That's ridiculous!" I jumped up. Maybe Thomas was going to back down, but I wasn't. "Don't do that. They're no threat to us."

My frustration with the man never ceased to amaze me.

"You're the expert on security now?" He raised an eyebrow sarcastically.

I couldn't stand it anymore. Just because Richard was the king, just because he was my father, it didn't mean he had the right to walk all over people.

But as I opened my mouth to reply, I made the mistake of looking to my mother for support. Her teary expression nearly startled me. Her auburn hair fell in waves around her pale face as she rubbed her temples. I realized she was warding off another headache. The last thing she needed was for Richard and me to get into it.

I closed my mouth and sat back down, ending the argument before it could really begin. As I waited for the show to start, I stared at the disappointed looks on those little boys' faces as they were escorted from the theatre. I deserved to see their pain and feel the guilt creep through my body. I had let it happen.

The lights dimmed.

And it's my cue to leave.

I jumped up and muttered something about the bathroom as I hurried out of the back door. Two of our security guards peeled off the wall to follow me. Of course, I was expecting that. But I had years of experience dealing with these guys. All I needed was one moment of distraction and I could slip away.

As soon as I was out in the hallway, I realized my mistake. The whole area was completely empty.

I should have realized this during Richard's outburst. Cursing myself, I had only seconds to try something else or I probably wouldn't get another chance.

I decided to take a different tactic.

"Chill out," I stopped and allowed the guards to catch up.

The men studied me for a minute, then relaxed. I was the prince, and we'd been through this many times before. Just let me use the bathroom in peace!

I walked away, rounding a sharp corner. I passed by the men's bathroom and headed toward an unmarked door. I hoped this was the right one. I quietly slipped inside, locking myself in.

The woman waiting was younger than I expected,

probably nineteen. She was also much prettier than I would have imagined. I guess I'd wrongly assumed spies weren't beautiful.

The black dress she wore hugged her small, curvy body. Her smooth hair was long and blond. Her dark blue eyes sparked impatiently.

Wait, did she just say something? Well, I did always have a thing for blondes. No surprise here.

"Uh, what?" I stammered, bothered that the small janitorial closet was so brightly lit. I was probably blushing. Not a good look on me.

"Shhh! Seriously? Do you have it or not?"

She put her hands on her hips and raised an eyebrow. I noticed the way her red lipstick perfectly stained her full mouth and momentarily felt off balance. Was I too frightened to talk to a beautiful girl? I needed to get a grip.

I gave her my best grin and shrugged. "Maybe I do."

She sighed and moved toward the door. "I don't have time for your games."

"Wait, I'm sorry. I was just kidding—I have it."

She paused when I handed her the slatebook I had tucked in my suit jacket. I studied her carefully. Was she relieved or suspicious?

"You're doing the right thing." She smirked at the screen and swiped it with her index finger, turning it on.

"What do you want with it, anyway?" I asked, though I was pretty sure I could make an educated guess.

"To spy on him." She peered at me like I was dense.

"Okay, yes, I get that. But what are you looking for?"

Her expression grew unreadable. "Why would New Colony's only prince turn on his own father?"

All the times my father had nagged me to be a better prince flashed through my mind. The weeks my mother had locked herself in their dark bedroom with another headache. Or the way he always appeared kind and trustworthy to the public. The way he talked to his advisors about the country, as if the citizens weren't real people with real feelings and real problems—just people to be manipulated and used as he saw fit.

Surprisingly, none of those things would've caused me to turn on him. I wasn't just some child crying for attention, as this girl seemed to be suggesting.

There was something much bigger going on here. And my anger toward my father had gone beyond the merely personal. This wasn't about me.

"I've seen some of the things he's done. I know about the tests he runs." Fleeting images of the shadow lands came to mind, even though I hated to think of it. The way he'd been using alchemy in the rural areas was devastating to the people there. Many were left with nothing, or worse, dead. And it was all kept hidden from the rest of the citizens, brushed under the rug. It'd made me sick when I found out. But honestly, I couldn't say I was surprised. Richard was all about more power, more money, more control. If we were ahead of West America, keeping our borders secure from their democratic influence, then it was worth it.

"I want to change things, and your people can help me."

Her guarded expression relaxed into one of pity.

Great, she's sorry for me. Just what I need.

But I could understand the sympathy. My own father was a corrupt man. I was supposed to follow in his footsteps. It wasn't an ideal situation.

Still, I didn't want her pity.

I looked down at the slatebook in her hands. The device glowed as she maneuvered through the programs. She smiled knowingly. An icon appeared, indicating that a new program was downloading —although I couldn't quite make out what it was. Within seconds, the download was complete and she passed the slatebook back to me.

"All done. Make sure he doesn't figure out it was ever gone. Do you think you can handle that?"

I slipped it into my pocket. "Where's your faith in me?"

"Right. You'd better get to it, then," she said, the slightest crescent of a smile unmistakable as she moved for the door. I wasn't ready to let her leave.

"What's your name?" I slid in front of her and blocked the exit.

The heat between us was sudden and thick.

I expected her to do what other girls did. Right about now she'd either freeze up or lean into me. Instead, she held her ground. It was the kind of unexpected reaction I thoroughly enjoyed.

"How did you *really* get involved in all of this, Lucas?" she asked.

I considered how much to reveal. Ultimately, we were part of the same cause, right? Stopping the corruption that was happening within the Guardians of Color. The corruption of color alchemy that was slowly creeping across our country without the citizens being any the wiser.

"Your people approached me first. Turns out being a prince makes me someone of interest."

I never expected to end up here, but maybe I never had a choice. The memory of my first contact with the Resistance flashed through my mind.

The woman had approached me while I was alone.

I was running along one of the paths, working out. I stopped to catch my breath when a middle-aged lady practically materialized from out of the shrubbery. She was dressed like any other palace gardener. I figured she was just doing her job. But then she walked over and asked if I had done any new traveling lately.

As the only child of two distant parents, I tended to make friends with people around the palace quite often. Our conversation was no different. Every day for some time, she stopped me on my run to talk. I didn't mind it so much. It was always toward the end of the run, anyway. And she seemed kind, curious, essentially harmless.

But after a few weeks, she told me who she was.

She said she had been watching me for a reason. She'd studied my reactions to see where my loyalties lay and whether she could trust me. And after enough time, she felt comfortable asking me to join her cause.

Normally, I would have refused. Who was she kidding? This kind of thing wasn't okay. I would have called for a palace guard under normal circumstances. But there was something different about her. Trustworthy. And I was still livid at the way Richard had destroyed whole communities. On a short trip weeks before, my father had brought me to the shadow lands. It was just a "little experiment."

"You've seen things you wish you could forget, haven't you?" she'd asked. And then she told me what she knew about my father. About what the alchemists were really doing. She knew what I knew.

And she wanted to help me.

I needed more proof than that. Could I really align myself with these people so easily? It wasn't that simple.

The bodies. That's what did it.

She sent me a file of classified information, straight from the email server of Royal Officer Faulk. Faulk was my father's most trusted officer. How these people had an inside line into Faulk's computer, I didn't know. In the file were photos of the dead: adults and children. The color drained right out of many of them. Also attached were memos explaining what happened to these people. Essentially, they were murdered. They were test subjects. Failed experiments. The result of alchemy pushed to its brutal limits. And why? What was so important it mattered more than human lives?

My father, Faulk, they'd both ordered these tests. And then ordered more.

Before that experience, I didn't even know that the Resistance existed, or that anyone cared what the GC did. Sure, my father had enemies—lots of them, in fact. And our country had enemies, too. We'd been on the brink of war with West America for decades. But this was different. This was about magic, about an evil that was consuming the palace from within. Not the other way around.

So when this woman told me that the Resistance was a nonviolent group, I wanted to believe her. If they were violent, wouldn't I have heard of them before? She said they were people committed to making change happen quietly and without bloodshed. They wanted to do this the right way. For everyone involved.

Was that still the case?

Looking at this girl now, I couldn't help but wonder. How had she became a part of all this? Had someone approached her, too? Did she know the woman who'd disguised herself as a gardener?

"But why would they trust you? You're the last person I would trust. No offense."

"I already told you. I know what's going on. I know what my father is doing. It needs to be stopped civilly. I've been promised that assassination isn't something your group supports. That better be the truth, or I'm dead, too."

Yes, I was a traitor. I could admit that now. But it was for the right reasons. I wasn't turning on the people. I was turning on my father. And it wasn't like I wanted Richard dead. But there was murder on his hands. I hated that truth. And knowing that I likely had decades before Richard would step down, allowing me to rule, I needed to find another way to stop him.

The girl stared back at me. "I guess you have more on the line than me, after all."

She ran her hand through her hair and brushed it away from her face. The motion sent a waft of sweet perfume into the air. Was that citrus or vanilla? "Anyway, thank you. You did a good thing today."

"You still haven't told me your name," I reminded her. We were still just inches apart.

She smirked and kissed my cheek. I felt the thick mark of her lipstick stain my skin. One small movement and I could have my mouth on hers.

"Play along, little prince," she whispered. Abruptly, she laughed aloud and pushed past me, opening the door and stumbling out in the hallway. I followed behind, amused but somewhat irked by her "little prince" comment.

What did she mean, "play along?"

"There he is," a voice called from down the corridor. The two security guards appeared, their blue uniforms now uncomfortably rumpled. "Some bathroom break, huh?"

The girl continued to laugh. "Oh, Lucas, you're trouble!"

She grabbed my tie, pulled me in, and kissed me hard on the lips.

Before I could get control of myself and kiss her back, it was over. Not that I exactly minded the surprise. I still didn't know her name.

Giggling, she skirted down the hallway, stumbling as she went. This girl, whoever she was, could seriously put on a show. I'd given her exactly what she wanted. And what did I get in return? Nothing.

The guards seemed embarrassed but not at all suspicious. For all they knew, I had been hooking up with some girl who'd had a little too much to drink. Not really my style. I preferred my women sober. But they didn't have to know that. *Nature calls, right boys?*

I winked at the pair of guards and coolly shrugged before heading back down the hallway to my parents.

■

My father didn't even bother to look in my direction as I sat in the plush seat beside him. I assumed he was angry with me for taking off. What he would do if he knew where I had been?

I was justified in my actions. This was my first assignment, and I'd done it without hesitation. I had to.

You crossed a line, a small voice rang in my head.

No. Richard crossed a line. I can't let myself feel sorry for him.

I peered over at my mother, who had gone from gently massaging her temples when I'd left, to furiously rubbing her forehead. It was always hard to watch her unsuccessfully fight off a headache. She noticed me and shot a glare in my direction. *Ah, finally, some fire out of the woman!*

But I'd done it. I'd actually pulled it off.

Normally Richard banned me from using my slatebook at events. But he failed to notice when I'd so easily made the switch and stolen his own identical device tonight.

I guessed correctly that he wouldn't pay attention to it. Richard always made a point of *not* using his slatebook while he was in the public eye. He wanted everyone to love him, feel that he was one with the masses. To an extent, anyway. It wasn't like having the whole upper level of the auditorium to ourselves could be perceived as normal.

Most people didn't have access to luxuries like our family. Even though this was the wealthiest country on the planet, our people didn't live like royalty. They had slatebooks, sure. But not like the technology we carried.

He doesn't suspect a thing, does he?

When I was sure no one was watching, I discreetly slipped his slatebook back into the pocket of his suit jacket. It was simply lying over the back of his chair, exposed. It was almost too easy and that made me uncomfortable.

I had made a bet. My family would never suspect anything out of the ordinary. Not from their own son. So far, it turned out I was right.

And just like that, the stakes got higher.

■

I spent most of the ballet nodding off. Sure, it was nice, but it was the same orchestral music and sweeping jumps across the stage, times ten, which got boring fast. At the very least, I was grateful for the dark auditorium.

Maybe I could sneak in a nap?

I tried to focus on the ballet, hoping it would get better soon. The dancers were talented. I'm sure they were the best of the best, or something like that. After a long piece involving a lot of identically costumed women running around, the lights dimmed and a girl dressed in violet stepped out onto the empty stage.

As she began to move to the piano's melody, I leaned forward in my seat.

Of course, she was technically trained but she also had something else. Something about her motions couldn't be taught. This girl was born to be a ballerina, even an unappreciative guy like myself could admit that much.

I was momentarily surprised by my reaction. Who knew a dancer could have such a magnetic effect on me?

Just as I was about to come to my senses, the tempo increased and I was pulled back into her dance. I joined the rest of the audience, mesmerized.

She began to twist into a series of spins. Her delight flew off her as if it was contagious. As her moves accelerated, she was transformed into a blur of purple.

And then all at once, the colors changed.

Is that what I think it is?

She just kept going. Apparently oblivious to the swirling cloud of purple that was lifting out of her costume. She continued to dance.

So did the color.

She was free, alive, the hues exploding around her like wildfire.

The audience was stirring now, something pulsed like a collective heartbeat. Fear? Of course I had seen color alchemy countless times, and I certainly knew quite a bit about the magic behind it, but most of the audience didn't.

Color alchemy had taken our country to the top. The wealth, the prosperity, the magnificent advances in technology. I'd spent much of my education studying alchemy. I knew all about its powerful uses. And its negative side effects.

Which is how I knew that the sheer amount of power coming off this girl was staggering. It was bright, moving above and around her, dancing with her. Her costume was completely gray at this point, which meant she had taken it all, removed all the color. In only a few seconds. And from an artificial item no less. Remarkable. I wondered if she knew how to harness that power and actually do something useful with it.

Then something strange began to transpire. The purple colors slowly separated. Shifted. Together, spinning with lavender, were shades of blue...and red. The two colors that combined to make purple had actually separated. And there it was. Red.

How is she doing that?

This girl was about to change *everything*. Her level of talent was absolutely unprecedented. To separate the colors down to the primary sources like that? It was rare enough to find someone who had the ability to harness color at all, but this display of skill was unfathomable.

My father erupted from his seat, shouting instructions to his operatives. The audience snapped out of their trance. Calls of confusion pummeled like a tidal wave. Most people hurried to exit the theatre, practically crawling over each other. Others stayed frozen in their seats. And a reckless few actually pushed their way toward the stage.

The girl finally stopped moving. She stared wide-eyed at the spectrum still whirling around her body. I could see her features better now. She was young despite her height. Wispy, tall, and uncommonly beautiful. Her pale skin contrasted nicely against her dark hair and large eyes.

I studied her expression and looked for any indication that she knew what was happening. Would she take control over her alchemy? But she was utterly stunned. Just as the curtain began to descend, her knees buckled and she dropped to the floor.

THREE

JESSA

I woke lost to the world. Floating in a foggy void.

I was lying on a hard surface in a nearly pitch-black room, my eyes focusing in and out on a sliver of light coming from under a door. Was someone there? I tried not to come undone as the images of my most recent memory flooded me.

Oh yes, I'd been dancing. And I had felt so good. Alive. Free.

And then, in an instant, it had all shattered to pieces.

What have I done?

I tried to sit up, but a ring of pain enveloped my wrists. I was tightly handcuffed to a hard surface. I laid flat again and waited for someone to notice I was awake.

No one came.

I tried not to drift back into sleep, but I didn't know how much longer I could keep my eyes open. If it wasn't for the small red light, I'd question if I was awake at all. Despite the disorientation, I didn't mind the darkness. As uncomfortable as this featureless room was, I was more afraid of what would happen when the lights came on. Then I'd have to face the truth.

As if my very thought triggered the action, the room exploded in a burst of fluorescent light. The walls, the ceiling, the floor, everything was chalky gray. The door opened, and a man in a matching gray lab coat walked in. His face was mostly covered by a doctor's mask. Two pale blue eyes, and that was it.

"Where am I?" I asked, trying to keep my voice calm.

He walked right to me, peering down.

"Relax, this doesn't have to hurt."

Before I had a chance to respond, the needle pierced my arm, and a burning ache shot deep through my bicep. He stepped back.

"What did you…" I blinked, stunned, as the words were lost.

■

The color behind my eyelids was a warm, inky red. I couldn't open them.

I pushed and pushed, willing them to part, but they didn't move. Wasn't I supposed to be somewhere? The heaviness of sleep was too strong for me to finish the thought as I drifted. Just before it overtook me, a man's voice spoke.

"Let me see her."

■

The echo of a door slamming bounced through my memory.

You've been drugged. Wake up!

I'm trying. I don't know if I can.

But no matter how hard I fought, the darkness pulled back

even harder. I was just too tired.

There was a clatter of footsteps.

Again, I tried to open my eyes, but I gave up easily. The voices began to speak near me. It took all my energy to comprehend what they were saying.

"What do you intend to do with her?" The voice of a younger man asked.

"It's none of your concern," the deeper voice responded.

"You wanted me to get more involved. Well, here I am."

There was a pause before a woman's voice jutted into the conversation. Something about the sharp lilt in her words rang familiar to me.

Did I know her?

"Not only has Jessa broken several laws—she lied about her alchemy. I advise you to keep her here. I don't trust this girl."

"That would be a bad move," the young man interjected. "She could be a huge asset to the Guardians of Color. She has abilities we've never seen before. And that's without proper training. Just think about it. What could a few months with the GC do for someone with that kind of aptitude for color alchemy?"

"You don't know anything about her. She is a liability. She's dangerous and too old to start training. It's too late. The best thing would be to keep her under lock and key."

"She's incredibly talented. It's as simple as that. And it's not your decision, anyway."

"Nor is it yours. I will not be lectured by some boy about the intricacies of color alchemy. You don't know what it takes to properly train an effective alchemist. Years of hard work and dedication are required to hone the magic. This girl is already a teenager. She's too volatile. She's had time to come forward with this. Where was she ten years ago?"

"I'm hardly a boy. And I know enough about color alchemy to know that she deserves a chance."

"Enough," scoffed the deeper baritone voice. I tried to recall how I knew him. Was he the one from earlier in the conversation?

"I have final say over what happens to this girl. Not either of you. And my son is right. She accessed red. And that means we need her. *I* need her." Nobody bothered to contradict him.

Everything inside was screaming that this was too important to miss, to hold onto this conversation. Instead, I fell closer to the darkness.

■

I opened my eyes. The room was dark again. Bits and pieces from the earlier events floated into my drug-induced sleep.

I knew something important had happened, but I couldn't remember exactly what. A conversation between three people about color alchemy. About me.

The door swung open and two armed guards, dressed in blue uniforms, entered the room. Dread tumbled down my spine. They turned on the lights and I was reminded that the room had no color. It was a cube of gray. No windows. One door. One light.

They released my handcuffs from the metal bed and roughly pulled me up, barely giving me a chance to catch my balance. Before I could console my aching wrists, I was handcuffed again. They yanked me from the room.

"Where are you taking me?"

They didn't answer. I started to repeat my question, louder this time, but stopped when I got a better look at the men.

They were clearly in control here. But despite their

dominance, there was a bit of stray emotion pulling at their faces. Fear.

What did men like these have to be afraid of?

I caught the shifting eyes of one, and then I knew. *Me*. He was afraid of me. A very large, heavily armed New Colony guard was afraid of me. A ballerina. I would have laughed if I hadn't been so bewildered. I looked around for a way to escape. I needed to get away from them. I just wanted to go home! But it was no use; the men had a firm hold on me.

■

We walked through a maze of gray hallways lined with closed doors. The handcuffs still in place, one of the guards pulled out a thick blindfold and wrapped it around my eyes. They were treating me like a violent criminal!

I'd thought Lacey was the alchemist. But I'd been so wrong. And the fact that I had to find this out about myself in front of hundreds of people? What luck! My eyes returned to the darkness under the blindfold and that's when I understood the reason for the gray room. I didn't realize it before. I hadn't been around color since passing out at the ballet. If I somehow wanted to use alchemy as a weapon, I didn't have any ammunition.

This is not necessary!

I bit my tongue to prevent myself from yelling the string of obscenities that was running through my mind.

If someone would just talk to me, they would know that I was not a threat. What happened was a mistake. I was just a teenager. I wanted nothing to do with color alchemy. All this time, I thought it was Lacey who was the alchemist. No. It was me. *How could I have been so stupid?*

At least Lacey wasn't in my place right now. I would never

want this for her. I hoped she was home safe with Mom and Dad.

It wasn't long until the air around me shifted and I was guided up a staircase and into a cool room. The blindfold stayed snugly in place, keeping me in darkness.

"Where am I?" Again, silence. "Please don't hurt me. It was an accident. I swear. I'll never do it again!"

Still nothing.

"I promise. Just please say something. Anything! What is going on?" We continued to move. The men pulled me by my elbow, much faster now. Still no one uttered a word.

I thrashed out, resisting the rough hands that pulled me forward. I still couldn't see anything, what did they expect?

I tried to move away, but my strength was nothing compared to theirs. The men simply lifted me up and continued forward. Jerks!

"Stop it!" A door slammed and we abruptly stopped.

"Let her go!" Someone boomed from behind.

They dropped me and I slammed to the ground. Pain erupted across my jaw and the taste of metal warmed my mouth. Blood.

Footsteps rushed forward. Someone gently removed my blindfold.

"Idiots," a male voice mumbled.

I took in the boy kneeling before me. Stormy gray eyes stared back, framed by disheveled dark hair.

For a moment, neither of us made a move. No one said a word. I just stared at him, trying to figure out why *this* guy was staring me down like I was a wanted criminal. I knew him.

Prince Lucas.

Is this really happening right now?

He was barely a breath away. His height, lean athletic build, unruly hair, and striking charcoal eyes made him almost too perfect. Painfully gorgeous, actually. All the girls—and women—of New Colony were basically obsessed with him. Did he know that? Yes, of course he did. From the way his mouth turned, he probably knew what I was thinking.

How embarrassing.

He stood up. My hands were still restrained behind me. He carefully helped me stand. His closeness bothered me. I didn't want to think of how disheveled I must look after all that time drugged and confined. Mortified, I looked away, willing him to do the same.

"Take off the handcuffs and don't treat her like that again." I was surprised by his kindness and thick anger toward the guards. Both looked chastened. Ashamed, even. *Good!*

"What were you thinking? You could have set her off. Don't forget, she's deadly."

Well, so much for chivalry!

Once my wrists were free, I gingerly rubbed at the tender bruises. I nearly jumped when Prince Lucas reached toward them. He stopped short, his expression unreadable.

"We'll have someone take care of that," he said, eyes still studying me, drinking me in.

Unsure of what to do or say, I stood motionless. He had just warned armed guards that I was dangerous, but he didn't seem to fear me himself. At the same time, he seemed uncomfortable.

"Why am I here?"

"Excellent question. You and I need to have a discussion." He nodded to the guards and added: "In private."

■

Moments later, he took me to a nearby parlor room and

motioned for me to sit down. From the ornate décor, I immediately knew we were in the palace.

I can't believe this is happening!

Prince Lucas wasn't someone I ever thought I'd set eyes on in the flesh. Certainly not so close. I could touch him if I wanted. Not that I would! But still, I could. Weird.

New Colony's palace was more than just a royal residence. It was a huge set of connected buildings that housed the most exclusive government agencies, including the headquarters of the Guardians of Color.

Even though the elegant room had large oil paintings, plush rugs, and mahogany trimmings, it still managed to exude coziness. A fire crackled in the large fireplace.

Does he want me to remain calm?

Well, I was anything but calm. The hard sheath of material didn't help the matter. I was still wearing the lavender ballet outfit from that night in the theatre. I looked ridiculous wearing a costume in here. At least it was back to its original color.

I frowned down at myself. The spattering of crystals across the bodice had rubbed at the soft insides of my arms. *Did no one care enough to let me change out of this?*

"I know who you are," I said. I attempted to betray no emotion and ignored the nerves that bubbled inside.

He laughed. "And I know who you are, Jessa."

So he knew my name. I could only conclude that Faulk, or one of the other officials, had told him all about me. Had they studied me? Followed me?

"Jessa, are you okay?"

I didn't respond. Instead, I stared at the floor, breaking his eye contact. I didn't know what to think of him. Was he also afraid of me? Did he think I was star-struck to meet him? Impressed because he was the crown prince?

I could feel him give me the classic guy once-over. I was slender, yes. But that shouldn't be mistaken for weakness. I was strong and healthy. My long brown curls had come loose from my ballerina bun, returning it to its natural bird's nest. I doubted that I looked very threatening.

"Jessa, are you hungry? Do you want some water?"

"Why do you care? But since you're asking, yes, I'm hungry. I haven't had much to eat in a while." Placing a small hand across my stomach, I glared at him, as if this was all his doing.

Whoever was assigned to guard me obviously didn't care about my stomach. Anger churned in my belly as I tried to figure out how long it had been since I'd had a meal.

He pulled out a very thin, very expensive slatebook and dialed a number. Within seconds, he ordered someone to bring in food and water. I continued to glare at him. He wasn't going to bribe his way into my good graces.

"Send in a healer while you're at it, please," he added. We both stared uncomfortably at my chafed wrists. Somehow the bruises looked even worse now. "And some women's clothing too, please."

Finally, I can change from this ridiculous costume!

I still didn't trust him. Why should I?

"Listen, we need to talk about a few things. I am not going to hurt you. Actually, I want to help you."

"Am I supposed to thank you?"

"I—I don't need any thanks," he replied, faltering.

"Look, I know you're the prince. What on earth would a prince want with me?"

He didn't respond.

"No one will tell me what's going on!" I jumped out of my seat. "Why are you even talking to me? I thought I was a prisoner. Since when do princes talk to prisoners? I just need someone to tell me the truth. Why am I here?"

He sighed and stood.

"Fine. If you want to do this now, then we can do this now. But you should be thanking me. Stop being so defensive. If it weren't for me, you would still be stuck in that prison cell, probably for the rest of your life. First of all, you broke the law. Second, you put a whole building full of people at risk when you pulled that stunt at the ballet two nights ago. You could have gotten yourself killed."

"It was an accident."

Two nights ago? So I've been drugged for two whole days…

"It doesn't matter. You don't know how to control your abilities, and that's dangerous. I don't care what your reasons are for hiding the truth. You're in a lot of trouble!"

I tried to stay calm but how could I? He didn't get it!

"I didn't know…it was an accident." I tried to steady my voice. I frowned and sat back down. I was about to cry and felt sick at the thought. That was the last thing I needed right now.

Don't cry. Come on, Jessa, get it together.

Lucas sat down next to me, putting his hand on my arm. I stiffened as a wave of heat rolled across my flesh before I pulled away. He was too attractive for his own good. I hated it.

Now is not the time to be acting like such a girl.

"I'm dangerous?" I asked, holding back the tears.

"Yes, but we can change that. That's why I got you out of prison as quickly as I could. I want to help you."

"Why?" I asked.

"I've been studying alchemy my whole life. I know dozens of alchemists and have worked with many on different projects. I've seen remarkable things, but none of their talent has even come close to what I saw the other night.

41

Yes, you're dangerous, but only because you're untrained. With the right direction, you could become a huge asset. You could help a lot of people."

I studied him and waited for a flicker of deception to cross his face. We sat in silence as I considered his words. Why did he care so much? What was in it for him? He was charming but I wasn't sure I could trust him.

Then I asked the question I was pretty sure I already knew the answer to. The one that scared me the most. "Will I have to join the GC?"

The Guardians of Color were the only alchemists legally permitted to use their abilities. Those who didn't qualify for the GC were usually incarcerated, and apparently some were drugged and strapped to tables. I could testify to that.

I didn't know a lot about color alchemy. I did, however, understand that it was a delicate art that could quickly become deadly if it wasn't controlled. Being a member of the GC was an honor. Only the best of the best were able to reach the level of skill necessary to join. And the ones that weren't up to par? I wasn't sure what happened to them.

I was heartbroken to think about my prospects. Guardians were forbidden from having other careers. They didn't live in normal society. They lived apart from their families. Did they even have children? Get married? I had never known an alchemist, so I knew they didn't lead public lives. The GC had always been a foreign group. In my sixteen years, I had yet to meet a guardian. Alchemists were so rare.

"You're not going home," Lucas said. "We need you here."

"And do I have a choice?"

His silence told me all I needed to know.

I didn't know why he was here. Or what it was like to be a guardian. But I knew for sure that nothing would be the same. No more dinners with my family. No more sleeping in my bed or retreating to my room to be alone with my thoughts. I wouldn't get to talk to Mom and Dad about my day or have arguments with them about normal things like homework and curfews.

I would be absent as my little sister grew up. I wouldn't be there for the milestones, broken hearts, fits of laughter, conversations about school and which teachers to avoid. When the moments came that Lacey needed to confide in someone, just needed someone to listen to her fears and secrets, to console her through her first heartbreak, I wouldn't be there.

Long ago, I promised myself I would never give up on my ballet dreams, but now I would never dance on stage again. Why would New Colony care to have a ballerina when they could have an alchemist?

My friends, my family, ballet, *my life*. They would all become memories.

"Just tell me. Do I have to become a guardian? Do I have to live here now?"

"It's not so bad. It's the highest civilian honor."

A pain unlike any I'd felt before dropped into my chest.

How could this be?

My vision blurred.

Oh no, I can't breathe. This can't be happening to me. No!

Lucas was speaking, but I couldn't hear him. I couldn't process anything outside of my body. My fears were taking over, amplified.

Am I having a heart attack?

Did I even care? What would be the point of living now, anyway? Maybe it would be nice to die, to be free from all of this. If there were such a thing as an afterlife, would I get to visit my family? Maybe I would get to watch Lacey grow up, after all. I relaxed into the thought, allowing the darkness to spread through my vision, pulling me under.

Don't give up! This is not the end!

I stood and staggered through the room, desperate to get away. But then I tripped. *I never trip!* And I fell in the worst possible direction. The flames of the fireplace seemed to reach out as I let my palms take the impact.

White heat caught my hands. I screamed and pulled myself away from the crippling pain. In the same moment, a burst of brilliant energy shot from the fireplace. The room was illuminated in a bright yellow glow. The fire exploded with an ear-piercing shriek before becoming nothing but dark billowing waves of smoke. I clutched at my blistered hands. After a moment of intense agony, I realized what had just happened. Lucas reached for me, but I shoved him hard, screaming in agony.

Unbelievable. I used color alchemy. Again.

This time it must have come from the color of the fire. After a second to calm my nerves, I looked around for Lucas, hoping he'd know what to do to take away the pain ripping through my hands. But Lucas Heart, the beloved prince of New Colony, the only heir to the throne, was lying on the floor, limbs awkwardly twisted.

He was completely unconscious.

FOUR

LUCAS

I was only out for a minute. Okay, maybe two.

I opened my eyes to green energy swirling around my vision and weaving through the air. Bright, fluid, and filled with sparkling neon light. It wasn't a typical green. It was vibrant. Alive.

I sat up and rubbed my head. *Well, that was unexpected.*

A calming warmth of the green energy filled my body. It tingled every sense within me and tasted faintly of sugar. A tinkering sound danced inside my head, like far away wind chimes. An overwhelming feeling of peace expanded across my chest.

Everything is going to be okay.

My whole body relaxed as my mind cleared. The green energy that was once so bright, so powerful, so real, was gone. The pain that would have racked my body for days had dissipated, just like the green. Carried away in a moment.

I took quick stock of my surroundings and breathed in deeply.

An older woman knelt in front of me. She had twinkling

brown eyes and long gray hair that was braided down her back. An eclectic collection of long necklaces draped over her loose clothing. I noticed she'd brought one of the potted plants closer. She must have pulled the green from it to use for her alchemy.

I was surprised to find that she was not dressed in the typical guardian attire. They usually wore black from head to toe. Her skin was tanned and wrinkled, like worn leather. Despite her wizened appearance, I liked her. *I knew her.* She turned to Jessa, who was just next to her, also leaning over me.

"You're both okay now," the woman said, laughing at Jessa's expression. "You had a panic attack, dear, plus burned yourself and he passed out. What did he say to you?"

Neither of us responded. She studied the fire, which still crackled as if someone had tossed water over the embers. She could probably guess the answer.

Yes, lady, that's right. I was just knocked out by an untrained color alchemist.

"It's okay," she said to Jessa. "You'll adjust. We all do." Her smile was magnetic. Maybe this woman was the perfect person to get through to Jessa. *Should I keep her around to help me?*

"I'm a color alchemist. Primarily, a healer," the old woman continued. "I used the green color of this plant to heal your wounds, as well as calm your panic attack. Not to mention, wake up Prince Charming here." She laughed at her lame joke. "You'll be fine, but if you need anything else, you're welcome to ask for me. My name is Jasmine." She held out her hand and shook Jessa's.

"Thank you," Jessa replied.

"By the way," I added as I brushed off my suit and stood. "Jessa is not getting into trouble for that, because we aren't

46

going to tell anyone."

I peered at Jessa. "But please, try not to do it again."

"Everything is going to be just fine now," Jasmine said. "Do you need anything else, Prince Lucas?"

"That's all, thank you." I was grateful for her perfect timing, of course, despite the embarrassment. Jasmine curtsied to me before leaving the room. I reminded myself to have a conversation with her later.

As soon as we were alone, Jessa and I were immediately transported back to our earlier tension.

"What just happened?" she asked as I sat next to her. "One moment, I was sure I was having a heart attack. I tripped. I *never* trip. And I burned myself. Then the next moment, you're on the ground knocked out. That lady comes in here and makes it all go away as if it was nothing. Using color. Green color, from a plant right? I didn't even catch the whole thing—I was too shocked."

"That was only a little bit of healing. Jasmine used green color alchemy. It healed you and woke me from whatever you'd done to me with that fire. I have to admit, you're the first alchemist I've met who's actually touched fire like that."

I meant it as a joke, but she wasn't laughing. She sat speechless, staring at her healed wrists and hands. She probably never suspected alchemy existed on this kind of level. Maybe she'd heard of other alchemists, but if she'd seen one before, she certainly didn't look it.

"It's just a glimpse of what's to come, Jessa," I continued. "Before long, you'll be able to do that, too. And more. Welcome to your future."

At that, she was ready to listen. *What can I say? It's a good line.*

I couldn't admit that what had just happened with the fire had bothered me. I'd never seen anyone react the way she

47

had. I certainly hadn't been expecting her to fall into the fire, let alone pull the orange energy out. Again, I was reminded of how lucky we were that Jasmine had already been on her way in. I had called for a healer, and apparently they'd sent only the best. Now...where was that food and clothing?

As I racked my brain, I realized that Jasmine's face was familiar. I was pretty sure she'd been a GC staple at the palace for years. But since I typically avoided their area in the palace and really had no purpose for healers, our paths hadn't crossed much. Was she one of the guardians who regularly attended to my mother? There were well over two hundred guardians by now. I didn't know them all.

Despite Jasmine's rescue, Jessa's emotions were still all over the place. *This is the danger with untrained color alchemists,* I reminded myself. I had to keep her calm while I explained the situation.

I momentarily wondered if I should summon the guards back in. But I decided against it. I needed to gain her trust if this was going to work. Given Jessa's unprecedented power, it was clear that my father wanted to use Jessa for his own ends. I needed to get close enough to her to stop that from happening. I didn't just *need* to gain her trust, I *had* to. She was the tipping point. Perhaps she could even help the Resistance. Maybe together we could save New Colony from my father.

"You're struggling with this because you're a little late to the game," I explained, trying not to get too far ahead of myself. "The fact that your abilities weren't discovered earlier is astonishing."

"It really *was* an accident."

"Was that actually the first time?" I asked, pushing thoughts of her beauty from my mind. I didn't need the distraction.

She hesitated, but I didn't want to irritate her and risk another accidental blast of power. She shook her head. "It was the second."

I paused to consider that. The first time it happened, she should have turned herself in. This must be why General Faulk was so bent on keeping Jessa locked up. We had to make examples out of people like Jessa. But I had no intention of punishing this girl. Luckily, Richard had seen my logic for once. He'd even put me in charge of seeing she got the training she needed. That was normally a royal officer's job, but ever since I turned eighteen, Richard had been bringing me in for more and more work. His orders had enabled me to be in this room, talking to this potentially dangerous girl.

"Color alchemists are born, not created. There are different degrees to their power, and some only have abilities as children before they quickly grow out of it."

"They're lucky."

"Yes and no," I replied. "Yes, because they usually are able to integrate back into their families. We keep tabs on them, but in most cases, they seem completely normal. But many who are discovered with this power become strong enough that they must fight to have control. They join the GC because it means they've trained enough to handle their abilities. It means they know what they're doing can make a difference. Those that can't control it—" I paused to consider how to say this. "Let's just say it's not very appealing."

Her gaze held me, a trace of pain buried beneath her eyes. Was she recalling the brief time spent in the isolated prison, with its dull gray surfaces? The first time I'd seen her up close, she had been drugged and asleep. I felt a twinge of empathy, remembering the way she'd been so helpless.

"To be a Guardian of Color is an honor. Most of the alchemy the GC does is kept secret from the public. People don't usually accept what they can't understand. But I can testify that their magic is remarkable and instrumental to our kingdom."

Her brow furrowed skeptically, but she didn't interrupt.

I took that as a good sign and continued. "You already know that New Colony is the only country that takes care of its people. Many have returned to the Dark Ages. Why do you think that is?"

"Standard answer? Because when natural resources dried up, the rest of the world was holding onto their democracies. But no one agreed on anything. They didn't take care of what they had. They were too busy fighting with each other, which meant no one got anything done. So we broke away. Our monarchy created stabilization. The kingdom was named New Colony, and your family became our royal family decades ago, in our last ever election."

Each word sounded like it had been lifted verbatim from a history book. *Richard would be proud.*

"Yes, initially that's how we survived. But what did alchemy have to do with it?" As I suspected, she didn't have an answer. She wouldn't. Regular citizens knew very little about color alchemy or the guardians. They only knew to report anything suspicious. That was it. My father and grandfathers before me had gone to great lengths to keep our secrets well hidden from our enemies. Our biggest weapon? We knew why alchemy worked—*and* how to harness it.

"Did you know that throughout history, color alchemists have been persecuted?"

"There aren't very many of them. Didn't they hide it?"

"Sometimes they did. And sometimes they were murdered, burned alive with accusations of witchcraft. More civilized societies would just throw them in prison. That's only if they were lucky enough not to accidentally kill someone, which ended in execution."

From the horrified expression on her face, I could tell this was new information.

"There's a lot about the past that New Colony has kept from society."

"To keep us safe?"

Typical obedient civilian answer. "To keep the citizens safe, sure. But it's also been for you, to keep the color alchemists safe from the people. You saw the way those people in that auditorium reacted to you. They were the wealthiest, most educated and elite citizens in our nation, and even they were ready to create a mob. Normal people don't understand you, Jessa. They never will."

She flinched at the word "normal."

"So what makes you royals so different? Why is the GC located here at the palace, of all places?"

"Generations ago, our family created the GC to study color alchemy. We housed it here, right in plain sight. Instead of fearing it, we've used it to our advantage. New Colony has not only survived, but we've thrived. What Jasmine did today was only an ounce of what she's capable of. Before the GC, we had scheduled blackouts, poverty, and a lot of unhappy people. And that's what still happens outside of our borders."

Jessa still looked pained. Was she conflicted? If she believed me, then she understood why her power was so important. We needed her. She could never go back to her old life.

"If I join you, what happens to me? What about my family? What about ballet?"

"I wish I had a better answer for you, but I don't."

"Don't pretend to feel sorry for me," she murmured.

Why did I have to do this to her?

"Please, if you know so much about it, can you help me

51

turn it off? I could have my life back." She held off tears. "Please just let me try."

"There's no turning it off. It's impossible." It took everything in me not to go over to her and hold her. I couldn't risk revealing my unwanted feelings. I was angry with myself for even acknowledging them at all. I needed to stay in control.

Guilt threatened to rise to the surface knowing how I'd lied. She'd asked if she could turn off her powers and I said no. Alchemy wasn't exactly impossible to turn off. It was just *nearly* impossible. Sure, she could try. I know it had happened once before. An alchemist was able to do it. Turn it all off.

But I couldn't tell her that. I'd never tell her that.

I kept my face still. She was too valuable. I suspected the Resistance could use her to stop Richard. She wasn't indoctrinated by the alchemists yet. Clearly, Faulk hated her. Maybe we could gain Jessa's trust and get her on our side.

"You can't make me do it. You can't make me do anything. I don't want to be a Guardian of Color."

"You don't have a choice. Besides, we can't just let you go. You'd hurt someone. Would you rather sit in that cell for the rest of your life?"

She scowled at me. "What does any of it matter to you?"

How was I supposed to get through to this girl? Was she hearing a single thing I was telling her? So stubborn, so frustrating!

And that makes you like her more.

Just then, the heavy oak door opened and a woman dressed head-to-toe in a white uniform walked in the room. The white alone meant she was part of the special forces group that governed the Guardians of Color. I recognized her immediately though: Royal Officer Faulk. She was the head of that department, and she loved every controlling

52

minute.

My body contracted. I still hadn't figured out why Faulk cared so much about what happened to Jessa, besides the obvious "make an example of her to the people" argument. There had to be something more.

Faulk was flanked by several palace guards. They were dressed in the standard blue uniforms. I identified another as a guardian, because he was dressed in the typical sleek black GC getup. He was more relaxed than the others, more sure of himself. He was also the youngest in the group. If I had to guess, I would have pegged him for seventeen, not much younger than me.

His arrogance was irritating. Who was this kid? He was staring at Jessa with an appreciative boyish gaze, unlike the regular palace guards, who were obviously afraid of her. He clearly saw her beauty. Her potential.

"Hello, General Faulk," Jessa said, eyes downcast.

If Faulk was the one who'd questioned the Loxley family just a few short days ago, then Faulk was the one Jessa had lied to. Not the smartest choice.

Faulk didn't return the hello. She gave me a slight glare and a small bow before moving into the room. To her, I was insignificant to the conversation. But we both knew this wasn't true. My father wanted me here. Ever since I'd confronted him about the deaths he had caused with alchemy, he'd wanted me to learn more about this world. To understand his reasoning, I supposed, though I would never agree with his tactics. *Never.* But still, I had authority that even Faulk didn't have.

"I've heard some of your conversation," Faulk said. Jessa frowned, confused, and rightly so.

I caught the proud expression on the young guardian's face. He looked a little too pleased with himself.

I recognized him. He had strong abilities in communication, which meant he could intercept conversations. Certain shades of blue could be used to replicate powerful listening and surveillance devices. Blue was a tough magic and highly useful. I looked at the boy with a newfound respect, despite myself.

Jessa was at a loss for words, and just when I was about to intervene, Faulk moved in closer.

"I would have you locked up for your crimes," she said. "But the king has other plans. So you will do what you are told, or I will make sure your family loses everything."

I wondered just how much of our conversation Faulk had heard because of that annoying kid! But I guessed she didn't know about Jessa's earlier accidental alchemy with the orange color from the fire. Otherwise, it would have been the first thing out of her mouth. She wouldn't be the sort to withstand yet another violation of the law.

"Lay off, Faulk. Jessa knows what has to be done. There's no need to threaten her family. You can leave them out of this."

"They're innocent," Jessa said to Faulk. "I swear they had no idea. It was all me."

"So you admit you lied?" Faulk asked.

"I'll do what you ask. But please, leave them out of it." Going after family was a low blow, which of course was why it worked.

"Your family will be fine," I said, shooting a dangerous glance at Faulk. She needed to ease up on the threats before Jessa had another breakdown. "Jessa, you'll be staying here as my guest," I continued, nodding toward the guards. "I'm sure Miss Loxley is tired. Please show her to her room."

Jessa practically gaped at me. Was that gratitude or suspicion reddening her cheeks? I knew she still had a barrage of questions, but she kept them to herself. Now was not the time. Smart girl.

She stood up and quickly followed the guards out of the room.

Faulk watched the whole exchange silently. She turned on me once Jessa and the guards were gone. "How dare you dismiss that girl when I clearly had unfinished business with her!"

I was unfazed. "Jessa has been through a lot. And quite frankly, you're not going to get anything out of her tonight. Just let her get some rest. We can start her training tomorrow."

"It's not your call."

"Actually, if you'll remember correctly, it *is* my call. Your king, my father, put me in charge of overseeing Jessa's training. Not you," I said.

"That may be true," Faulk responded. "But he wants her in the GC. And as the head of that program, I'll also be making sure that this girl stays in line. If she doesn't get through the basic training, there will be no initiation."

I doubted that. If Richard wanted Jessa in the GC, it would happen.

"And how are you planning to keep her in line?"

The younger guardian stepped forward, smirking. I frowned, having forgotten that he was still in the room.

"I'm Reed. I'll be working with you both from here on out."

"He's my eyes and ears." Faulk said. "Your father already approved it."

Great. Faulk's spy kid was going to be following us around. That was the opposite of what I needed right now. If I was going to get Jessa to help me, Reed needed to be out of the picture. But what choice did I have? As much as it bothered me, I knew this wasn't a battle I could win. At least not right now.

"So, Lucas," Reed continued boldly, "when do we start?"

I studied them both before turning on the kid. "You'd be advised to call me Prince Heart. We'll start first thing in the morning. I'll find you."

I turned and strode away before I lost my temper completely. It was only once I was out of the room that I let myself consider the implications of everything that had just happened in there.

There were a few things I knew for sure.

First of all, Jessa was dangerous and talented. She wasn't afraid to put up a fight. She had a fierce spirit and, despite everything, it still wasn't broken.

Second, I wasn't the only one who wanted something from the girl. Faulk, Reed, and my father all had their hooks in her. She was a valuable resource. She had separated purple into primary colors, which was unheard of. Alchemists could access variations of five of the seven colors: purple, blue, green, yellow, and orange. And all the shades in between. White and red remained a mystery. Black, as well. Jessa had accessed red that night at the ballet. This could change everything.

Moreover, it was possible that separating color wasn't the only remarkable talent hidden inside Jessa.

I admired the fight in her. Her vulnerabilities echoed my own. But she had no idea what she had gotten herself into. The last thing was hard to admit, if only to myself. I wanted to protect Jessa Loxley with my life.

Man, what in the world has gotten into you?

■

I found Jasmine in the now-empty GC dining hall. Realizing

that Jessa must still be starving, I quickly ordered some food to be sent directly her room. Jasmine watched me with curiosity as I stood in the doorway.

I slid the slatebook back into my pocket and walked over to the old woman. She picked at her salad, distracted.

"What do you do for the GC?" I asked, sliding into the chair next to her.

"I teach. And I heal. I used to help out with your skinned knees as a child. Boy, did you get those a lot. I even fixed your broken arm once. Do you remember that?"

I laughed. I'd forgotten all about those experiences. But they came back instantly. "Actually, now that you mention it, I do remember."

Jasmine was so different to me now. Back then, her hair had been brown instead of gray. And she'd dressed in the customary GC black, instead of the casual clothing she now wore. I still wondered how she'd managed the trade.

"But you grew out of your clumsiness. So you stopped needing my help."

That was a point we seemed to differ on.

"Why do you want to know what I do here?" she asked.

"I was really impressed with how you handled Jessa just now."

"Thank you. I was just doing my job."

But it was more than that. She cared. She put Jessa at ease in a way that I just hadn't managed yet.

"You teach? Can you tell me about that?"

"I'm a strong healer, so I focus on working with green. Teaching others to heal is a delight. These young children that come here—they don't know what's going on. They're practically babies. Their minds are so open and vulnerable. I always do my best to teach them the difference between right and wrong, to teach them to use their gifts for good."

She glanced at me quizzically. "That's what the GC is all about, isn't it?"

"Yes," I said, though I knew differently. I knew it was really about the royals being able to control the kingdom. "That's what it was designed to do—help people. And I was wondering if you would help me."

"What do you need?"

"I'm not an alchemist, but I've been tasked with training Jessa. Yes, I have extensive knowledge on the subject, but I can't possibly do it alone."

"And nor should you. The royal officers governing us guardians aren't alchemists, either. That's why they have people like me teaching. *Someone* needs to know what they're doing."

I thought I heard a hint of something troubled in her voice, but I could have imagined it. "Yes, exactly. We have an alchemist named Reed assigned to help us. But I don't trust him. He's working for Faulk, and I certainly don't trust her."

"Trust is a delicate thing."

"So that's why I want you to join us in Jessa's training. She likes you. I could tell immediately that you would be the perfect mentor for her. Will you do it? Will you help us?"

"What's so important about this girl? She is probably too old to be starting this process."

"Yes, she's about ten years late. But she's special. When she was discovered, it was because she'd accidentally stumbled upon purple alchemy. But what was remarkable about it was that she separated the blue and the red."

"Red? But no one has red alchemy."

"Yes, I know," I said. That was a color that seemed to be untouchable. "She didn't actually do anything with the red, but she accessed it. It was there. Right there. I saw it myself."

"I can imagine your father wants to get to that."

I nodded but didn't say more. I needed to tread carefully.

Jasmine looked down at the plate of barely touched salad, a small smile tilting her mouth upward. When she hovered her open palm just above the green leaves of lettuce and spinach, delicate tendrils of emerald magic danced in the air. It was like watching light take on a physical form. It swirled and played beneath her fingers, haunting and mysterious.

"Yes, Lucas. You really do need my help."

We sat in silence for a long minute.

"How's your mother doing? Another headache today?"

How did she know?

She lifted the green even higher into the air before allowing it to fall back into the leaves below, like raindrops.

"Are you the one who helps her heal?"

"I try," she said. "It appears to be a chronic condition, unfortunately. We haven't found a cure, as you know. But I help with the pain."

"You're probably with her often, then?" I asked, trying to push for more information. I should know this, but hated to admit that I avoided my mother. It was just too hard to see what she'd become.

"Too often. She's a good woman. With a kind heart. Don't ever give up on her, okay?"

Before I could comment, Jasmine stood up and nodded.

"We'll be seeing each other soon."

FIVE

JESSA

After Faulk's threat against my family, I decided to keep my mouth shut. Fuming on the inside, I forced myself to stay calm.

Alone, I was now lying on a large bed, trying to process the many thoughts battling inside my head.

After finishing my conversation with Faulk, I'd been led to a guest suite. When the tray of food arrived a few minutes later, I'd devoured every last bite. Then I took a long shower, wrapped myself in a plush bathrobe, and curled up like a kitten under the heavy white duvet.

I wasn't content, but I could breathe steadily again. Did I have Lucas to thank for that? He confused me. He didn't seem to care about what I wanted, and yet he'd ended the conversation with Faulk for me. Also, he had told me he was the one who'd gotten me out of prison. The memory of the short time spent in the dark room wasn't one I wanted to revisit.

I had to admit that this room was much nicer than anything I expected. Faulk would have put me up in a dank closet somewhere if she'd had a say in the matter. Luckily for me, Lucas was the one who gave the orders. Once again, he'd come to my rescue. A part of me questioned his motives, while another part warmed at the thought that Lucas was on my side.

The suite was large, with dark, polished wood floors and trimmings. The walls were a soft white, and a large four-poster bed sat next to a wide floor-to-ceiling window. The drapery and linens, also white, contrasted nicely with the rich wood.

The bathroom itself was larger than my bedroom. The glass shower was sleek and modern, with an expansive set of buttons on the wall. Most exciting was the claw-foot bathtub, cutting an impressive figure in the center of the white marbled floor. The entire place was calm and luxurious.

But I still couldn't decide how I felt about all this. Part of me felt guilty for enjoying it. The gorgeous amenities were unlike anything I'd experienced. Sure, we were well taken care of in New Colony. We had a nice home. Anything we needed, we had. How could I enjoy this suite when all I longed for was my own lived-in bedroom?

The palace was beautiful, yes, but it was not my home.

I didn't know who I was anymore. Nor did I know what I was capable of. Tomorrow I would start my training. Maybe then I would be able to find answers. With no idea of what to expect, I stared blankly out the window. The bright moon floated in the darkness. It was full tonight, and watching it made me feel extra lonely. The tears came back again, pooling on my pillow. It wasn't until the early hours of the morning, when the black night began to turn blue, that I finally fell asleep.

■

"Slow down," *the sweet voice calls behind me as my child-self runs through the grass. My bare feet press into the lawn and leave small tracks as the blades fold in on themselves, a cool imprint of my movements. Instead, I move faster, my little legs rubbing together.*

"To the special place! To the special place," I singsong, calling behind me to the girl following. She catches up quickly and grabs my hand. Instead of stopping me, she runs with me, fueling my excitement. A head taller, her blond hair streams behind her like ribbons of light in the sea of blue sky.

"Okay, Jessa," she says, "let's go to the special place."

She leads me out from the back of the lawn and into a thicket of trees. They stand tall, their trunks papery white with branches that reach out to the sky. The leaves dance together, making a sound like fluttering wind chimes on the afternoon breeze. Once inside the cropping of trees, we are hidden, the shadows our only playmates. But that's okay. These games are played in secret, anyway.

"Show me the magic," I say, whispering.

She always wants me to whisper.

She smiles and picks a dandelion flower peeking through the grass. Its stem separates from the ground with a little pop. Holding it in front of her face, she fixes her shiny blue eyes upon it, concentrating. When she squeezes, the yellow petals stain her fingers.

And then the flower's color begins to fade, as the hues of yellow puff out into a cloud of smoky light. It floats on the air, waiting for her command.

"Can I touch it?" I ask.

She smiles and blows. The color drifts to me as I eagerly reach out to meet it.

■

I floated through that place between sleep and waking. Exhaustion pulled me down. My body was heavy, my mind dense. Somewhere, the world was going on, moving, without me. I wanted to stay here in this garden, in this happy dream of giggling children, but a stark thought jolted me back into consciousness.

Where am I?

I sat up, my eyes adjusting to the strange surroundings. Then the flood of memory filled me, and I fell back into the sea of pillows with a groan. This had been happening too much lately!

Since when did I start remembering my dreams?

Someone lightly knocked on the door. Before I could respond, a girl dressed in a maid's outfit shyly entered the room. She was young, petite, and carrying a tray of breakfast items. The salty smell of bacon wafted through the air. Bacon, like most meat, was a luxury food that my family didn't often eat. My mouth watered as I imagined the taste. Since I was still wearing the bathrobe from the night before, I considered excusing myself to quickly dress, but my stomach growled in protest.

The maid placed the tray on a small table in the corner of the room, peering at my rumpled appearance. "Excuse me, would you like anything else?"

I gaped at the feast of eggs, potatoes, cheese, pastries, fruit juices, and, of course, crispy bacon.

"It's perfect."

Skipping to the closest chair, I reached out a hand and introduced myself to the young maid. "I'm Jessa. What's your name?"

"It's Eliza, miss."

"Well, Eliza, you don't have to call me that. Just call me Jessa."

She smiled, eyeing the plate of food.

"Would you like some?" I asked her.

She blushed and looked down. "I couldn't."

"Yes, you can. Here." I lifted the basket of pastries. "Take one."

She gingerly took a chocolate-filled croissant and nibbled at the edge. I laughed and grabbed some bacon. When she grinned back, I wondered if she'd be bringing me more meals. *Maybe she could be my friend.* My mood got lighter than it had been since this whole nightmare began.

A heavy knock sounded on the door, and it abruptly swung open. A guardian dressed in black marched into the room. I immediately recognized him as the one who'd come in with Faulk. He was young—probably around my age—with sandy blond hair, dark-brown eyes, and, I had to admit, adorable dimples.

"There *is* such a thing as privacy," I said. I was in my bathrobe, after all.

"I knocked."

Actually, he'd knocked once and then walked right in. But I decided not to belabor the point. Given his inviting smile, maybe he wasn't as bad as Royal Officer Faulk. But still, I knew I couldn't trust him. Or anyone else in the palace, Lucas included. When all was said and done, fancy room notwithstanding, they were my captors and I was their prisoner.

"Whatever. Why are you in here?"

"On behalf of Faulk and the Guardians of Color, I'll be overseeing your training." He smiled even more widely. "I'm Reed."

"Already? You don't waste any time."

"Well, you do need to learn how to control color alchemy, and I happen to be a great teacher," he replied, practically laughing. Was there a joke here? Maybe this was Reed's idea of flirting but I wasn't having it.

"I'm not ready," I said. "I just woke up."

"I've been waiting all morning for you to get ready. I guess you're a stereotypical teenage girl. Sleeping all morning long. You'll probably need two hours just to do your hair?"

I stood from behind the table and folded my arms. *Judge much?* But I immediately regretted the gesture when I felt the cool air on my bare legs. Reed drank me in, stepping back. He scanned my under-dressed body.

On my tall frame, the bathrobe I'd slept in was entirely too short. As a dancer, I was used to people looking at my body. But the way Reed was staring at me with his flustered boyish expression was different. Embarrassing.

"Can I help you?"

"It depends on what you're offering."

Eliza stood off to the side during this whole exchange. She coughed on her croissant and scurried out of the room without a goodbye or an apology.

I eyed Reed, annoyed again at the interruption. I was making a new friend in Eliza until he had shown up and ruined it.

"I'm not offering anything. I was forced to be here. Or did you forget about your little eavesdropping stunt already?"

I hadn't forgotten that he was the guardian with Faulk last night. They had listened in on my conversation with Lucas. I was still not sure how he was able to do it, given the seemingly impervious walls and the fact that I hadn't seen any visible devices that would've clued me into the possibility of spies. As much as I didn't want to care, I was curious.

"Impressed?" He plopped down into the chair across from me. He tried to reach for the last piece of bacon, but I slapped his hand away.

"Hey! Where are your manners?"

"I'm a growing boy. I need my second breakfast."

He grinned, snatching it up, then split the bacon in half and handed me a piece. Somehow, I found myself laughing.

■

I let him eat with me while I questioned him. He was seventeen. He'd lived primarily at the palace for eleven years now, training in color alchemy. Soon he would be sent out on long-term assignments. When I asked him what that meant, he clammed up and changed the subject.

Just as we were finishing up, there was yet another knock. Prince Lucas stepped inside. He was dressed casually in dark jeans and a black t-shirt. The shirt was cotton, and on a body like his, it created the perfect male contrast of soft and hard. As much as I hated to admit it, he looked incredible. The royals always did look great though. Most often they weren't dressed so casually. In newspapers and on the news feeds I'd always seen him in his royal uniform.

"Are you ready?" Lucas asked.

I couldn't read his blank expression. "Wait, are you training me, too?" I looked from Lucas to Reed.

"I'm overseeing your progress," Lucas said. "I've assigned one of our healers, Jasmine, to train you. Reed here will also help."

He spoke of Jasmine as if I hadn't already met her. I guess because of the fact that I'd knocked Lucas out, which was still a secret. Was that even possible with someone like Reed following me around?

I got up and started to stack the plates before realizing I probably didn't have to clean up after myself. I noticed the two boys staring at my bare legs.

Seriously, are there no girls in this palace?

Reed grinned with enjoyment, but Lucas looked bothered.

"What is your problem?" I said. "It's not like I was going to sleep in that costume again."

Lucas shook his head. "You have a closet completely stocked with clothing."

He walked over to the dark-wood wall and pulled on a handle I hadn't noticed before. It slid open to reveal about six feet of wardrobe space. Each hanger had an item. Most of the clothing was black. Was all that for me?

Well, okay then.

Reed doubled over in laughter. "The look on your face right now is priceless."

I glared at him and tilted my head toward Lucas. "And how was I supposed to know that? I heard you called for clothing last night, but it never came. I figured someone forgot."

"Well, you're obviously not ready for training," he said.

"Thank you for pointing out the obvious."

He glanced down at my appearance again, and I pulled the robe, attempting to cover up as much as possible.

"Guardian." Lucas stopped Reed's laughter short. "Please allow Jessa some time alone to prepare herself. We'll meet in an hour to begin our training. It's a nice day, isn't it? Let's spend it out in the royal gardens."

"Your Majesty, we should begin her training somewhere more appropriate. Those gardens are hardly guardian headquarters. If it's greenery you're looking for, we've got plenty in the GC area."

"The royal gardens are exclusively used by the royal family and our guests. I'm sure Jessa would like to get a breath of fresh air. It will be just the three of us and Jasmine. No one else."

I breathed a sigh of relief and nodded.

I loved the outdoors. And something about the idea of being amid the lush gardens and their beautiful flowers reminded me of my childhood.

Didn't I have a dream about a flower?

"Too macho to hang out in the gardens?" I asked Reed.

I bit my tongue before I could say anything more. I didn't want Lucas to think I was flirting with Reed.

Both of these boys were attractive, but I wanted no part in that game.

Instead, I tried to focus on the matter at hand. Namely, how was I going to get myself out of this palace? As exciting as all this was, alchemy wasn't my plan. It wasn't dancing, and it took me away from my family. I had no clue how any of this could work in my favor, but I had to try, at least.

I'd been so lost in my thoughts I hadn't noticed Reed and Lucas were still here. *Hello? What are they waiting for?*

"Hey guys, you can go now."

They mumbled a string of awkward goodbyes and left the room. I wanted to go back to bed but knew it was time to get ready for the day. Hopefully I wouldn't embarrass myself.

◼

Reed was waiting for me when I left my room an hour later. We engaged in trivial conversation as we walked down to the gardens together. When we came out onto the palace steps, I stopped short.

I don't know what I was expecting, but this wasn't it.

It wasn't just a garden. It was beautiful greenery that stretched for what looked like half a mile, and beyond that was a towering stone wall. Picturesque rose bushes, symmetrical flowerbeds, perfectly trimmed hedges, marble statues, beautiful fountains, stone paths, and vast lawns sprawled out around me.

We approached a bench where Prince Lucas sat waiting. He gave me a polite smile but didn't bother to acknowledge Reed's small bow. I got the feeling that Reed was only doing it out of obligation and nothing else. I wondered if I was supposed to curtsy, but before I got the chance, Lucas stood and waved at someone behind us.

"Jasmine. I'm glad you could make it."

Again, the older woman wasn't dressed in the black uniform that Reed wore, even though she was GC. Did the Guardians of Color have a little more freedom than I'd originally thought? Or was it just her?

"It's my pleasure," she said.

"I didn't know you were helping out today." Reed frowned.

"I'll be helping every day."

Lucas stood and led our group down one of the paths, a few of his guards following at a distance. Lucas must have been listening, but he didn't join in on the conversation. I could tell the two guys disliked each other. And yet they seemed so alike to me. They could probably be friends if the egos involved weren't so big.

After several minutes of navigating the garden, Lucas stopped at a charming pavilion and sat down at a small table. We were secluded, surrounded by the tall trees. Spindly green vines covered the delicate white structure. The spring air was breezy, and the pleasant scent of freshly cut grass wafted through the area.

"Before we start testing your abilities, it's important that you're educated on the intricacies of alchemy," Lucas said.

He motioned for us to join him at the table. Reed and Jasmine sat across from Lucas, leaving me no other place than right next to him. Strangely, I felt vulnerable there. I still couldn't believe the wild situation I'd found myself in.

"What better way to learn than by practicing?" Reed asked Lucas. "If you're not too afraid."

I wasn't sure if the comment was directed at me or at Lucas. Either way, I was definitely not ready to take another crack at color alchemy.

"Jessa is different," Lucas said to Reed. "She's older, so her magic is strong, but she's also very new to this. She's better off understanding what she's doing before she tries again."

Lucas was right. I was not ready to do any alchemy. The three times I'd done it, I'd had no control. The experiences with Lacey's blood, the ballet, and the fire last night had been terrifying.

I'd rather just talk, even if it meant listening to Lucas and Reed bicker. Sacrifices, right?

"Okay, I like your plan, Lucas. And I do have a lot of questions."

"I'm sure you do, but let's start by explaining the basics. After we're finished, we'll try to answer some of your questions."

I nodded as he pulled out his slatebook, the same high-tech device he'd used the night before. He typed in a quick password, and the screen pulled up a search engine.

"There is a lot of information out there about color alchemy, but most of it is only speculation. You probably believe all sorts of false rumors. We don't like to correct the public, because the less they know, the better for us. New Colony is the only country we know of that uses alchemists as assets. We don't accuse you of witchcraft, and we don't publicly execute you."

Wow, how nice of you.

I didn't like to think about it, but it made sense. After a number of crippling wars and most of the planet's natural resources in scarce supply, the world wasn't thriving anymore. People resorted to desperate measures as they were struggling to survive. Having a scapegoat gave people an outlet for all their rage. Was it misdirected? Yes. But it happened. New Colony wasn't at war anymore, but we knew our government used alchemy to take care of us. I'd heard other countries wanted the information. Why wouldn't they? West America probably wouldn't be able to agree on what to do with alchemy anyway. Still, with such powerful magic at our disposal, I was certain we had ways to keep our secrets.

Lucas typed something into his slatebook. "That's why most of the real information about alchemists and guardians is banned from public access. We don't want our foreign enemies learning our secrets."

Besides West America, who exactly are our foreign enemies?

"But couldn't it help? If people are struggling, wouldn't this be valuable information for them? Maybe they could train their alchemists and live the way we do here."

"And then we'd be back to more world wars," Reed argued. "There are still plenty of people out there who want us to return to the old ways of democracy. What makes you think they wouldn't use alchemy against us?"

Democracy? I didn't know much about it except what I was told. In the old country, called America, people voted for their leaders. But that only led to more disagreement, hatred, and division. We split off, becoming New Colony. Things were better now.

Lucas placed the screen face-up on the table. "That's a discussion for another day. But if I were you, I wouldn't repeat your sentiments to anyone."

He winked, and I realized my mistake. Had I sounded treasonous?

"Anyway, if you have a very high level of security clearance, like I do, then you can access this." He pointed to the screen.

It was an image of a colorful drawing. A man was sitting, his legs crossed, with his palms open on his knees. From the crown of his head to the base of his spine were circles of color. Together they made a rainbow, moving from white at the top to red at the bottom. Although the image was on a modern screen, it still had an ancient quality. Unlike anything I knew.

Reed's eyes glittered. "Whoa! I know what this is, but even I've never seen it before."

"This is a very old document. It comes from a time even before America was established. Possibly from before there were people on this continent. Its teachings are ancient."

I tried to imagine this, but I didn't know what he meant. The history classes I'd taken never went back that far.

"This document gave my family huge clues on how to control color. We've succeeded, while so many others have failed. What we're looking at has many names. Some texts refer to this concept as chakras, others as the wheels of light. We refer to each sphere as an energy center." He nodded at Jasmine to explain.

She put a hand to her head. "White." Then she placed it on her forehead. "Purple." She moved her hand to her throat. "Blue." Her heart. "Green and pink as well." Her upper torso was yellow, her stomach orange.

Jasmine motioned to her pelvis. "Red."

I peered at the drawing. "I don't understand."

"Energy exists in some way or another in all things. Humans have seven main energy centers. You wouldn't know that because you can't see them, but I promise you, they are there."

"We're not sure why, but some humans are born with the

ability to tap into their own energy centers and connect them with other energies. That's where color alchemy first begins."

Lucas peered at me. "When you were dancing, what were you feeling?"

It hurt to remember. I'd been full of joy, and that was all gone now. But I needed to understand, so I decided to push my feelings aside and talk about that night. "I felt like I was exactly where I was supposed to be. I felt sure of myself. I was free. I knew what I was doing. I've practiced that a million times, so I just let all my thoughts go, and I danced. It was like breathing."

I held back my tears. I'd allowed myself to cry last night. I couldn't do that anymore if I hoped to gain any respect.

"And that's why you were able to use alchemy so strongly." Reed grinned.

"In that moment, you were most connected to your violet or purple energy, the ball of light here," Jasmine said, pointing to the man's forehead. "This has been historically called the third eye. That's because the brow is associated with self-knowledge, intuition, spirituality, and self-reflection. I suspect you were also connected to other energy centers in your body, but I can't know for sure."

Reed stood excitedly. "This is where it started. Do you understand?"

No, I couldn't say that I did.

This was confusing. They may as well have been speaking a different language. What I didn't get was how this so-called energy center in my head caused the show of color alchemy. My dress had become gray, while the air around me sparkled in an electric cloud of purple. Almost like physical light.

"What color was your costume?" Reed asked.

"It was dark purple and lavender. Yes, it was similar to

that." I pointed to the sphere of purple around the man's head.

"Exactly," Lucas said. "In that moment you let go, that perfect moment when you were dancing, something happened. One of your energy centers, the one in your forehead, was activated. The energy was so strong that it needed a way to escape. So what did it do? It connected with the object that corresponded to its color. One you just happened to be physically touching. Purple."

"My dress."

"Yes! The energy connected with your dress, and the color released. Do you remember the dress briefly turned gray? That's exactly why. What's even more extraordinary is that your dress isn't exactly a living organism. It's made of manufactured fabrics. Most alchemists can only connect with organic things, like plants. Our strongest are able to connect with nonliving things, but that takes years of training. You went beyond that without even meaning to!"

So physically touching the color was part of the process. I remembered Lacey's blood and how, when I touched it, the red had seeped away from the liquid, turning it gray. According to them, my power had been responsible for the brilliant display of color alchemy that had followed. I shook my head in disbelief.

"So what happened to the color after my dance? I passed out, remember? When I woke up the next day, my costume was normal again."

"Even for a natural like you, it's not easy." Reed smirked. "You have to know what to do with it once it's out. Or else it goes back to where it came from."

"Yes," Lucas said, "but that's complicated. Best to see it for yourself. Since we're not ready for that yet, I think it's best we stop here for today."

I didn't want to stop the conversation. I needed to know more. What did the other colors mean? How were they contained? What did the New Colony want with them? Why did they need me? And was Lacey really okay after what I'd done to her? After all, the blood I'd changed had remained gray, as Faulk had shown us. What had happened to the red? Where did it go? Had we used it somehow? The questions were endless.

"Why don't I get you a copy of this?" Lucas pointed to the screen. "You can study it today and come back with questions tomorrow."

"Can I get a copy, too?" Reed asked.

Lucas paused. Just when I was sure he was going to deny Reed his request, he sighed. "I can grant access for all of you with a temporary copy only. So I suggest you study it well. I'm going out on a limb for you, so please don't break my trust. Do not share this with anyone. And printing it is illegal, so don't even think about it."

We nodded.

"Jessa," he added, "I'll make sure you receive a slatebook today. You'll need it." He powered off his own and stood to lead us from the garden.

At his words, a heavy load of weariness slowly lifted from my chest. Of course our family had a slatebook at home, everyone did. Sure it wasn't nearly as high-tech as the ones here at the palace. So what? It still worked! I knew immediately what my first order of business was. As soon as I got my slatebook, before I studied the energy centers, before I did anything else, I was going to call home. I was going to talk to my parents. They would know what to do.

SIX

LUCAS

Reed immediately wanted his copy of the old chakra drawing, and without a good excuse to keep it from him, I emailed it to his device. It wasn't ten minutes later that Officer Faulk found me in my study. Coincidence? Doubtful. Not bothering with a polite "Your Highness," she stormed in unannounced. "How dare you undermine me!"

I turned from my bookshelf, already wishing she would leave. "I assume this is about Jessa?"

She really had it in for the girl, and something about that made me want to defend her even more. So what if Jessa had lied? It wasn't the first time someone had tried to hide alchemy, and it certainly wouldn't be the last. How was this girl any different from so many others? She deserved a break.

"Giving her a slatebook with outside call access? You may as well just give her complete freedom. And apparently the two guards posted at her door have been ordered to let her come and go from her room as she pleases. Have you lost your mind? She is a prisoner and a criminal! She is not a guest."

I could only guess that Reed must have gone running to tell Faulk about the slatebook and Jessa's housing situation. He'd put up a front of wanting to be Jessa's friend. She probably thought he cared for her. I was stupid to believe he would be anything other than another one of Faulk's golden boys.

"As much as you don't approve of my approach, I'm in charge. If you have a problem, then you can take it up with my father."

We both knew she hated that I had the reins. She was ordered to assist me with what I needed, but to essentially stay out of my way. I also suspected she had been tasked to report the efficacy of my methods to Richard.

"Don't think I won't be telling your father all about this. He knows as well as I do that the Loxley family is trouble."

"What do you mean, her family?" I asked, my heart jumping to my throat. There was something going on that Faulk wasn't telling me about. Was there more to why she was so strict with Jessa?

But she only stared at me for a minute before briskly turning on her heel and leaving my study. With the slam of the door, my suspicions were confirmed. She was hiding something. And it was highly likely she'd be following my every move, reporting it all back to my father.

I walked over to the door and made sure it was locked this time.

Going back to the bookshelf, I found what I was looking for. Pulling out the non-descript title, I opened the large leather-bound book. The one with the hidden compartment. I'd altered the book years ago, looking for a place to hide the access to my unauthorized research.

This is where I'd hidden my undocumented flash drive. The slatebook attachment held electronic information that couldn't be found on any computer or information cloud.

Information I was sure no one expected me to have. I was only eighteen, but I'd been collecting it for years.

Granted, alchemy was a very important part of New Colony's success. My great-grandfather was the one who had created the GC. But over the last few decades, Richard had built an empire based on the extraordinary uses of color alchemy. He'd dived into the project as no one else before him, looking for the most talented alchemists and taking their skills to the limit. I'd seen myself how they'd depleted some of our rural areas of color. What was left could only be described as utter devastation. To keep everything quiet he'd enlisted only the brightest minds to become royal officers... like Faulk. Their job was to make sure things ran smoothly and that no alchemist stepped out of line.

Even if he would never admit it, I suspected my father would have done anything to be an alchemist. Since he wasn't, the next best thing was to control those who were. And just to make sure no one became more powerful than the royals, he'd created strict laws governing the guardians. Appointing non-alchemists to police their activities and oversee training was just one more way to stay on top. People like Faulk only had power because he said they did.

I think it helped that guardians were first brought to the palace at such a young age. Color alchemy was something that developed quickly. Not in infants or toddlers, but in young children. Most of the GC didn't have many memories of their families. The palace was their only home.

But things couldn't be all bad or else guardians would rebel, wouldn't they? So in return for their obedience, they were provided with lavish lifestyles, not too unlike us royals. They mostly resided in the palace, in their own immaculate areas. GC headquarters were off limits. I, of course, could go there. A prince could pretty much go anywhere. Despite that, I had intentionally avoided anything GC outside of special assignments from my father.

I was in a delicate position. I had too much knowledge of deadly repercussions of alchemy, but not enough power to actually change anything.

After a few more minutes browsing through my research, I found what I was looking for. On the sleek screen was the list of names I'd slowly compiled of those alchemists who had been incarcerated. Most of them had been locked up because they weren't able to control their dangerous talents, but some were on this list because they had refused to join the GC. These were the ones who had rebelled. And if there was one thing I knew about my father, rebellion was squashed immediately.

Next to each name, I'd noted what information I'd uncovered, if any. I began searching for something to indicate why Faulk had said the Loxley family was trouble.

Marissa Levi: Lost control of her mind, became increasingly violent with each attempt. Entered training at age 5, was placed in custody at age 11.

I knew that "custody" was the polite way of saying that this Marissa girl was sent to a mental institution. Had she really lost her mind?

Jackson Spears: Repeated refusal to use his abilities. After three attempted suicides, he was placed in isolation, deemed a danger to himself and others. Started his training at age 8, joined the guard at age 15, incarcerated at age 16.

I remembered him. Jackson had been a natural talent,

but he'd hated to use his powers and he couldn't control his mind. He had turned out to be deadly. In fact, he'd almost killed another alchemist in the final suicide attempt that had landed him in solitary confinement. I often wondered if coming here at eight years old had been too late for Jackson. If they'd gotten to him sooner, would he have been happier?

The list continued, reaching back through the last fifty years since the formation of the Guardians of Color. I'd added anything I could find about people not being able to control it and what happened to them.

I was looking for something—anything—that would lead back to Jessa.

The public believed that color alchemists popped up at random. That was true sometimes. But most often, color alchemy could be tracked through DNA. The problem was that many people were born with the trait and never developed any powers. But they were marked at birth and then watched closely. All citizens were now required to submit to genetic testing as infants. That was probably my father's idea. I wondered how Jessa had kept herself hidden for so long. Maybe she was telling the truth.

About 30 percent of the population had the genetic trait, but less than 0.1 percent ever needed to be taken into custody by the GC. The trait usually stayed dormant. Like it had with our family. We actually were part of the 30 percent, but not the 0.1 percent. I suspected my father had tried to find a way to somehow activate alchemy in himself, but with no success.

I continued to comb through my research.

Since it ran in families, it was very likely that somewhere along the line, Jessa had a family member who was an alchemist. All I could hope was that we'd known about them. It would provide tremendous insight into her training. Just as regular talents were passed down through families, so were specific color-alchemy abilities. Maybe she had a family member out there who knew more about her alchemy than she did.

Someone who could help us understand how she'd separated the purple into red and blue. As it stood, none of our trainers could do that.

My records included information about people who were trained but never actually initiated as members of the GC. While this information was technically off limits, I'd found ways around that problem. Sure, it took time, but I'd been at this for years.

I continued to scan my notes until I found it.

Francesca Loxley: Training began at age 5, initiation into the GC at age 6, and went missing from guardian custody at age 9. Whereabouts unknown.

Whereabouts unknown?

Whoever this girl was, she was young while she was at the palace. That was not unusual. She would have been trained by the GC, as everyone was given a shot. I wondered why they had initiated her so quickly. Six-year-olds were not ready to be full-blown guardians, at least not that I was aware of.

Unfortunately, I had nothing else on file for Francesca except a few dates. But dates were valuable.

Francesca went missing eleven years ago. If she was still alive, then she would be nineteen. Jessa would have only been three years old when Francesca was taken. Even if they were related, Jessa probably wouldn't remember her—assuming her parents had kept the whole thing a secret, which was possible. I knew there had to be more to the story than Faulk and Richard were telling me.

Could I question Jessa's parents? Find out if they knew Francesca? The easier solution would be to sneak into the royal officer's computers and find the information myself. I'd done it a few times over the years. But with Faulk watching my every move, I wasn't so sure of myself.

Francesca was my clue as to why Faulk was so distrusting of Jessa and her family. I couldn't be sure yet, but I suspected that Francesca was Jessa's older sister. A sister who was also an alchemist.

That begged the question: Where was Francesca now?

Either Jessa was as clueless as she acted or she was hiding something even bigger than I could have imagined.

A long-lost sister.

■

I needed someone in the GC on my side. I'd worked with different guardians on random assignments, but never one-on-one like this. Not how I would be working with Jessa. She would be taught by other guardians, of course, but those guardians weren't allowed to actually oversee the whole process. My father had always put his best non-alchemist royal officers—a mixture of scientists, soldiers, and the government's various "secret weapons"—in charge of those matters. But I still didn't understand why Richard had given me the assignment of working with Jessa. Why not Faulk or someone else with more experience? I had resolved that keeping Jasmine around would be best for me, and I wanted to make sure Richard would stay on board with that.

I found him alone in his large office. This surprised me, as my father typically spent his time in other, less private, areas of the palace. He was leaning over a map on the desk, concentration etched into his brow.

"What do you need, son?" My father motioned me into the room.

I took a seat in one of the large chairs and glanced at the map. There were red pins stuck in clusters around the edges of the country. I recognized the areas to be shadow lands. Places where our overuse of alchemy had destroyed everything. Crops, animals, even people, all gone.

"What are you going to do about that," I said, pointing to the map.

Richard didn't bother to look up at me. We'd already had this argument. He wasn't going to change his mind. He didn't care what sacrifices were made for power. He thought I would see his side soon enough.

"It's nothing we need to talk about right now, Lucas. What do you need?"

I sighed, pushing down my anger, knowing I was doing something.

"I want to know why you assigned me to Jessa Loxley," I said, changing the topic.

He looked up from the map and leaned back in his chair. "You don't want the assignment?"

"I didn't say that. It just seems more important than any of the ones you've given me before."

"And this concerns you?" He laughed. "Well, that's a bad sign."

"Just tell me why."

"Your mother has been wanting me to give you more responsibilities. And since you turned eighteen, I've been looking for something. When you came to the prison in defense of the girl, I figured it would be a good place to start."

Could it really be that simple?

I'd essentially been my father's apprentice since I was

a young boy. I'd go on little errands with him or sit in on boring meetings. As I got older, I went on trips with him as well, but nothing exciting ever happened. It wasn't like we were going to fight wars or anything. They were usually just marketing campaigns to sway public opinion.

Most of my time growing up was spent with tutors, reading, playing games with my nannies, or running around outside. Sometimes I'd find the other children in the palace, all guardians in training, and we'd play. But as soon as my parents figured that out, they stopped it. I cried for hours the first time they separated me from my friends.

They told me I was above the alchemists and that I would never fit in with such strange children. I was forbidden to play with them from that day onward. It had broken my heart, and I'd gone back to being lonely, a child in a world of busy adults.

Mom probably felt guilty about that, because as I grew up, she started bringing in other children for me to spend time with—the offspring of government officials, celebrities, and her society friends.

As a teen, I demanded more. I tried to get permission to go to a public school in the city. But Richard wouldn't allow it. As their only child, I was too valuable to leave the palace. So instead, I had to be content with my personal tutors and the occasional pre-screened play date. But once we started going to parties, I began connecting with other teenagers. Email, phone calls, and video chats kept things going between meetings.

It had worked out okay in the end. By the age of thirteen, I had decided it was better to keep others at a distance, anyway. By fifteen, everything changed when girls started taking notice. Actually, they became obsessed with "winning" the prince. I used it to my advantage when I wanted, and when

I didn't, I ignored them.

But then everything in my world changed. I'd started to suspect that maybe Richard wasn't who I thought he was. And recently, I learned about the shadow lands, and then the email came about the deaths. It was what I needed to make a decision. If I was going to change anything, I had to work with the Resistance. And maybe Jessa was our way to change things.

"There are plenty of things you could assign me to. But overseeing the training of Jessa Loxley? I mean, the girl pulled from lavender and then shifted it into primary colors. It's a big job. I can do it. I know I can do it. But…"

"What are you trying to say?"

"Why are you suddenly taking an interest in me?"

There had to be a catch. Only a couple of months ago I'd found out about the extremes my father was doing with his color experiments. I didn't want to believe them, but I think I'd always known, deep down. After making contact with the woman from the Resistance, the one I'd met in the palace gardens, she'd confirmed it. There was no life left in the shadow lands. There was nothing.

"I've always had an interest in you," Richard replied. "But do I need to remind you that you were the one who came out to see her? You defended her."

He was right. The image of her falling to the stage flashed through my mind. So did the way she'd collapsed when those guards had dropped her, handcuffed and blindfolded. I realized that something about Jessa reminded me of myself. Sure, we came from opposite ends of the social spectrum, but we had one thing in common: our lives weren't our own.

"Yes. I did defend her."

"Why did you do that?"

"What do you mean? I told you, she's worth too much to

just lock up." It wasn't a lie.

"You've never taken a particular interest in color alchemy before. So why this girl?"

"She's not a regular alchemist. She has something more. I'm just not exactly sure what it is yet." I paused. "I know Mom's condition is chronic, and the doctors have said that we can only treat it, not cure it. But what if…"

"What if Jessa could heal her?" He frowned.

"I've wondered. Maybe there's a way."

"I agree that Jessa's powerful. We've already seen her separate the primary colors from purple. That alone could prove to be invaluable. But your mother's migraines aren't going anywhere. The best doctors have all confirmed this. All we can do is keep Natasha comfortable."

Something about his tone bothered me. It was cold. Final.

"So then what do you want Jessa for?" I suspected I already knew the answer. Even if he wasn't going to tell me, I still had to ask.

He smiled, pressing clasped hands to his lips. "To make this country stronger."

Hope laced his every word, and I had a sinking feeling we had two distinct definitions.

"I need you to be a part of this," Richard said. "As my heir, I need you to fully comprehend why we do things the way we do. I think Jessa is the key to fixing everything."

Except his own wife. I looked away, attempting to ignore the ache. What could he possibly want fixed outside of that? New Colony was already the most powerful nation on Earth.

I glanced at the map and its clusters of red pins. They reminded me of what I was fighting for. Whom I was fighting against. Could I be the only one? I knew of the Resistance, but even they seemed so small. How many people out there knew what I knew? How many would be willing to help us?

Richard caught my eye, caught me staring at the red pins.

"One day, Lucas, you'll understand."

No. I wouldn't. I got up to leave.

"Don't mess this up. You won't get a second chance."

"About that. You know that Faulk assigned a young guardian to help with Jessa's training?"

"Reed is an asset. What's the problem?"

"No problem, except that I don't think he's got enough going for him to help someone like Jessa all on his own. I've asked another alchemist, Jasmine, to also step in and assist."

"I know who she is. She's one of your mother's favorites. Are you asking for my permission?"

"No, actually, I'm not."

I turned the corner and walked down the hallway of our secluded residence, intending to find a distraction. Maybe go for a run?

But there was someone I needed to talk to first. I switched direction and headed instead for my parents' bedroom, knocking gently on the door before entering the darkened room.

"Mother, are you in here?" I whispered. I slowly walked toward the canopied bed and found her lying in a heap, with several pillows propped up behind her. A cool washcloth was draped across her pale forehead. Her auburn hair was fanned around her like a fiery halo.

"Lucas," she smiled. "How are you, sweetheart?"

"I'm good, Mom." Something about that word felt comforting. The last few years, I'd taken to calling her by her name, Natasha. So much about her had changed over time. She used to be spirited, fun, playful, and nurturing. But all of that had disappeared as her illness took over.

"What do you need?" she asked.

"I just wanted to check on you. How do you feel?"

"Oh, you know. It comes and goes. They've been worse lately, but farther apart. So that's good."

"I don't know if I'd call that a good thing."

"Well, at least it allows me to get back out into public when I'm feeling up for it. I'd rather have really good days and really bad ones. Not being stuck in here with the lights off constantly."

"I guess you're right." I stood up from the edge of the bed, not sure what else to say. This conversation was depressing, and I wanted to get out.

"Will you call for Jasmine to come to me?" she asked.

"You know Jasmine well?" I was curious about their relationship now, since my mother had never mentioned her before, but Richard had.

"Oh, yes." She smiled. "I'm afraid I'm not much use around here. Jasmine helps with the pain. We've become friends these last few years."

Friends? I wondered how my father felt about his queen being friends with a color alchemist. I studied her, holed up in this darkened room. My heart sank as I realized that maybe Richard was right. Maybe there was nothing we could do to help. But somehow, I knew I wasn't ready to give up just yet. I needed to get Jessa trained and figure out what powers she actually had. And to do that I needed her to trust me. I knew it was wishful thinking, but I couldn't help myself. Maybe Jessa could not only help the Resistance, maybe she could save my mother.

"Something's wrong." Mother grabbed her head, pushing her palms against her ears.

"What is it? Are you okay?"

"The pain is *on purpose*. Someone is hurting me."

What was she talking about? If someone was hurting her, I needed to know who it was.

"I can't remember. I can never remember anything."

"Who's hurting you?" I asked. Urging her to have a moment of clarity. *Please, Mom, don't go silent on me now.*

But her face cleared again, and she peered up at me. The moment was lost. Those few words clung to me: *on purpose.* They changed everything. This wasn't just about chronic migraines. Was something darker going on? Of course, I had failed to see it all these years. Someone was *causing* her pain, stealing her away. It had to be alchemy. How else could it be done? But the bigger question wasn't what was happening, it was who was doing it, and why? Jasmine was with her often, but so were other healers. My father, Faulk, and a few of the royal officers saw her daily. Plenty of people were around her. She was Queen Natasha after all. So why would someone want to ruin her mind?

I wasn't sure exactly why this was happening, but I was sure someone was hurting her, using her. I would have to be more observant than ever. Just as I left the room, she called out to me in an even voice, "Be careful, Lucas."

SEVEN
JESSA

By the time Eliza delivered the slatebook, I'd learned something new about myself. I was a seriously impatient person. I sat in my room, picking through my dinner halfheartedly, waiting hours until I finally had the brand new device in my hands. It was square and thin, but strong and smooth, made entirely of glass.

I couldn't believe it was mine!

I turned it on, pleased by how easily I could navigate through the options. I found the telephone icon with no problem but decided on the video chat instead. Just as I was about to call home, I paused to reconsider.

What would they think of me, their daughter, the alchemist?

I wrung my hands out, then sat on them to stop myself. Would they even want to see me? I could only imagine their disappointment when they'd learned the truth. I wasn't the person they thought I was.

By now, they'd probably figured out that I'd been the one to tamper with Lacey's blood. Was she still okay? I remembered Officer Faulk's nasty threats against my family. If I didn't follow her rules, they would be the ones to face the consequences. It was possible they could lose their home, be relocated out of the capital city. They could end up in jobs they hated. Lacey might not have a good school anymore. Those thoughts terrified me. Despite my pride, I had to make sure they were safe.

Sitting on the edge of the bed, I took a deep breath and made the call. The device was so advanced it had holographic capabilities, but I was happy to use the traditional video chat option. I studied myself in the shiny reflection of the screen while the phone rang. Even though I felt different, I looked the same. The same pale skin, the same large blue eyes, the same wavy mess of brown hair.

After what felt like ages, the shiny screen changed and my mother's face materialized across the glass. Her equally curly hair was a disaster. Her dark eyes were swollen and red-rimmed.

Guilt swept over me, washed by the pain of utter homesickness. I wanted to cry too, but I resolved to hold it together. For her sake and my own.

"Jessa?" she asked. "Where are you? Are you hurt?"

My body tensed. Did she really have no idea? How could they have left my parents in the dark? It had been days.

"There have been royal officers standing outside our doors, but they won't answer any of our questions. We didn't know what to think."

"I'm okay, Mom," I said, my voice shaking. "I'm in the palace. I'm safe now."

She sighed slightly before calling out, "Christopher! Lacey! It's Jessa!"

My father and Lacey quickly appeared behind her. They peered over her shoulder, getting a better look at me.

"What happened, Jessa?" my Dad asked. "Are you all right?"

"She's in the palace," my mother said.

"Like a princess?" Lacey clapped.

Oh yeah, it's definitely been princess treatment so far.

Lacey's smile was a lifeline for me. It was the only thing keeping me from breaking down in front of my family. She was dressed in her favorite pair of pink pajamas, ready for bed. Her blond hair was dark, wet from the bath. She was tucked comfortably against Dad's chest while he held her with one strong arm. The familiarity of that bedtime embrace nearly broke me.

Who am I kidding? I can't hold this in anymore.

"I'm so sorry. I tried to stop it. I tried, but I wasn't even sure about what was happening. I didn't know what to do."

"So it's true, then?" Mom asked, her hopeful expression deflating.

"Why didn't you tell us, honey?" Dad asked, puzzled.

I wiped at my tears. "I know I should have told you. But I was scared. I didn't want to ruin everything. I didn't want it to be real."

I spent the next few minutes explaining what was going on. When I told them I wouldn't be coming home for a while, my mother started to cry again. I couldn't bring myself to let them in on the truth, that I'd likely never get to spend any significant amount of time with them again. I was lost to them.

"Come home, Jessa," Lacey whimpered. "I miss you."

"I miss you, too. I know it's going to be hard, but somehow I am going to turn this whole thing around. Right now I have to be at the palace, but only so I can find a way to come home later."

Was that true? I wasn't sure. But it was the only plan I

could hope for.

"You promise?"

I hesitated. Could I make her that promise? Her eyes, normally full of innocence, were filled with a grown-up sense of knowing.

I looked her straight on. "I promise."

Mom and Dad exchanged a quick, almost imperceptible, glance. I had a feeling they'd already discussed this. I immediately detected doubt.

Do you know something I don't? I bit my tongue. Maybe they just didn't want me around anymore. They probably didn't want to risk having an untrained color alchemist near Lacey. I didn't blame them. As much as I wished it wasn't true, I wasn't safe.

Lacey fought back a sweet yawn as she rubbed her eyes with her small fists. She was too young to understand, but she was smart enough to know that something was wrong. She wanted to be treated like a grown-up, and that stung. All I wanted was for her to stay little and happy, like a six-year-old ought to be.

"We have to go, honey," Dad said. "It's past her bedtime."

With Lacey still in his arms, he waved a quick goodbye and they disappeared. I could hear Lacey's exhausted whine that she *wasn't tired* in the background.

"Goodbye, dear. Always remember, we love you." Mom stared, as if she wanted to say more. "You're there, but we're here. We can't help you right now. You need to help yourself. Please, be smart. We love you more than you know."

The screen went black.

"I love you, too," I said to the empty screen, the empty room.

I'd missed my chance to schedule our next call. They hadn't told me anything about what their lives were like now.

Did they still have the same government-assigned jobs? Had Faulk done anything to punish them? Were they afraid for me? Afraid for themselves?

Maybe I was just being overly sensitive, but it felt like they'd already given up, already dismissed me from their lives. How could that be? I was their daughter. They loved me. I loved them.

So why did they act that way? Why did she say those things?

The brief call home wasn't what I was expecting. Family was family. We would always have each other. My parents taught me that. They were my flesh and blood. Perhaps they weren't ready to fight for me, but I was going to fight for them. I didn't know how yet, but I would return home. I would keep my promise to Lacey. I would get my life back.

■

Sleep wouldn't come easily. It was too early for me to be in bed. At home, I was always the last one to go to bed and the first one to wake. Besides, the conversations of the day—earlier in the garden and recently with my parents—had been turning over and over in my mind.

I got up and slid open the door to the huge closet, filled with elegant clothing. I pulled on the simplest jacket I could find and headed for the door.

But when I tried to turn the knob, it didn't budge. I had one of those surreal moments where something that should have been obvious to me became suddenly clear. Of course they had locked me up. Just because it didn't look like the gray room from the prison didn't mean I wasn't a prisoner. The evidence was right in front of me.

Frustrated, I raised my hand to bang on the door,

demanding to be let out. But before my fist reached the dark oak, it swung open and I nearly punched Prince Lucas in the face.

"Well, at least you didn't use color alchemy this time to try and knock me out," he said, catching my wrist with a swift hand.

He moved into the room, still holding onto me as he softly closed the door behind us.

"Can I help you?" I asked, flushed with embarrassment.

He laughed, seemingly taking pleasure in my discomfort.

The fact that he was amused only made the heat burn deeper in my cheeks. A large smile filled his face, reaching his steel-gray eyes. They darted from my face to my wrist, which he still held in his grasp. He ever so slightly caressed my skin with his warm thumb before letting go.

Did he mean to do that?

And then he winked.

Yes. Yes, he did.

So the stories were true. Lucas was rumored to be a huge flirt. Maybe he couldn't help acting the part. Maybe he was so used to the effect he had on women that he saw me as just another ordinary girl who would succumb to his charms. But that wasn't me. I needed to get back home to my family. The last thing I needed was some lame fling, even if he did get a rise out of me.

"Why am I locked in here? I thought you said I was a guest."

"You were, and as far as I am concerned, you still are."

"Explain the locked door then."

"Faulk tattled. She got upset about your arrangements and told my father. He wanted us to come up with a compromise. It's stupid. I'm sorry, but for now, you'll only be able to move freely around the palace when you're accompanied."

"So, no alone time anywhere but here?"

"I'm sorry."

"Why are you here, Lucas?" I stood as tall as I could, looking him squarely in the eye. So what if he was famous, royal, and attractive?

"That's a loaded question," he said, holding my gaze.

The heat built between us, and I didn't know how to respond. If I opened my mouth now, who knows what nonsense would come stumbling out? The silence stretched before he laughed again, breaking the tension.

Why is this happening? I don't want to deal with this right now!

"Don't worry, I don't bite," he said, before adding, "usually."

I froze and he laughed again.

"If you're just here to tease me, then you can go."

"Oh, relax, Jessa. I was just coming to check on you. It's been a depressing evening, hasn't it? Were you wanting to go somewhere?"

"Yes, it has. And yes, I was. I have been cooped up in this room all afternoon. I want to go for a walk. Checking out where I am going to be staying wouldn't be so bad. But I guess that's off the table."

"Sorry about that. You should consider yourself a student here. And even the students have rules. They're mostly kept sequestered in their areas, too. In the GC wing."

"Looks like I'm still a prisoner then."

"You can leave your room if you're with someone who is comfortable enough to spend time with you. Or if you don't mind guards following you. Being such a dangerous alchemist, well, it limits your options. However, you're in luck. I don't scare easily."

"Gee, thanks. But I don't need a babysitter."

"It's not like that. Anyway, soon enough, you will become

a guardian. You'll be living with them and will have much more freedom to do what you want. But for now..." He turned and opened the door, pausing at the entrance. "Well? Are you coming?"

"You really want to take me for a walk?" Was he willing to spend time with me only because he felt sorry for me? Or because something in him felt the same way I did—drawn to the other despite better intentions? I wasn't sure which answer bothered me more.

"Sure I do. Unless you don't want to be seen with me?"

This huge palace was my home now. And however temporary it would be, I was dying to check it out. Before I could talk myself out of it, I summoned courage and followed him out of the room.

∎

We strolled through the labyrinth of hallways as he pointed out different areas. Libraries, ballrooms, guest suites, and government departments were all located here. The palace was by far the largest building I'd ever been in. In fact, it was multiple buildings strung together. Even the theatre where the Royal Ballet was housed couldn't hold a candle to this place.

The main building had three stories that stretched wide across acres of land. It was comprised of a delicate hodgepodge of old and new architecture. The original building was part of the old country's capital building. I think it had been called the White House. But as New Colony grew, the royal family had leveled all of the surrounding buildings and new wings had been added to this property. The rest of those old buildings didn't correspond to the new ways of thinking, so no one had really protested their removal. At least, I didn't think they had. A small part of me was starting to question everything I'd been taught.

Some areas were built to match the old southern style, with tall ceilings, marble pillars, and beautiful oak trimmings. And some were built in the current modern way, with clean lines, white shining surfaces, and walls made entirely of glass.

Despite the clashing styles, none of it felt jarring. Actually, there was a delicate flow to the design that felt both regal and industrial. Somehow, it worked. I had to admit the palace was beautiful.

We approached another hallway. At the end, guards were posted by a padlocked door. A couple of men had their backs to us. They were let in without a fuss. They were dressed in the same black uniform Reed wore.

"Is this the Guardians of Color headquarters?"

"Yes, they have that whole wing." Lucas cleared his throat. "But we're not going in there tonight."

Oh, thank you! I didn't question him. It wasn't a place I was ready to visit yet, anyway. Instead, we turned a few more corners and descended the stairs to the ground floor.

From the look of this palace, I may as well have been transported to a different country. But I knew it wasn't the case. The thought kept popping into my head that we were still in the capital city. Which meant I really wasn't that far from home. Only a twenty-minute ride on the high-speed train would put me a block from my suburban doorstep. It hurt to entertain even a glimmer of hope, but I held on tightly to the thought anyway.

As soon as the scent wafted through my nostrils, I knew.

"Let me guess. This is your favorite spot in the whole palace, right?"

He laughed. "You got me there."

He opened the double doors, revealing a huge kitchen. Correction: kitchens. There were multiples of everything we had at home, plus lots of things we didn't. Between all the diplomats, guardians, advisors, guests, and staff who inhabited the palace, there were probably several hundred people here at any given time.

It was late, so all the cooks had already retired for the day, leaving the entire space quiet.

"Why is this your favorite room in the palace?"

"The area where I live with my parents is pretty nice, no doubt. But I don't like to hang out there too much. I spend my free time in my study, outside, or down here in the kitchen. I appreciate the ordinary things in life, and yes, the unlimited access to food is a nice perk. Besides, I like people. I like the workers. They've always been kind to me. I grew up knowing many of them."

I wondered what that must have been like. I'd never considered that Lucas wasn't close to his parents. But perhaps his life wasn't as good I'd thought it was. Maybe he was lonely.

We went over to a row of large refrigerators. He opened one, with a sly smile on his face, as if he knew the contents would surprise me.

"You're kidding?"

Lucas grinned and grabbed the largest piece of chocolate cake I had ever seen. He used his other hand to pull out a slice of cheesecake. "Aren't you going to help yourself?"

It was amazing. Desserts, sweets, puddings, and delectable items I didn't even recognize filled the fridge. I spotted carrot cake and moved in for a slice. I'd had it once at a ballet banquet, so I already knew how sweet it would taste. The memory of cream cheese frosting wetted my taste buds.

Lucas rummaged through a nearby cupboard and pulled

out a handful of salted caramels twisted neatly in waxed paper.

"Oh, wow." Any kind of sweet treat was a rarity in my life…in the lives of all of us beyond the palace gates. We were accustomed to having more than enough, but simplicity was the norm. Caramel was basically sugar, so it wasn't too hard to make when we had some extra rations. But these certainly didn't look like the ones we made at home. These were perfect.

As with everything in the palace, the food was presented very neatly. The plates were in clear containers to keep the desserts fresh and moist, ready to be served tomorrow. I stared down at the cakes in our hands and tried not to squeal with delight.

"It's been a long time since I had anything like this." Something about all this food felt naughty and exciting. And to be honest, an emotional eating session seemed appropriate after everything I'd been through.

"Well, that's good because we're going to share. Come on."

■

We ended up back in the gardens, and even though I wanted to see the rest of the palace, I took solace in this area. The air was warm, and the sky still clung to the last bit of light. It was the perfect summer night, not too hot and not too cold.

Walking through the near dark, I worried about tripping and knocking the delicate cake from my hands. Somehow, though, we both managed to make it to the empty lawn and sat down on the manicured grass. The light from the palace was behind us, and the last rays of the setting sun were quickly disappearing.

Lucas pulled a couple forks from his back pocket, and

together, we dug in. The flavors were incredible, better than anything I ever tasted before. I could only imagine the amount of fat and butter wrapped up in each bite, but I didn't care. This was heaven.

"So, do you always eat this late?"

"Not always, but I like the kitchens, so I end up eating more than I should," he replied, reaching for a caramel.

Following his lead, I took one. I popped the warm silky sugar into my mouth and sank back into the grass. The caramel melted around my tongue.

"Why do you like the kitchens? You don't seem like someone who cooks," I asked.

"No, I don't cook. I've never had a reason to, although it might be one of my undiscovered talents. Maybe I'll take lessons."

I noticed he hadn't answered my question. I was beginning to understand something about Prince Lucas. He liked people, but spent a lot of time alone. "Are you out here often?"

"Yes, quite a lot. I come running out here every morning. I usually eat lunch here, too. It's just my place, I guess. Except for winter, when I hole up in my family's library. Sounds stupid, maybe, but I generally like to distance myself from all the politics."

"But isn't that something you should get used to? I mean, you are going to be the next king."

As soon as the words were out of my mouth, I regretted them. Perhaps I was being insensitive by prying.

"Basically, yes."

He started in on the rest of my carrot cake and dropped all conversation.

I let it go, focusing on enjoying a few more pieces of caramel. Soon, I found I couldn't eat another bite. Lucas, in typical boy-fashion, didn't slow down until every last crumb was gone. I looked at him with strange admiration. From his lean physique, I would never have guessed he could put food away with so much gusto. He must exercise *a lot*.

Lying on the grass, I allowed a gentle peace to sweep over me. It was something I hadn't felt in a long time. Not since before Lacey's accident months ago. I gazed at the first stars peeking through the clear sky, thinking of my family. Were they watching the same ones? Stargazing was a favorite pastime of ours, and I could almost imagine myself with them, enjoying this warm night.

Lucas turned back to me for a few minutes, then moved the plates aside. When he lay down next to me, I bit back a small smile.

He didn't touch me, but he was close enough that I could feel the heat of his body against my arm. The urge to look over at him was so overwhelming that I almost gave in. But I didn't. I was afraid he'd be looking back.

And I was more afraid he wouldn't.

"I'm always being watched." Lucas's voice was calm. "Ever since I was born, I've been the property of New Colony. Everybody wanted something. Everybody thought they knew who I was. They still do."

I could tell he wanted to say more, but he fell silent. I didn't know how to respond. I was more surprised by his openness than anything else. So I just waited, ready to listen.

"I guess that's why I come out here a lot or go downstairs to the kitchens. To be alone, or at least be around people who won't bother me. I'm trying to figure out who I am. I don't like all that other stuff getting in the way."

In that moment, I wanted to say the perfect thing. I wanted to tell him that I understood, but honestly, I wasn't sure I did. I had always known exactly who I was, exactly who I wanted to be and what I wanted to do. And even though people were telling me I couldn't be that person anymore, I couldn't let her go. That girl on the ballet stage was more real to me now than ever.

Maybe Lucas wasn't such a bad guy.

Without stopping to think it through, I reached out and laced his fingers through mine. It was intended to be an act of friendliness, support, solidarity.

But when he stiffened, I shut my eyes tight. I was sure he was going to laugh or push me away. But he didn't. He squeezed my hand tighter and rolled toward me.

My fear of looking at him, and what could happen if I did, was no match for my need to see his face. I had to know if the electric chemistry between us was real. Did he feel it too? My eyes fluttered open and caught myself in his steely gaze. His charcoal eyes held mine, intense, like smoke from a wildfire.

He moved in closer, ever so slightly raising his chin, parting his lips. I knew what was about to happen. I knew he was going to kiss me.

And I was going to let him.

"There he is!" a female voice echoed through the night.

Lucas shot up, letting my hand—and the moment—go.

She was coming from the direction of the palace, her laugh ringing out, sultry and comfortable. I sat up and saw the silhouette of a petite girl flanked on either side by four palace guards.

When my eyes adjusted, insignificance burned through me. Her beauty was obvious. She was perfect in all the ways I wasn't. While I was too thin, she was softly curved. While I had unruly brown hair, hers was long, glossy blond, and neatly styled. Her smile was so infectious that I couldn't help but return it, despite my embarrassment.

She sashayed over to Lucas and practically yanked him to standing. He didn't look at me when she wrapped her fingers through his and spoke in a sweet singsong voice.

"Baby, they wouldn't let me into your room. I thought we had a date. You didn't tell me you were working."

Working? Did Lucas have a girlfriend?

I was so stupid. Obviously, they were together. She was the type of girl he would date. Of course she was!

Why don't I follow the gossip feeds?

"You know I hate it when you work all the time," she continued, pouting.

Was that what I was to him? Work? But something in me didn't believe it. He was going to kiss me before this girl came along. *And so what? That doesn't mean he cares about you.* Apparently, his reputation was justified. He played around. He was a flirt. And he got into girls' hearts.

Well, he wasn't going to get to mine. I wouldn't be so naïve again.

"What are you doing here?" Lucas asked, his voice cracking. I almost laughed. He probably thought he'd been caught cheating on his girlfriend. *Almost* cheating. Strangely, this girl didn't seem to care.

The palace guards stepped forward. "Sir, is this woman bothering you?" one asked, motioning to the girl and shining his flashlight on us.

She looked close to Lucas's eighteen years. Given her casual indifference to the question, I was sure they were dating. That, or something else I didn't want to think about.

"Don't be rude." She playfully slapped Lucas's arm. "Don't you remember inviting me over tonight? Seriously, Lucas, you need to start writing things down."

He paused and then relaxed, still never looking down at me. "I forgot. I'm sorry," he said, pulling her into an intimate hug. "You're right. I was working, but we're done now."

Are you kidding me?

Lucas had his back to me, and the girl smiled over his shoulder and curled herself into his embrace. When she looked down, I was taken aback by her expression. It wasn't angry, accusing, or predatory like I was expecting. Instead, she looked sorry for me.

And that made it even worse.

I jumped up, brushing the grass from my clothes. Politeness took over, and before I knew it, I was gathering up the dirty dishes.

Lucas turned to me, puzzled. "Jessa, you don't have to do that. The guards will call someone to take care of it."

I carefully handed them to the nearest guard before meeting Lucas's gaze. "You two have a wonderful night," I said, before giving them the most sarcastic curtsy I could manage.

Then I turned and walked away.

"Wait, Jessa, let us walk you back," Lucas called.

I refused to stop or turn around. I stumbled across the lawn, eager to make it to my room before anyone could see the tears blurring my vision. Why did I care so much? I just met him! He shouldn't matter to me anyway. All my focus needed to be on getting out of the palace. He would only get in the way of that. I had to find a way to prove to these people that I wasn't the alchemist they wanted. I needed them to give me my old life back. I would not let these stupid tears fall. Enough was enough. I was done with crying.

EIGHT

LUCAS

"Sorry about that," the girl said, letting go of my hand after the guards left. "I guess I never properly introduced myself. I'm Sasha."

The name suited her. It matched her exotic qualities. Her timing. The reason she was here, the Resistance. Yes, she was very mysterious, but I couldn't help my frustration at our situation.

Sasha had just interrupted something I wanted to happen, despite my better instincts. And yet my feelings didn't matter. I should've been relieved that I didn't kiss Jessa, but I wasn't. At the same time, my desire was foolish; kissing her would have made things too complicated.

"Sasha." I shook her hand. "Nice to see you again."

She was the woman from the ballet, the representative that the Resistance had sent to install spy software on my father's slatebook. She carried herself like a woman of society, but she looked almost as young and innocent as Jessa.

"What are you doing here?" I asked. I couldn't imagine how she got access to the palace, let alone, to me.

"Is it safe to speak out here?" She was all business now.

I considered going farther into the gardens, since our voices might carry out here. But then again, anyone could easily hide in them.

"It's not safe to speak to you anywhere." This place was always crawling with people. At least we were alone outside. "Let's just keep it down and hope we'll be fine."

She raised an eyebrow. "Again, I'm sorry about your friend. I told the guards that you are I are dating. It was the only way I could find you. One of them remembered me from the other night and agreed to bring me here."

It made sense. And she was so stunning that nobody would have been surprised. Just a few days ago, I was attracted and intrigued. It's likely that I would have tried to casually date her. But right now, those feelings just weren't there. I suspected that had a lot to do with Jessa and the feelings she brought out in me. Feelings that would be better served to keep to myself. "Honestly, you just did me a favor. And it's actually a good cover. We'll go with it."

"It's the only believable one." She glanced around one last time. "I've been relocated to the palace, to join the guardians here, so it should be easier to communicate."

Relocated? That could only mean she was one of the guardians who'd been assigned to a different location. I would say that it was a convenient coincidence, but more than likely, the Resistance had pulled some strings to land her here.

"You're a color alchemist? You're GC?"

She nodded and then looked around, searching for something. She held up a finger, then skipped off in the direction of the nearest flower bushes. After a moment, she jogged back with a silky flower held snugly between her fingers.

Immediately, she manipulated the color, pulling a bit of the delicate blue out of the flower and into the open air. It danced between us. Even in the darkness, I could discern her talent. After a moment, she released the color into us and placed the flower gently behind her ear. Must mean she had blue alchemy.

"Shhh," she whispered. "It's a secret. Wouldn't want the officers to know about that little trick." She was good. How had the Resistance gotten her on their side? Before I could ask the question, she explained.

"I was sent to the northeastern edge of the kingdom when I was still really young. Too young." She stared off into the night, a mixture of longing and fear etched across her face.

I frowned. I didn't remember her. I'd been involved with the guardians ever since I was a child. It was my father's most important project, and he included me in their work now and again.

But that didn't mean I should know her. There were a few hundred guardians at the palace at any given time. And most of the ones living full-time in the palace were the children, teenagers, and their trainers. Older guardians were sent on assignments all over the kingdom.

"Tell me about the Resistance. Why should I continue to align with them?" I was eager for information. It seemed that the more I worked with them, the less I knew. And I was beginning to worry I'd jumped into bed with them *way* too quickly. If I didn't get some solid ground with them soon, I would have to pull out. What other choice did they leave me?

"There's a lot you probably think you know. But you don't." She returned her gaze to me, her eyes stoic. Maybe there was a lot I didn't know, but I had my secrets too.

"The thing is, Sasha, I can't be led on forever. I need some concrete information about who you people are and what you're planning. It's too risky for me to be in the dark much longer. I need to know I am doing the right thing."

The warm breeze caught her hair. A warm, flowery scent brushed by.

"Oh, you're doing the right thing. I honestly don't know what I can tell you at this point. But I can tell you this. We're the good guys."

"I hope so. So why are you here with me now?" Her vague responses were starting to get to me. Yes, they wanted to stop the deaths happening in the shadow lands. But beyond that, how could I really know what they wanted?

"Listen," she said. "I don't know if I can trust you either. My life is on the line here. But we came to you first, and I've been told that you're the real deal. But seriously, Lucas, you're the crown prince. How do I know you're not going to turn on me? How do I know this isn't just some boyish vendetta against your father, and tomorrow you'll wake up and change your mind?"

Of course, I already knew she was risking her life to be here, talking to me. But when I'd first met her, I'd told her that I'd also been to the shadow lands. I'd seen what was happening up there, too. I saw the death, the destruction. We had that much in common—wasn't it enough for her to trust me? "I'm not changing my mind unless the Resistance gives me a good reason to. I know why I'm here."

I sometimes felt suffocated by my own secrets. There were so many layers to my identity; I was constantly concealing myself. First, I was the New Colony prince, the boy who would one day be king—loyal to his people, forever in service to crown and country. Then there was the supposed playboy—the one the media loved to create, always looking for the smallest flirtation to spin into a full-blown romance.

Whose heart would I break today?

I cringed. This was the persona Sasha knew above all else. It was what everyone saw. And Jessa was the most recent person to witness it firsthand.

But under all the layers of masks and secrets and lies, in the dark corners of a beautiful palace, lived the truth. And I would have to spend the rest of my life trying to make up for those empty spaces, hiding the real me.

I couldn't tell Sasha all the reasons I was working with her. The Resistance was an underground organization with a mission to overthrow the monarchy and return the country to the democracy we had once been. And even though that meant I wouldn't be king one day, I supported them. Because what Richard was using alchemy for was wrong. And honestly, I was afraid what being king would do to me, who it would make me become. Would I be like him? No, democracy had to be the better way.

The members of the Resistance were well hidden. If Sasha was telling me the truth, they were nowhere and everywhere at once.

At least we had the same end goal: we wanted to stop Richard from harming more innocent people inside and outside of our borders. And we didn't want civil war or execution to be the means for making that happen.

"I know what my father is capable of. I've been where you've been, remember? I heard the rumors, read the reports. And then I saw parts of it for myself."

"The shadow lands?"

I nodded and she frowned. I was grateful that this was enough to satisfy her. But I didn't want her pity. I was here to do something about the problem. And I was willing to betray my family to do what was best for the people. I couldn't sit back and watch my father take innocent lives, just to get a chance at stronger alchemy. It didn't matter what his reasons were.

"Fair enough," she said, as if to seal the deal. "Let's trust each other."

I sighed, hoping I wouldn't regret letting this mysterious girl in.

"There's something I need help with. It's my mother. I think someone is using alchemy to hurt her."

"Her headaches?"

"How do you know about those? Are you guys doing something to her?"

"No, it's not us, I swear. But, we've had our suspicions. We don't know who's doing it to her, Lucas. Is it getting worse?"

"Yes, they're not as often, but each one is worse now. Can you help me? She's losing her memory...her mind. I can feel it."

"I'll talk to my people, see what more we can do. And I'll keep a look out myself. We'll let you know if we find anything."

I hoped that would be enough. I didn't know how much more of this my mother could take. And I was scared to talk to anyone in the palace about it, clue them in, in case they were the culprits. What if my father was the one behind it? I didn't want to entertain that thought. I needed to find the answer soon. "I need to save my mother."

■

I promised myself that the next time I saw Jessa, I would apologize for leading her on. I never wanted to hurt her. I didn't know if she'd forgive me, but at least I could try to smooth things over. But when I knocked on her door the next morning and let myself in, she wouldn't even look at me.

"Listen, about last night. I never meant for any of that to happen."

"Nothing happened," she quickly cut me off, pretending to be interested in whatever was going on outside her window. Which I knew was just a side view of the lawns.

Neither of us said anything for a while. I didn't know what to do to get through to her. Should I just apologize? An apology would be disingenuous. I had wanted that kiss to happen. This whole mess wasn't her fault.

"I need to take a shower. Can you please leave?"

Of course she didn't want to see me. I didn't deserve anything more from her right now. As I left, I uttered the only apology I could give her. "You can have the day to do as you please."

"Are you serious?" she asked, turning to me with wide eyes.

Was I? I wasn't sure how I'd explain this one to Faulk and Richard. But then again, it was just one day. She'd be happier for it. *And that's better for her training.* "Yes, but stay within the grounds. Obviously." She perked up. "Oh, and tonight you'll be accompanying me to a palace party where you'll officially be introduced to the Guardians of Color and my parents."

Her mouth dropped. "Won't you be taking your girlfriend?"

I blinked at her. I hadn't thought about Sasha being my date when my father had announced the party plans over breakfast. But it was the perfect place to get some real traction for our cover. Sasha was a guardian, after all. But Richard had told me to escort Jessa myself.

"Sasha will be there, yes. But I'm taking you."

"Sorry, but contrary to what you thought of me last night,

112

I am not the other woman type of girl."

Unfortunately for her, when Richard gave an order, he gave an order. Period. For her sake, it was better I forced this issue instead of him.

"I'll pick you up at seven," I replied, quickly leaving the room.

I stood outside her door and inhaled deeply. *How am I going to do this?* I had to escort Jessa tonight and, at the same time let everyone know that Sasha and I were together. It was a totally bad maneuver either way. I needed Jessa to trust me. But I also needed an easy excuse to be seen with Sasha.

I wasn't looking forward to this evening.

■

Faulk's office was at the top entrance of GC headquarters. All the royal officers' offices were here. The area itself was the most modern of the palace, and the most recently constructed. Everything was charcoal gray and stark white, but it also felt lived in. Busy. People spent a lot of time there.

A few guardians came out of a nearby doorway, their voices light as they echoed through the corridor. The younger guardians were still in training, while most of the teens were official initiates. I didn't know these faces well. They barely took notice of me as they disappeared around a corner.

I tended to stay away from most of the guardians. My parents preferred I didn't make friends with alchemists, and personally, I no longer wanted to. They weren't bad people, but they wielded powers that my father worked hard to control. With such small numbers, he could. He treated the few hundred guardians well in return for their obedience. But, no, I didn't fear them. I just chose to stay away.

I walked into the GC headquarters, eyes peeled for my target.

Faulk was essentially in charge of the GC, second only to the king. So I went to her office. Of course, the sleekest, biggest, and nicest one had to be hers. As I walked through the area, the royal officers stopped their work to watch me. This wasn't a place I customarily frequented.

It looked almost like a normal office. Except for the modern glass, which covered most of the surfaces. And the fact that I knew what these people actually did for a living. Royal officers were anything but normal. Their whole existence revolved around controlling the GC, and thus, the kingdom.

I stood there for a minute, still looking for Faulk. An older man got up to greet me with a bow and a smile: Thomas. "Prince Lucas. How can I help you?"

He was my favorite officer. I returned his smile. "Why do you work here Thomas? Aren't you tired of all this?"

"I wouldn't know what else to do. I've been committed to this post for decades now." His tone was kind, unlike most of the other royal officers I knew, who were cold and unemotional—all business. Still, it bothered me because I was sure *he knew the truth*. He had to be involved in the shadow lands project.

"When my grandfather was king, didn't you have Faulk's job?"

He frowned, nodding.

"So what happened? Why did Faulk replace you? No offense to her, but I like you much better."

"Well, I appreciate that. But Richard wanted to make some changes. I guess there are things he and I don't always see eye to eye on. But that's okay, Lucas. I do what I'm told. I'm loyal to your family."

I couldn't be sure what he meant by all that.

"I need to talk to Faulk. Is she here?"

He pointed behind and above me to her office. It was at the top of a set of industrial stairs. It was no surprise to me that she'd set herself at an elevated level; whoever worked up there could watch what everyone was doing. *Royal Officer Isadora Faulk: General* was written in big bold letters across a heavy glass door.

As I moved for the staircase, he quietly added, "Be careful, Lucas. Remember who you're dealing with." He turned and walked away. Was he trying to intimidate me or warn me?

The office was made entirely of opaque and clear glass with wide sweeping views of the back gardens, an area used for guardian training and recreation. This was all exclusive GC territory.

I entered quickly, wondering how Faulk felt about people barging in on her. I didn't care either way. After all, she'd done the same to me yesterday. Faulk was busy typing furiously on a slatebook. She continued for a moment, ignoring me.

"Lucas, please have a seat," she said, still typing.

I sat back in one of the uncomfortable chairs and waited for her to look at me. After a few long minutes, she finished up whatever she was working on. She wanted control. And she hated me for taking some of that away from her. I assumed her indifference was all part of her game.

"What do you want?" she asked, finally breaking the silence.

"I came to inform you about Jessa. She's had a rough couple of days, so I gave her the day off. Except for tonight, of course. Richard is throwing a party in her honor."

Faulk's chair screeched as she stood up. "You did *what*?"

"Do you have a hearing problem?"

"Who do you think you are? We have a schedule for that

girl!"

"Who do I think I am? I'm the crown prince of this kingdom. The *only* prince of the most powerful country on the planet. Who do you think you are?"

"I am a royal officer, the First General of the Guardians of Color, *not* you. You have a long wait before you get to be king. And that is only if your father steps down. My guess is that he'll stay on his throne until the bitter end, especially knowing he has you as a successor."

I observed the vein in her temple as it pulsed with every word.

Maybe she was right. Maybe my father would never step down for me to take control of New Colony. But that didn't change the fact that he had charged me with overseeing Jessa's training. Not Faulk.

"Look," I said, standing. "I didn't come here to fight with you. Yes, you are in charge of GC training, but Jessa isn't a guardian yet. She has to be initiated for that. And we both know I'm the one making day-to-day decisions for her right now. I came to tell you what I did out of courtesy, not to get your permission. Anyway, it's done."

I got up. Just as I turned to leave, I was startled by Jessa's blurred figure standing on the other side of the glass door. What was she doing here? I quickly opened it and pulled her inside.

"Do you have a built-in radar?" I asked.

"For what?" Jessa replied, her face flushed.

"For opening doors just as I'm about to walk through them?"

Faulk cleared her throat. "To what do I owe another interruption in your honor, Miss Loxley?"

Jessa glanced at me. "I've been trying to call my parents all morning." Her words were directed at Faulk. "It's their day off, and they're not answering my calls. I was wondering if you knew what's going on. Are they okay?"

"You just spoke to them yesterday," Faulk said. "We have royal officers stationed at their home, you know."

"Yes, I called them. But when I tried again, they didn't answer. That really isn't like them."

Well, this is interesting. I sat back down in the uncomfortable chair and pulled one over for Jessa.

"Yes, Faulk," I said. "What's going on with my trainee's parents?"

Faulk peered at us, tilting her head. "Whatever Lucas says, you should know this Jessa: I am in charge of GC security around here. Do you recall getting permission from me to call home?"

"I didn't know I needed permission to talk to my own family." Jessa's voice rose with each word. "They never did anything wrong. And I'm here, aren't I? Doing exactly what you've asked of me. We had our first training session yesterday."

"Let me be clear, Ms. Loxley. I did *not* want you here. My job is to put threats like you in prison. We need complete loyalty of our guardians. The only reason you are here right now is because the king has taken an interest in your alchemy. I've decided to agree with him and give you a chance. Don't think it means you're off the hook."

"Please," Jessa said, truly sounding apologetic. "I didn't want to lie. I didn't know what else to do. I was afraid. Please, I just want to know if my family is safe. Did they get punished for my crimes?"

"And what makes you think I would know?" Faulk asked.

I scoffed. Of course she had the power to answer Jessa's questions. She just didn't want to.

"I think it's your job to know. You've met them. You've

117

talked to them. And you just said you have royal officers stationed at the house. Just tell me, are they okay?"

I suspected Jessa's parents weren't as innocent as she believed them to be. I was still pretty sure they'd lost a daughter or some kind of family member to the GC years before. I studied Jessa's frustrated face. Did any part of her suspect that her parents had been harboring a giant secret from her? I was sure Faulk knew the truth. Maybe that was why she hated Jessa so much. Who was Francesca Loxley and how did she get away from the GC?

Faulk paused, her hard face softening slightly. "They're fine. It turns out you're a bit of a celebrity after your ballet stunt. We've had their phone number changed for their privacy, as well as yours."

A good reason, but I wasn't sure I could buy that simple of an answer. I mentally added "further inquiry into the Loxley family situation" to my to-do list.

"So I can call them? Do you have the new number?" Jessa asked.

"You cannot call them. You're the property of New Colony now. You're a huge asset and a huge liability. Part of your agreement here is that you will do as we say. Security is my top priority. I am not giving you permission to call home. Lucas never should have given you a line out. It is not safe, and I will not allow it to continue."

"What? You can't do that!"

"What does any of that have to do with security?" I shot back.

"Jessa has been trusted with classified information and will continue to be trusted with State secrets. All guardians must cut off outside relationships. No exceptions." She turned back to the work on her desk, excusing us.

"So that's it?" Jessa asked. "You expect me to give them

up, just like that? I won't do it. I won't join your stupid Color Guard. I won't help you."

Why couldn't Faulk see things my way? Jessa wasn't a young child that she could manipulate into forgetting her family. Giving Jessa an easier life here meant she would be easier to train. It was a simple, win-win situation. And besides that, I wouldn't have to watch her struggle so much. I hated to see her upset like this, knowing there wasn't much I could do.

"You don't have a choice," Faulk replied. "It's that or prison. Either way, you're not going home."

Jessa doubled over as if she was about to be sick. Was she just realizing what I had known my whole life? New Colony had all the power. She had none. It didn't add up, since she was the one with the powers they wanted. But that's how things were going to be.

"Fine, I'm not going home. But you're not going to keep me from my family. If you do, I'll make sure you lose your job."

And that's why I like her so much. No one stood up to Faulk. Except me, that was. I had to admit I was impressed.

Faulk laughed. "There's nothing you can do, Jessa. I make the rules and you follow."

"Actually, that's where you're wrong—the king makes the rules," I interjected.

"And what's your point?" Faulk squared her shoulders.

"My point is that my father wants her to help her country. And if he wants her to do that, then I'm pretty sure he needs us to help Jessa."

"Where are you going with this?"

"I'll help you," Jessa said. "I'll work as hard as I can. I'll do whatever you ask of me, but I won't give up my family. And if you take them from me, then you can explain to the king why I refuse to work. I mean it, I'll go to prison instead of staying here if you keep me from them."

Faulk and I both studied her determined face.

"You're bluffing," Faulk said.

"I don't think she is," I mused.

"Try me."

"Fine," Faulk said after a long pause. "After you learn how to control the color red, I'll give you a line out to call them. That is what the king wants most, you know—he wants red. That's all I can offer. Phone calls, twice a month."

"Twice a week," Jessa replied.

"*Once* a week."

Did Faulk just say red? No. No. No. Red? That's what he wants? Of course it is. How could I have been so blind?

My stomach dropped. I knew there had been a reason my father wanted Jessa in his custody. There was a reason he'd taken such a huge interest in her. *Of course* it was red. A memory flashed through my mind of the first time I saw Jessa. She'd used alchemy on the lavender of her ballet costume. And the colors had separated. Blue. And red. How had I not put two and two together?

We still didn't know what red could be used for. It was the only color on the spectrum that none of the guardians had any power over, besides white and black. They weren't even sure white or black were colors that could be used by alchemists. But red? Well, with a color that symbolic—representing everything from bloodshed to passion to *control*—it definitely had to be useful for someone like my father. I had no doubt he could get even more power once he could control Jessa.

Jessa stood and reached her hand toward Faulk's. For her, this was a done deal. I wanted to say something. To scream at her to stop.

Don't agree to this!

But what could I do? My cover would be blown if Faulk knew I had an issue with Jessa helping my father. I was supposed to be on the side of the GC, of the New Colony.

They shook on it. Their grip was tight and unforgettable.

NINE

JESSA

After a quick walk around the palace, I decided to go back to my room. Lucas had tried to delay me, but I barely gave him a second glance. I was still infuriated about his decision to take me to the ball without my consent. Besides, I needed to get to work and figure out how to access red alchemy. Unfortunately, I had no idea how to go about something like that. Even when I'd messed with Lacey's blood, I hadn't known what I was doing, or what it did to her.

I ended up sitting on my bed during the early afternoon hours, pondering how I was going to pull this off. If I helped Faulk, I would at least get to call home. And maybe I could sabotage my alchemy after that, show Faulk that she didn't need me after all. After what felt like an eternity, I realized I needed to distract myself from my own thoughts...thoughts about color alchemy, thoughts about my family and Faulk, and far too many thoughts about Lucas. About his smile. About the way his naturally tanned arms looked in that t-shirt.

No, those thoughts could only get me into trouble.

And then there were my parents to consider. When I called them last night, something wasn't right. I couldn't put my finger on it, exactly. It's not that they were afraid of me, as I had worried. Or even disappointed.

No, they'd been dismissive. Did they believe they'd lost me? Until I got privileges to call home, I'd have to wait to find out why.

An idea hit me with such clarity that I couldn't believe I hadn't thought of it before. There was only one thing that would serve to distract me from all this turmoil and clear my mind. It had always been the one thing in this world that could make me feel better.

I needed to dance.

A light tap sounded on the door, followed by the maid, Eliza. She was holding a tray of afternoon snacks. As appetizing as they were, I hated to dance with anything fresh in my stomach. If I ate now, I would need to wait an hour before dancing.

"Is there an empty ballroom somewhere around here?"

"Sure, which one, miss?"

Perfect. I felt like I could breathe again just thinking about it.

"Whichever one is empty and closest," I said, jumping from the bed and pulling Eliza into a hug. She squeaked in surprise, nearly dropping the tray. I laughed. We weren't exactly on hugging terms, but I didn't care. Right now, Eliza was my ticket to emotional freedom.

Tonight I had to attend a guardian event. I had to meet the king and queen. I had to be introduced to people who'd probably be my colleagues until I made it home. But this afternoon, I would dance.

It came back to me as if I hadn't been away at all. Had it really only been five days? Even so, I couldn't remember the last time I'd missed five days in a row of dance. So much had changed for me in such a short time. If I could erase the past week, I would. Then I'd be able to return to the core of what I loved. Of who I was.

As I moved across the marble floor, I felt immense gratitude for the moment. I counted my blessings that no one had dared touch me after my performance at the Royal Ballet. Thanks to that oversight, I'd still been wearing my pointe shoes upon arriving here. I didn't need the costume to dance, of course, but I was happy I at least had some shoes. They wouldn't last long. Pointe shoes never did. But I had them for now. I plopped to the floor to slip them on and lace them up.

The empty ballroom was all hard shiny surfaces. The white floors were polished like ice, but they were not too slippery for dancing. The walls were a beautiful well-oiled mahogany, dripping with antique tapestries. But nothing was as stunning as the gorgeous crystal chandelier that hung from the ceiling.

For some reason, the guards didn't follow Eliza and me in here. I was reluctant to admit that Lucas probably had something to do with that.

As I danced, I imagined a simple melody. Eliza stood at the far end of the room, peering out the back window. Even though I had told her she could leave, she had insisted on staying with me in case I needed anything.

"Are you trying to give me space or something?" I laughed, dancing over to her at the far end of the room. She paled, shaking her head. She was young and petite, like a mouse.

Too young to be working here. But her smile was sweet, and her innocence reminded me of Lacey.

"It's okay." I laughed. "You can watch. Or not. I don't mind. Like I said, you don't have to stay."

"Do you want me to leave, miss?"

"You can call me Jessa. And no, you're welcome to stay. But I don't know why you would want to sit around and wait for me. Unless you're supposed to?"

Eliza blushed.

"Are you supposed to be spying on me or something?"

"I'm sorry, miss." She couldn't even look me in the eye. "I sort of am. But I promise I won't tell them anything that could get you in trouble. I'm supposed to stay with you today. We can do whatever you want. Are you mad?"

Who was she working for? Lucas? Faulk? The king? But given the frightened look on her face, I decided not to push her. I liked Eliza. I didn't think she was out to get me. If she'd been appointed by someone to spy on me, she most likely didn't have a say. And being forced into something doesn't breed loyalty. I should know. "I believe you. And I'm not mad."

She let out a sigh of relief and smiled back.

"How long have you worked here?" I asked, hoping I wasn't prying too much. But I was curious about this young girl who was working her tail off instead of attending school. I didn't know people did that. I always thought all capital citizens lived the same way; taken care of, educated, assigned into the perfect job for their qualifications.

"Two years."

"How old are you?"

"I'm almost sixteen." She'd been working since she was thirteen?

"What about school?" I blanched.

"I home-school in the evenings. They have it all digitized. This way, I can work full-time."

I gaped at her. How was that fair when my teen years had been spent going to normal school and dancing all afternoon?

"I know what you're thinking. But I have to support my mother and little sisters. I'm all they have. My mother… she's very sick. She can't work. And my father…he died three years ago. That's when I applied for work-study."

"I'm so sorry." I didn't know what else to say. I didn't know work-study was a thing.

"It's not so bad. I like this job."

"Well, couldn't an alchemist heal your mother? I mean, I've seen it in action. It's pretty remarkable!"

"I don't know." She paled. "I am forbidden to ask anything of the alchemists that I serve. Please don't say anything."

"Forbidden? That's ridiculous. I'll ask Jasmine for you."

"No!" Eliza nearly jumped. I'd never seen her so anxious before. "I could lose my job. Please just…forget it."

I wanted to argue, but what could I say? I was fuming inside at the thought that she couldn't ask for help. Alchemists were right at her fingertips! If the GC weren't healing people like Eliza's mother, then what were they doing?

"What would you be doing if you weren't with me?"

"Probably cleaning somewhere. Maybe working in the laundry facility." She stared sheepishly at her hands.

"We can't have that! You're not going anywhere," I said, happy I could give her some time off from her duties. She responded with a laugh that was so sweet, it was contagious. It broke the fury that had been building in my chest and I couldn't help but laugh with her.

"Take a seat. I always did like an audience."

I pranced to the center of the room, deciding to start with

an old piece from a few years back. I closed my eyes and allowed every note to echo through my mind. The ballet was fun and fanciful, full of quick jumps and turns. I let my mind and body relax. Soon, the dancing slowed, and I began to move in my own way, taking each step as it came to me. I simply allowed my heart to guide my body, which felt incredibly freeing.

A deep sense of peace washed through every inch of me. I couldn't help but feel like everything was going to work out. *There must be a way to find myself again,* I mused. Because right then, I felt like that girl. The one with a life that revolved around ballet and family. The one who had lived with total trust in her world. How could I love something so much and not be meant to do it? It just couldn't be possible. Closing my eyes, the weight of the world lifted from my shoulders, and I was myself again. I wrapped my arms around myself in a soothing embrace. Dance was everything. It was all of me.

I was instantly rocketed back to my reality. The shrill sound filled every inch of the large room. The horrified, ear-splitting, gut-wrenching scream of pain was undeniable. I reached out, looking for the source. And then I saw her, Eliza. And I saw all the blood. Her blood. *Everywhere.*

What have I done? The color shattered my vision, and then it was gone. The blackness took its place.

■

When my eyes popped open, I sat up too quickly, causing a rush to blur my vision. I hurried to look around the room. I was in a hospital bed. Actually, no, this was still the palace. The view from the window was too familiar. It was the palace infirmary.

I lay back in a bed and put my hand to my head. Looking

at my reflection in the metallic surface next to me, my face was ghostly white. Aside from a few small cuts, I looked healthy enough. I tried to sit again, but the fog returned when I did. So I relaxed. *Why am I here?*

And then the memory returned to me. It was Eliza. I had hurt her. Maybe even killed her. I hadn't realized the power that had been building inside me during my dance. I thought bitterly of all those years of ballet without incident, and now it seemed that would never be the case again. And Eliza had gotten hurt in the process. Did I use alchemy again? I should have known better. I did know better. What kind of person was I? This had to stop.

Lucas strode into the room, concern drawn all over his face. "How are you feeling?"

I didn't answer.

"It was an accident. You couldn't have known."

I lifted my hand to wipe an angry tear. I didn't want to cry in front of Lucas. But I couldn't help it. I had done something unthinkable.

"Is Eliza dead?" I feared I already knew the answer. "I don't know what happened. We went to an empty ballroom. I was just dancing. That's all. I wanted to give her a break, so I invited her to stay and watch. Then, suddenly, she was screaming and there was glass everywhere. I saw it all. Then the…the…the…"

Lucas already knew what happened. I had accidentally used alchemy with such force that it caused the chandelier to fall. Somehow, it didn't land on top of me as it should have. No. It flew across the room, right at Eliza. I wouldn't have believed that was possible if I hadn't seen it with my own eyes. I was so lucky she wasn't killed on contact. But there had been so much destruction. And I'd passed out before I could help her.

I looked down at my clothing, looking for the source of color. But I'd been redressed in a gray hospital gown.

"What color were you wearing?" he asked.

"Orange t-shirt. Black leggings," I said. "Can orange do that? Move things? But...but it was so large. How is that even possible?"

"It can, given the strength of the alchemist. Maybe you should start dressing in black like the others. There's plenty in your closet."

"And what about Eliza?"

"They're doing everything they can. So far, it's touch and go. But there's still a chance..."

"Can I do anything to help?" I asked. But the look on his face said there wasn't anything I'd be helpful for. I didn't know how to control my abilities.

"I sent Jasmine. She's one of the best healers we have."

"I didn't mean it. I swear. I would never hurt someone."

Predictably, General Faulk burst into the room, furious.

"You're a danger to yourself and others," she barked at me.

I wish I could disagree with her. But she's right.

Turning on Lucas, she added, "And you should have known better than to let her dance like that."

In his defense, he hadn't known I was going to dance. Why couldn't I have gone to the library instead?

"I'm so sorry. I had no idea this would happen," I said.

"Only time will tell if that girl will survive," Faulk replied, folding her arms. "This is exactly why you should have come forward sooner with your abilities, Jessa. Can you image if this had happened at the Royal Ballet? You could have inadvertently thrown a theatre light at the crowd. Or what if it had happened in your home and your family got in the way? They were in danger for years with you under their roof. I warned you that you were a ticking time bomb."

I didn't try to defend myself. I knew I was broken. I couldn't cry anymore. There was nothing left for me to say. Faulk was right.

"If it were up to me, you would be back in solitary confinement until you got control. But fortunately for you, you're a rare breed. We've never seen anyone develop so much power this quickly. The king wants to keep you around, despite the danger. As you already know, we need you to access red alchemy."

Maybe I should have been relieved, but at the mention of the king, I could only be nervous. I didn't know if I'd be able to access red. And if I did, what if it was dangerous?

"Despite today's unfortunate events, you two are still required to attend the ball together tonight. It's a direct order from the king. Don't be late. And Jessa, for everyone's sake, wear black." She gave us both one glance before leaving the room.

"No," I insisted to Lucas. "I can't go. I could hurt someone."

"I won't let that happen."

"You can't control it any better than I can. I'm better off in solitary confinement. Faulk is right."

"It's not up to you."

"I can't be here. I can't do this. You have to help me."

"Help you do what? Lock yourself up? I can't believe what I'm hearing. I've been around a lot of color alchemists in my time, but no one asks to be put away. Who would want that?"

"I do. Please, talk to your father. Tell him it's the right decision."

I understood something about myself in that moment. I would rather spend the rest of my life alone than harm another human being. What had happened today had been horrifying. I couldn't be that monster.

"It's a noble idea, maybe," Lucas said. "But it's also a waste of talent. And anyway, Richard would never let you go so easily. Jessa, don't you get it? If you don't cooperate, he'll use force. He'll do whatever it takes to get what he wants."

"Then help me stop it. Help me bury the alchemy so deep it never comes back again." Then I could forget this ever happened and go home.

"You know I can't do that."

"You have no idea what it's like to feel the way I feel right now. Your life is perfect, and yet you find little things to complain about. Ways to feel like you don't belong. Well, that's all in your head. This—" I pointed to a larger cut on my hand. "This is real. This is my life. You can either help me or you can get out of my way."

My own words stung. Was this who I was now?

"I'll get out of your way." Without another word, he left the room.

Breathing deeply, I pushed the emotions back down, deep inside. Accident or not, I didn't want to cause another person to get hurt.

I placed my bare feet on the cool floor and stood. I pulled the short cotton gown tightly around myself and tentatively walked out of the small room. I found myself in a hallway lined with pristine beds. Palace guards stood at attention. I needed to get out of here. If I could break out, maybe I could hide. Maybe I wouldn't hurt anyone if I wasn't *forced* to be around alchemy all the time. But I knew it was no use. As I padded down the hallway, the guards followed behind. They didn't say anything, but it was obvious. If I tried to get away from this awful place, they'd lock me back up.

What was I supposed to do now? Without thinking, I instinctively knew where I needed to go.

■

Eliza was barely recognizable. I expected to find blood, but that was mostly cleaned away. It was her face that startled me. It was swollen, bruised purple, yellow, and deep blue. Besides that, she was pale from all the blood loss. Too pale.

I choked back a sob, biting my clenched fist. This was my fault.

"Step back." A nurse appeared.

Suddenly, I became aware of the others in the room. I'd been so narrowed in on Eliza that I'd failed to notice the four people staring at me. One appeared to be the doctor, two nurses, and one I recognized. Jasmine.

"It's okay," Jasmine said. "Nothing will happen again while I'm here."

Are the staff afraid of me, too? I didn't blame them. I was afraid of myself.

"Do you remember that I am a healer?" Jasmine asked.

"Yes," I said, focusing on my teacher. She was a healer. But all the same, I felt helpless.

Jasmine smiled and motioned me closer to Eliza. "We have many ways of connecting with the colors, but the most powerful is through accessing other living things." She held up her hand, in which she was holding a small potted plant. "So I am using my own life force, with the life force of this little plant here to support me. The green energy is healing. It knows where it's needed." She looked back to Eliza and closed her eyes, wrapping her fingers around the green leaves. At first, nothing happened. Was I missing something?

Slowly, little green wisps of light began to float from the small plant. They grew, multiplying by the second, and moved toward Eliza. The moment they reached her skin, it happened. Her complexion began to return to a normal flesh color. The green light washed over her, somehow penetrating her every pore. It was incredible. Unlike anything I could have imagined. Powerful. Beautiful. And somehow, orderly.

Then it stopped and Jasmine smiled at me. "Neat, isn't it?"

I didn't know what to say. The plant, so small and delicate, had almost returned to normal. Only one leaf had turned a milky gray, and Eliza looked exceptionally better than she had only minutes ago. Remarkable.

"How?" I asked.

"Honestly, I don't *exactly* know how. I just know that I have to touch the plant. And then I have to imagine where the color will go." Jasmine stood from her chair and put the plant on the bedside table. Next to the shiny medical instruments, it looked out of place. How could it have more healing power than all those medical instruments? I still couldn't wrap my mind around it.

"But I do know that color alchemy from living things is the only way I have ever been able to heal anyone. Very few alchemists can use man-made items. It doesn't take much. I usually carry a plant of some kind everywhere I go. Have you also noticed them in the palace?" Jasmine asked.

Actually, now that she mentioned it, I had.

"Green is the color of healing, vitality, and longevity. It's the easiest of the colors for me draw upon with my alchemy. The live plants make the green much more powerful. I set my intention. And the color seems to know exactly what to do."

Looking at Eliza, I saw what Jasmine meant. Eliza's eyes were still closed, but her face was her own again. Calm and peaceful. There was no hint of what she'd been through. She was in a content, deep sleep.

"She's going to be okay?" I asked, hopeful.

"Yes. We caught it in time."

In time? So she still could have died. I could have killed her. I almost had.

"Jessa, color alchemy is a gift. There is no need to be afraid. This is who you are. In time, you'll learn to control it. You'll do many amazing things."

I hadn't allowed my thoughts to go that far. To imagine what I could do, who I could be. If I did get to that point, I still wanted it to be on my terms. I wanted my family back. I wanted to dance. Was this possible for me? So far, I'd only seemed to be able to hurt people. Not help them.

Something about that thought reminded of my conversation with Eliza. Maybe there was something I could do for her.

"Eliza's mother is very sick. Could you heal her?" I asked.

"We have to be careful about where and how we use our powers. But yes, I would love to help. Do you know what's wrong?"

"No, just that it's been going on for years." Could I hope that this would make things better between Eliza and me?

Jasmine frowned. "I'm sorry, Jessa, but I can't heal chronic conditions. I can only treat wounds, pain…this kind of thing here. But I can't change something that's been an ongoing problem. Some things are fated, it seems."

"But what you just did—it was so powerful."

"We need to finish cleaning her up," the nurse said, interrupting us. "Time to go."

Jasmine only nodded at the nurse and moved us toward the door. "We'd better get going. You have to get ready for tonight."

"Tonight?"

"You've got a party to prepare for. Tonight is your introduction," Jasmine said with a knowing look.

Oh no! I'd almost forgotten. I couldn't believe it was happening so soon. And I was definitely not ready for that. "Can you do me a favor?"

"What is it, dear?" Jasmine replied as we left the hospital room.

"Lucas is supposed to be escorting me to this party tonight. But I'd rather go by myself. Is that a possibility?"

Jasmine smiled. "I don't know what is going on between the two of you, but I'll do my best to let Lucas know your guards will be dropping you off. I don't know if he'll listen."

After the argument we'd just had, I doubted he would put up a fight.

"It's not going to be so bad," Jasmine said. "Who knows? Maybe you'll enjoy yourself."

Unlikely.

I had so many more questions to ask. I wasn't ready for this conversation to end. "Is there any other way alchemy could have healed her…maybe by using another color?"

"Not that we know of. Why do you ask?"

"Just curious," I lied. If I had manipulated Lacey's blood that day on the playground, and I hadn't healed her, then what had I done? Because Faulk had shown up that morning on our doorstep with a vial filled with gray blood. Gray meant I had used the red for something. But what? And why did the king want it?

TEN

LUCAS

It was always the same people. Sure, the venues changed from time to time, but nothing about these events ever surprised me. That was…until that ballet. I still couldn't get the image of Jessa's dance out of my head. By now, everyone at this party had heard about her, which was probably why the atmosphere in the room was different tonight. It was almost electric.

The ballroom was elaborately decorated with lavender roses and dark purple tablecloths. In honor of Jessa's first alchemy, I assumed. As if on cue, she walked into the room, and I lost myself.

She was stunning. There simply was no other way to describe her. Everyone noticed, especially the men. How could they not? Her light complexion contrasted with her dark hair and full red lips. Her blue eyes were innocent and unassuming. She was fresh and refined.

She wasn't formally announced as she entered the room. That was because I hadn't introduced her, like my parents had requested. Apparently, as I'd been informed by Jasmine, she didn't want to be seen with me. I knew that would bother Richard but he'd just have to deal with it. Then again, he still hadn't shown up.

Unsure of what to do, Jessa stood frozen, wide-eyed and perfect in a form-fitting, floor-length, purple gown. Its open neckline left her neck and shoulders exposed and vulnerable. The dark color of the dress played nicely against her creamy skin. Her long curls hung loose around her face and back.

Seeing her discomfort made me uncomfortable, too. I brushed myself off and headed in her direction, unsure of what I could say to clear the air. I faltered, wondering if she would even talk to me.

But it looked like she wouldn't be alone, after all. Reed appeared at her side, smiling. He leaned in to whisper something in her ear, and when she laughed, her mouth melted into a grin.

I wanted to be the one to make her laugh.

As if she could feel my eyes on her, she turned and looked directly at me. Her expression went flat. Why couldn't I forget this girl?

"Hey there, stranger," Sasha said, appearing beside me. She casually put her arm through mine. I'd been wondering when she would show up.

"Oh, hey," I replied, taking her hand. We'd agreed that tonight we would appear as a couple for the sake of our cover.

Her small, curvy frame fit perfectly into her tight red dress. Normally, I would have been all over a girl like her. But with Jessa watching, I wasn't in the mood for flirtation.

"Want to dance?" I asked, already knowing her answer would be yes.

Taking her hand, I led her to the small group of couples in the middle of the ballroom. It seemed like a good place to start.

As we danced, I tried not to pay any attention to Reed and Jessa, but I couldn't help myself. I really didn't like him. I didn't like that he was working so closely with Faulk. I didn't like that he would be involved in Jessa's training. And I especially didn't like the way he was dancing with Jessa now. He was dominating her time, and I still hadn't gotten a chance to talk to her. I wanted to apologize for our fight, but not with Reed standing right there. It wasn't any of his business.

"What's wrong?" Sasha said.

"Nothing." I really didn't want to talk about this right now. Not with the girl who was supposed to be my girlfriend. The very fact that she knew we weren't *really* together meant she was probably the only one I could talk to. But I didn't know where to begin, because I didn't understand my feelings myself.

Why do I care so much about Jessa? This isn't like me.

"You can't be with her, anyway," Sasha said.

"Is it that obvious?"

"Well, I mean, you could mess around with her, sure. But you can't really *be* with her. A royal and a would-be guardian? It would never work."

"*You're* a guardian. Aren't we supposed to be together?"

She smirked. "Trust me, no one thinks we're that serious. Together, in our case, is a loose term. It's not like you've ever been monogamous for long before."

"Ouch. All right, you have me there."

"Seriously, this pretend relationship we have going on here can't last long. Who would believe that coming from you, given your dating history? And anyway, would your parents *really* let you be with a color alchemist?"

"I haven't thought about it before. But you're right. There

138

is no way my father would let someone with that much power cross the line into royal territory. We're on one side. And you're on the other."

"And that is why you should stop staring at Jessa. Let her go. It can't possibly end well. You and I, on the other hand, understand what is really going on between us." She winked.

"It's work," I agreed.

"Yes. We probably only have a few weeks before our *break up*, right? Better make the most of it." She pulled me close as the music changed to a slower tempo. I folded my arms around her.

"Why did you stay with the GC?" I asked. "Why did you decide to come back here if you knew what they were doing?"

She stiffened, but I continued.

"I've been thinking about this. If you're with the Resistance, you probably know someone who could get you out. There must have been chances to leave New Colony. To go into hiding or something."

"I can't talk about this."

"You knew what I was talking about with the northeast. You said you've been there. The shadow lands. You saw it too, right?" The image of gray skies and dead things leaked into my mind.

"Lucas." Sasha pulled slightly from my embrace. "This is not the time or the place. This conversation isn't our assignment."

"Our assignment?" I asked. "What's that supposed to mean?"

"Our assignment is to establish a reason to be able to see each other often, sometimes during late hours. We have work to do and we don't have much time. But we can't talk about that here, in public. It's not safe."

She was right. And this assignment of ours wasn't so bad. Sasha was beautiful—exactly the type I went for. Blond, curvy, petite. And she had a maturity, a sophistication, that very few of my previous girls had boasted. As if she'd been to more places and seen more things than even I had. She checked off all the right boxes. We could get away with our cover, at least for a little while.

I glanced across the room, not realizing I had been looking for Jessa until I saw her. She was still dancing with Reed. They were chest to chest. His face pressed into the hair at her ear, and her eyes were closed as she giggled.

Oh forget this.

"You're right, we have work to do. We better get started." Then I bent my head down and kissed her, hard.

She reacted the way they always did, returning the heat. I pushed thoughts of Jessa out of my head, enjoying the woman in my arms.

After a few minutes of taking my frustration out, I pulled away and looked around. Had we gotten the attention we needed? From the many eyes that kept darting between the two of us, I'd say the answer was yes.

Sasha was getting glares equivalent to daggers from most of the women in the room, but she didn't care. I liked that about her. She just smirked back and then laughed. It was our secret. According to everyone else, we were clearly a couple. I finally started to relax and actually found myself having a good time.

When the party got its busiest, Sasha pulled me outside onto a terrace. The few people out there scurried inside when they caught sight of us. Giving us privacy, I assumed.

"We've got some news for you," Sasha said softly as she pulled me farther into the shadows. There was no one around us now. "It's about your mother."

"What is it? Do you know who's messing with her?"

"Have you noticed that Jasmine is frequently with your mother when she's ill?"

I had. I couldn't imagine why Jasmine had a reason. But if she was responsible, I had no problem doing whatever was necessary to stop her.

"It's not what you think," Sasha said. "We still don't know who's doing it or why. But we've been watching Jasmine carefully, since she's your mother's main healer."

"And what have you found?"

"It's not Jasmine. She's never so much as raised her voice at your mom, let alone done anything to hurt her."

"So I can rule Jasmine out?"

"We think so."

This was good information. I wasn't completely sure I could trust it, but my gut agreed. Jasmine wasn't the enemy. *If not her, who?*

"Will you keep watching? Let me know if you find anything."

Sasha nodded. "Let's go back inside."

The dance floor was filled to capacity now, and we squeezed our way in with the others. After a few songs, I was aware that we were directly next to Reed and Jessa. Jessa was forcing polite nods as Reed talked. Actually, I was pretty sure he was holding a one-way conversation. Maybe she didn't enjoy his company as much as it appeared earlier. She didn't say a thing. Just stood there as Reed prattled on about his life with the GC.

"What are you thinking?" I heard Reed ask. Maybe the guy had finally realizing that Jessa might have a voice too.

"Can you introduce me to some of the other guardians?" Jessa asked.

Sasha peered up at me, whispering. "Is this the kid that's

working for Faulk?"

I nodded and she glared at Reed's back. "What a tool."

I laughed, and together, we turned toward the couple. Jessa crossed her arms, not meeting my gaze. Okay, apparently she was still angry with me. She was right, I had tried to kiss her just last night.

"I'll introduce you to some people," Sasha said, intruding upon their conversation. "But I'll warn you, I haven't been back here myself for a while, so I'm kind of the new girl too. I don't know if I told you my name. I'm Sasha."

Her smile thawed its way right through Jessa's defensives. The two girls smiled at each other and shook hands.

"That would be great," Jessa said.

"I can help with that," Reed said, grabbing her hand and leading her to a group of young people mingling by the buffet table. Sasha shrugged and we followed.

The group appeared to be normal teens. Some wore bookish glasses, and some were more attractive than others. But they all had perfect clothes and hair. They were all dressed in expensive outfits. They oozed wealth and privilege—perks of being a color guardian.

I wondered what Jessa thought of them. She had grown up just outside the capital city. She'd been in the same house, going to the same schools, mingling with the same people her whole life. Her parents had tested well enough to be placed in a middle-class neighborhood and had never fallen below the minimum requirements to hold their jobs.

That's how it worked. Everything was done via testing. An aptitude test would tell a teen what sort of professions they could consider. But we still believed in the power of the human spirit. So once every year, someone had the opportunity to try for a better job. Sometimes they got it. Most of the time, they didn't. As long as they passed the minimum for their current workplace requirements, they would get to keep their job. And those who didn't do so well weren't abandoned, only reassigned into something more suitable. My father prided himself on taking care of the citizens. So he said.

Each job had a certain standard of living attached to it. What their house was like, what type of school their children attended, whether or not they had the luxury of a car, if they had the opportunity for a once-yearly vacation to the capital city or countryside. Did they get the chance to participate in local entertainment? Well, it was all determined by their job placement.

And that placement, of course, was determined by strict government guidelines and the strength of the royal family.

I'd researched Jessa's life that first night. Her family had fallen somewhere in the middle. Just barely high enough that she could choose an activity to participate in after school. And she'd chosen ballet. It had been her ticket to a better life. Some artists were allowed to continue their art as their jobs. With her talents, I was sure Jessa had been on the fast track to professional dancing.

I was sorry Jessa had lost that. But then again, being placed here in the palace was the best anyone could hope for…even if living within the royal precincts was a double-edged sword.

We moved closer to the group of guardian teenagers, and they peeled apart to meet us. Their smooth smiles were almost icy. Forced. And nervous, which was probably because of me. I didn't spend too much time around these kids if I could help it.

Reed introduced everyone, but I barely heard him. I stood back from the group, watching the way they sized Jessa up. Obviously jealous. Every now and then, they looked at me, but I never met their curious gazes.

"Hello," Jessa said, extending her hand to the nearest member.

The girl's jaw jutted upward as she refused to return the offer. "I don't mean to be rude. But I don't think it's fair that you get your own party. We don't even know what you're doing here. You're not a guardian. You're not even training the way we do."

"Brooke," Sasha said. "Don't be like that."

"What?" Brooke looked to the others. "It's not like it's a secret. Everyone knows she doesn't belong. Not yet, anyway."

Jessa turned to Reed. "What is she talking about?"

"It's nothing."

Brooke laughed. "You're not safe. You have no control. No training. This party shouldn't even be happening. This is not how we do things here. It's not even how we do things in New Colony. You have to earn your place. Period."

A few of the group members nodded along. Brooke showed no sign of remorse, adding, "This whole charade is completely unfair. Do you have any idea how long the rest of us have to work before we get any sort of recognition around here? Before we even get initiated as guardians?"

"I'm sorry," Jessa stammered. "What do you mean, initiated?"

Brooke laughed, as if she found the ignorance of Jessa's question offensive.

"Come off it, Brooke," Sasha said. "Jealousy is not a good look on you."

Is this how guardians act, or just teenagers? I hadn't spent tons of time with people my age, but still, I'd never witnessed anyone being so openly rude. If this was the way these people acted at a party—in front of me, no less—then I could only image how ruthless they were in private.

Jessa's face had drained of color.

"Jessa *did* earn this party," I said, stepping into the center of the girls. "I've seen what she can do with my own eyes. You haven't. She has more potential in her than this whole group of alchemists combined."

Brooke and her gaggle of girls immediately hushed. I resisted the urge to laugh. Did they think I couldn't hear them? For a heavy moment, they stared at me, taken aback. But then Brooke curtsied deeply and walked away, followed closely by the rest of the group.

"Don't worry about it." Sasha put her arm around Jessa. "They're just mad because you're already a superstar and not even a guardian yet."

"They all heard about what you did at the theatre," Reed added. "That was some seriously impressive alchemy, separating the colors like that. Uncharted territory for everyone here."

"It's not like I planned any of it."

"We know. That's exactly why they're threatened," I said.

Jessa turned on me, angry. Again. "Why did you have to step in like that? I didn't ask for that. You just made it worse. Now they hate me even more."

"I was trying to help you." I stepped back, hands up.

"Don't you get it? I don't want to be a special case!"

I looked around. But when my eyes found Brooke and her friends, I saw that they had joined another bunch of young guardians. The whole group was whispering and staring right at us.

Jessa watched them, a scarlet blush sweeping across her face. I hated to see her upset. But I had to admit, she was cute like this.

"Okay, maybe you're right. I'm sorry. I'll never understand girls like Brooke. Just try to ignore them."

"Have you eaten?" Sasha turned to the buffet table and grabbed a plate. "There *is* one good thing about these lame parties. The food is amazing."

The four of us filled our plates with piles of pastries, fruit, meats, and cheeses before finding an empty table.

The atmosphere was unexpected. Jessa and Sasha were acting like best friends, which surprised me. I'd assumed the women would become rivals. Reed and I, on the other hand, couldn't even look at each other. I couldn't stand the guy. He kept finding ways to touch Jessa or to inject his opinion into the conversation. He was also trying to be funny. The thing about being funny is that you can't try too hard. *This guy has no game.*

All the while, I could sense that Jessa was still mad at me. I touched her arm. "Can I talk to you in private?" She shrugged as I took her elbow and led her to the least populated corner of the large ballroom. "Listen, I know we've had our differences, but we need to put them behind us." I wanted to sound sympathetic, but even I could admit every word felt forced.

"Fine."

Fine? That was all I was going to get? "Look, about Reed." I glanced over to Reed and Sasha. He was making her laugh, too. How was that possible? The guy wasn't funny!

"What about him?"

"He's working with Faulk, remember? Don't let him get too close. I don't think we can trust him."

She laughed. "Are you serious?"

"Why wouldn't I be?"

"Aren't you supposed to be on the same side as Faulk? Why do you care what I do? Anyway, what I do with my free time is none of your business. I can be *friends* with whomever I want."

"I'm just trying to watch out for you," I said, and then I bit my tongue to keep from screaming out that Faulk and I were definitely *not* on the same side.

"I can take care of myself."

"Really? Because from the looks of it, you can't. Reed has been all over you tonight. You don't even know him. You don't know what his true intentions are. He spied on us just a few nights ago, remember?"

"I know what I'm doing. And anyway, you have no room to talk. You and Sasha were the ones making out in front of everyone. Or have you already forgotten about your girlfriend? You seemed to have forgotten about her last night."

She stepped back, folding her arms and taking me in. She was right. I wasn't being fair. But she didn't know the whole story about who Sasha really was to me. She *couldn't* know.

"Fine. Do what you want. But remember that I am in charge of overseeing your training. Reed is involved with it, too. It's a conflict of interest to get close to him."

"Are you kidding me? You are such a hypocrite! And like I said, Reed and I are just friends. I'm not like you."

"Like me?"

"I don't go from one guy to the next overnight. It's not so easy for me to play games," she said, turning and stalking back to the table.

The image of last night at our garden picnic played through my head. She was right. I was unintentionally playing with her emotions, and it needed to stop. I wasn't going to let Jessa get under my skin anymore. As far as she knew, Sasha and I were together. I had to keep it that way. For her sake, and for mine.

There wasn't any point in following her. There was nothing left to say. I stayed where I was, hiding out in the corner of the room, unsure of what to do with myself. I was beginning to feel annoyed that my parents were no-shows. This morning, Richard had been insistent—so where was he now? Fashionably late? Maybe. Making a point? Likely. I was sure it would come to light soon enough.

I spotted Jasmine and wondered if she had any new insight. She wore a simple black gown. Her gray hair, no longer braided down her back, was brushed out in waves around her shoulders. Her brown-sugar eyes held a knowing glint.

"Good evening, guardian," I said.

She turned to me and smiled. "Good evening to you as well, Prince Lucas."

"I was wondering if you know where my parents are. Should I go look for them? They're not being very gracious hosts, I'm afraid."

Jasmine frowned and stepped in close. "Your mother's headache got a little out of control today," she said confidentially. "It's the worst I've seen her. She won't be coming. I was just with them. Your father should be here soon. Thomas, Faulk, and some of the others are going to stay with her until we're sure she's stable."

"I should go to her."

"No, Lucas, she's sleeping now. There's nothing you can do for her."

I was tired of hearing that. I hated being so useless. I turned, finding myself looking for Jessa before I could catch myself. She'd gone back to the table where Reed and Sasha were bantering in light conversation. Apparently, my mother wasn't the only one who didn't seem to have any use for me.

ELEVEN

JESSA

Oddly enough, I was enjoying the party. Reed and Sasha were entertainment enough as they bantered, explaining the inner workings of guardian training.

It turned out that most of the older guardians were out on assignments. The rest were here for training, which they did often. Guardians started out as novices when they were young children. Each alchemist was trained a little differently, depending on the abilities they had and how quickly they learned to control them. But most trained for several years before they were initiated into the GC and given actual assignments.

Initiation wasn't something I would learn about until later, it seemed. But as it happened sometime during adolescence, I figured it couldn't be too bad. After that point, some left the palace, but most didn't get stationed elsewhere until age eighteen. It was similar to how job placement worked for citizens.

And yet, here I was. The sixteen-year-old newbie

alchemist.

"You'd be surprised how seldom guardians actually get to use color alchemy while out on assignment," Reed said. "It's nice to come home and get some real work done. Training is the best."

Home? I couldn't even imagine calling this place home. With its endless hallways and ever-changing guest roster, the palace was anything but homey. Despite my best efforts to ignore him, I couldn't seem to get Lucas out of my thoughts. After our argument, I'd gone back to the table with Sasha and Reed. Apparently, Lucas had decided to make himself scarce. The whole notion that I was supposed to be his date at this party was laughable. He had a girlfriend... who was charming and kind and beautiful. Despite my initial reaction to Sasha, I couldn't help but like her.

Dressed in an exquisite red mini dress, she was physically the complete opposite of me. She was curvy and sultry... in a word, *womanly*. I felt childlike and gawky. No wonder Lucas was dating her. They looked great together. Like they existed in the same world. And I wasn't about to become one of *those girls* who hated another girl just because she had good things in her life.

Focusing on Reed, I allowed myself to feed off his infectious energy. His charisma helped ease my nerves. And of course, he was pretty good-looking. His sandy-blond hair, tanned skin, and brown eyes gave him that wholesome quality. *Oh, did I mention the boy has dimples?* Plus, he was definitely attractive in a suit. I didn't mind his casual flirtation. I knew it wouldn't go anywhere, though. I wouldn't admit it to Lucas, but he was right. Reed wasn't someone I trusted. Not yet.

"Are you having any fun?"

I decided to answer Reed's question honestly. "Some. I

mean, I guess I'm okay. This just isn't my idea of fun. I guess I'm a little too introverted. "

"This is your party," Sasha said.

"You might as well have a little fun," Reed added.

"You know what?" I said, looking around at all the people enjoying themselves. "You're absolutely right." And he was. This party was being held in my honor right?

"I know something that could help," Reed said, turning to Sasha. "What do you think? A little orange bubbly for the party girl?"

Sasha laughed. "I guess a little wouldn't hurt."

"What do you mean?" I asked.

"You'll see." Reed smiled. "It just enhances your personality a bit. That's all."

I suspected it had something to do with color alchemy. Couldn't I avoid alchemy for just one evening?

"This party is all white and lavender." Sasha frowned. "Don't they normally have orange accessible at stuff like this?"

Orange! I didn't want to even think about orange right now. Not after my day with Eliza. Sasha got up, flagging down one of the servants laden with a large tray of drinks.

"What are those?" I asked, nervously.

"It's not quite what you think," Reed said. "There's no alcohol in the drinks at guardian events. No need for it."

"I knew they had something." Sasha brought a champagne flute back, holding it up for my inspection. It was filled with a clear, bubbly liquid. A single orange flower petal floated gently on the surface. It looked like it had once belonged to a tiger lily. Fire-bright and full of color.

"On second thought, maybe we shouldn't have her do it," Reed said. "She doesn't have the best track record with alchemy. No offense." He smiled apologetically at me.

151

"None taken," I replied. Despite my better judgment, I was intrigued.

Sasha placed her hand over the glass, the tip of her finger barely touching the flower. She smirked as the color from the lily seeped into the liquid, turning the whole drink a glowing orange. "Drink it," Sasha handed it to me. "But only half."

"Don't worry," Reed added, "all you're doing is enhancing your own orange energy center by drinking this. It's a little trick alchemists have been using for quite some time. Consuming color right after manipulating it tends to draw out those attributes in ourselves."

"And orange does what?"

"A number of things as it taps into base emotion and passion, but mainly, this is going to allow you to have fun." He took his own drink, now orange as well, and drank it quickly.

This was surreal. Could this work? This was a flower petal. One measly, albeit lovely, flower petal.

I picked up the glass and took a few sips.

It was light, citrus. Just as I'd imagined orange would taste. It tingled as it slid down the back of my throat.

Immediately, my body warmed. Anxiety lifted from me. Something welcoming bubbled up inside. Joy. My eyes began to water. But a smile pulled at my cheeks. I hadn't felt this since the night at the ballet, *before* the disaster.

I was light and effervescent, just like the bubbles in my glass. Looking around, I realized that I just wanted to dance! I jumped up as a loud, upbeat song blasted through the speakers that lined the ballroom.

"This is my song," I yelled to my new friends, pulling them to the dance floor. This wasn't ballet, not that kind of passion. I felt safe giving it a shot.

Ten minutes later, the three of us were dancing in the

middle of the room. Most of the party guests had joined us, and the whole atmosphere had lightened up considerably. It was actually starting to feel like a party, not a stuffy palace event.

Sasha was becoming my friend. And Reed was handsome. He knew how to have a good time. He was arguably the best dancer on the floor. Maybe I could have fun with Reed? I could enjoy a fling. Honestly, I had only ever kissed a couple boys before. Nothing exceptional. I'd always been too focused on ballet to care about dating. But ballet was gone, and everything, including me, was changing.

I smiled as the music blared and the crowd danced. I wondered why Lucas had left. He'd been gone for at least an hour now. Where was he? And where were his parents?

I frowned. He could be having fun with us. He could be dancing with his beautiful girlfriend. But he wasn't. He was avoiding me.

Ugh, why do I even care?

There was a hush among the crowd, and the blaring music scratched to a silent thud. The crowd stopped pulsing, and parted, everyone bowing low.

The king had just entered the room.

And he was coming straight toward me. *Oh no! I'm not ready for this.* I joined the others and fell into a low curtsy. My head felt light, and I willed the orange joyous energy to leave my system. I wanted to make a good impression. *This is the king!* Reed had said this was different from alcohol. He must be right. The second I wanted the orange haze of excitement to lift, it did. *Thank goodness.*

"I think it's time we formally introduced ourselves, Jessa." The king stopped in front of me as he spoke to my downturned head. He slowly said each syllable of my name, provoking a chilling sting to run down my spine.

153

Oh yes, the orange is definitely gone.

His black shoes were so reflective that I caught a glimpse of my startled expression. I imagined how I must look to him, bowed low. A rare bird, now captured and placed in her cage. What tricks could he teach me?

"Your Highness," I said, standing back up. "It is an honor to meet you. Thank you for throwing this party."

With a flick of his wrist, he motioned to the onlookers to go back to dancing. They obeyed, obviously. "Don't mind me. I hope I didn't interrupt too much fun."

I reached for a smile that didn't seem to come. This was the king, the most powerful person in the world. I couldn't help the intimidation burning a hole through me.

I stepped away, hoping to excuse myself. Technically, it was my party, right? I'd be happy to get back to it.

"You and I need to have a discussion," the king said, grabbing my arm before I could slip away. "Why don't we have a dance and talk about…things."

I didn't know how to respond. He wanted me to dance with him? Reed was still standing by my side, but he nodded to the king and disappeared. Sasha was nowhere to be seen. And where was Lucas?

Laughing, the king said, "Don't worry, it will be all business."

The music returned, much more subdued than before.

I noticed Lucas was back, finally. He was standing rigid in the far corner of the room. I caught his eye.

What does your father want with me?

A flash of confusion crossed his face as his eyes narrowed. Sasha appeared next to him then and whispered in his ear. He nodded, and together, they watched us with blank expressions.

"Welcome to the palace, Jessa." The king pulled me into

a slow dance. It felt wrong to be touching him, even if we were at least a foot apart. He wasn't just *a* royal, he was *the* royal. The leader of our country. And he was *old*. The father of Lucas, whom I'd been reluctantly crushing on all week.

I didn't want to be near this man. But what choice did I have?

"How are you coming along with your studies here?"

"It's going okay, Your Highness," I replied. "It's all so new. There's a lot to learn. I've just barely scratched the surface. We've only had one lesson."

He considered me, staring down. His gray eyes resembled Lucas's so strongly, and yet...they were different. They lacked something. Kindness?

"No need for formalities. Call me Richard. And that's good to hear. I can only hope we've barely scratched the surface with you."

I gulped, unsure what to say to that.

"You're old for a trainee. Especially for a novice. Normally, someone your age wouldn't be given a chance. Late developers are usually not strong enough to control their abilities. Lost causes. But somehow, you seem to be different, don't you? I think we can help you."

"How am I different from any other alchemist? I don't understand what's so special about me."

"Your power is strong, yes. But we have many strong guardians. We can do more with you. The alchemy you did with that purple the first time you were discovered was very different."

"What do you mean?" I was unsure how I felt about his excited tone. Something about it was unnerving, darkness threatening to surface.

"You used alchemy on purple and separated the blue and the red. How did you do that?"

"I don't know." And that was the truth.

His large hand tightened on mine, squeezing my knuckles together in a painful vice. I bit my lip, holding in the pain.

"You must learn how to control it. We need the red."

"Faulk told me…why red?"

"It's because color alchemists haven't been able to use it yet. You just focus on getting that color. Then we'll see what we can do with you, shall we?"

I thought about Lacey and how I had been able to pull the red from her blood. I could tell him about that, but I'd vowed not to bring her into this. Just the thought of him implicating Lacey made my stomach drop. He wanted red. But I would have to find another way to get to it. There had to be an alternative that didn't involve blood. Something about the very idea gave me the creeps. I hoped separating colors was the way. I'd done it before. I'd just have to figure out how to do it again.

As if reading my thoughts, he continued, "You are the only one in quite some time who has shown any progress in this area. Without even trying, it seems. Lucky girl."

"But *why* do you want red?"

He stopped and stared down at me.

"It's very likely we can use it to help people. To advance this kingdom. We won't know until we try. But we can't try until we figure out how to get to it. Until *you*, Jessa, figure out how to get to it."

"So you need my help?"

"Ah…that, my dear, is where you are wrong. *You* need *my* help." His grin lightened his wrinkled face. It was a truly handsome face. A politician's face. The older, weathered, mature version of Lucas's. "I believe today was an example of just how much you need us," he continued. "It was your maid, was it not?"

The image of young Eliza, lying under the broken chandelier, the shards of crystal and glass everywhere, snapped through my mind. Blood had poured from her head. Her cries had pierced the room before she'd lost consciousness.

How could I let myself forget, even for a moment, what I did to her?

"You're dangerous. You need discipline, focus, and training. Before you kill someone." Impossibly, his grip tightened on my hand.

He was right. I knew he was right.

"The guardians are the only ones who can provide that to you. So, you see, you need us. You need me."

"Okay," I whispered. It was all I could manage. The only word I had.

"You'd be smart to remember who is in charge here. Help me and I will help you."

All I could do was nod.

"I can't help but wonder, why didn't your parents turn you over to us sooner? Surely they are law-obeying citizens."

It was a threat; I knew it the moment the words came out of his mouth. "They didn't know."

"Strange. I think most parents know their children, secrets and all."

"What are you saying?" I couldn't care about pleasantries any longer. I wanted him to spell it out for me.

"Nothing yet. Just that you'd be smart to fall in line here. Get yourself in control of your abilities. Get a handle on the red. Do that, and I think I can overlook your lawless parents."

I gaped, pushing down the urge to spit out a string of angry words.

"Father, may I cut in?" Lucas interjected.

Lucas put his hand on my back, but I skirted away from

both of them. My fingers were still locked in the king's tight grip. Up close, the resemblance between Lucas and his father was stronger than ever.

So, how could they be so different? Or were they?

The threats against my family were tearing me apart. No, these men, this family, these people here…they were ripping me in two.

"Actually, I think I am done for the night." I turned my back on Lucas as, thankfully, the king released my hand. "Thank you for the dance, Your Highness."

I quickly curtsied and turned, promptly fleeing the ballroom. I'd had enough politics for one night. Enough guardians. Enough alchemy. Enough royals. Enough.

It wasn't until I was back in my bedroom that I noticed the sharp tingle in my right hand. The pinprick of sensation filled me as blood slowly returned, one by one, to my bruised fingers.

■

The next morning came too quickly, and I was back to work. I woke early and dressed in casual clothing for another day of training. I wondering if we would be returning to the gardens or heading into guardian territory. The very idea of the latter left me shuddering with nervous energy. Lucas picked me up at my door. When he opened his mouth to say something, I shook my head.

"Not today, okay?" I was tired of his apologies.

Thankfully, he only nodded and led me down the hall. From the direction we were headed, my fears were confirmed. Training would be spent at the GC headquarters. A nervous flutter arose in my belly and I willed it to go away. I could do this.

We rounded a hallway and walked through the guarded doors. I knew it was GC not only because of its modern design, but because of the people dressed in black. One by one, they all turned to stare.

Let them stare. I don't care anymore.

We walked down to the ground floor.

There were even more people, which meant more gawkers. Hadn't they seen enough last night? Of course, there were others here who hadn't been at the party. Younger ones. There were a *lot* of small children. Most of them couldn't have been older than Lacey.

They're practically babies. My heart ached for their forgotten parents.

I could tell who the trainees were, because they were dressed in gray. The actual initiated guardians, who were mostly teens, were dressed in black from head to toe. And again, I recognized the royal officers dressed in their white uniforms, the same style Faulk wore.

Didn't they believe in color around here? Apparently, they used it for alchemy but didn't actually wear it. Maybe my emotional experiences yesterday were the reason. I too was wearing black.

Lucas led me through a few of the hallways. It seemed that the farther in we went, the more the rooms were empty. We passed a large gymnasium filled with people working out. It had glass walls, so we could see inside.

They looked beyond fierce. Fighters.

What—are they trained soldiers, too?

"There she is." Reed bounced into step with us. He was dressed in the black uniform that he always seemed to wear with pride.

"Where to, boss?" he asked Lucas sarcastically.

Lucas only glanced at him and continued walking.

"More studying?" I asked, catching up to the prince.

"There's a lot to learn."

"I bet you're tired of reading about energy centers." Reed laughed. It was true. That was the only training I had done since the garden. And quite honestly, I hadn't made it through half of what Lucas had assigned me.

Lucas led us into one of the glass classrooms. It was filled from top to bottom with plants. The humidity was dense, and right away I could tell it was an actual greenhouse. He flipped a switch, and the glass wall facing the hallway turned opaque, giving us privacy. I'd never seen anything like it. I walked over to the switch and flipped it a few times.

"Your mouth is hanging open," Reed observed wryly.

"What was that? Did that have anything to do with alchemy?"

"No," Reed replied, walking over to me and wrapping his heavy arm around my shoulder, "just good old technology."

Something about Reed's touch bothered me. He was too confident.

"Are you two done yet?" Lucas asked.

"Knock knock!" Jasmine opened the door and joined us. She was dressed casually, in a simple cotton dress. *Why does she dress differently?*

"Good, the gang's all here," Reed said sarcastically. I think he liked being the only other alchemist here before Jasmine showed up.

"Before we get started," I said, "I have some questions. We never got to go over them the other day. Can we do that now?"

"Sure," Lucas replied. "We can, but it's already hot in here, so just a few for now."

Where do I even start?

Images of Lacey flashed through my mind. Of gray blood.

Of the way she hadn't remembered what I'd done.

"I've seen things lose their color and turn gray. Why is that?"

"The color has to go somewhere, doesn't it?" Jasmine said. "When an alchemist uses their abilities, whatever we're using as the source of color gives itself to us. We can choose where it goes. For example, does it go back to the original plant or does it go somewhere else?"

"Okay, but it wasn't like Eliza turned green when you healed her."

"That's true, but the green just transforms into matter. The colors are also very pliable, living in so many small little cells of light, that they can move into almost any matter easily."

"I don't understand."

"In science class, did you ever learn how cells work? What about atoms?" Reed interjected. "Everything that we think of as matter holds space, as well. Nothing is actually solid."

I thought about that for a second. I actually did remember learning that. The teacher had pointed to his chair and said there were particles small enough to pass through it.

"Okay, so the green went into Eliza—or the empty spaces in her atoms? How did it heal her?"

"All living things have energy centers," Lucas said. "And we can all access them, all the time. It's alchemists who can also access energy centers outside of ourselves. So in the case of Eliza, Jasmine used her own green energy center to draw out the healing properties of the green plant, and then she gave them to Eliza. Eliza then accepted them, drawing those healing properties into her own green energy center. From there, it took over." He placed his hand on his heart.

"And she was healed," Jasmine finished.

My mind was spinning. As much as I hated to admit it, so much of this felt...well, spiritual. We'd never gone to church when I was a kid. Church was allowed in New Colony, but very few families participated in my area. I hadn't ever contemplated anything as esoteric as energy centers. Could it be that there was a whole world beyond the one I could see?

"Okay, I think I'm starting to understand. But the gray—what does that signify? What happened to the plant? I saw part of it change."

"It died. It gave its energy away." Reed stepped forward, pointing to the lush greenery all around us. "But it's just a plant. There's plenty more where that came from."

I'm in trouble. I always thought that maybe I'd done something to help Lacey when I'd changed her blood. But actually, it was the opposite. I could have killed her. If Reed was right, I could have sucked the life right out of her.

I took a step back, processing this information. Should I tell them?

"I think we'd better move on." Jasmine smiled.

"So it seems you showed Jessa what we primarily use green for, then?" Lucas asked Jasmine.

I nodded, remembering again the way the green had flowed from the plant and into Eliza, healing her.

"It's pretty amazing stuff," Reed said.

"Reed will do another demonstration," Lucas replied.

"On what?" Reed scoffed, motioning to the room full of lush plants. "It's not like you took us to the medical ward. There's no one to heal."

Lucas raised an eyebrow, then reached into the back pocket of his jeans and pulled out a small, shiny pocketknife. The blade popped up thin and razor sharp.

"Are you going to cut yourself?" I asked, shocked. Lucas shook his head.

He handed the knife to Reed. "Go ahead, Reed. Cut yourself."

TWELVE

LUCAS

"You're crazy," Reed flared. "I'm not doing that. We can practice on something else. Someone else, if we have to."

I considered how to handle his reaction. Part of me knew I was being childish. I knew we had other options. But after Reed had told Faulk about the slatebook and after the way he'd danced with Jessa, I was more than willing to let my childish tendencies lead our session.

"If you're scared, then I'll do it," I said moving the edge of the blade to the palm of my hand. I would, too. Jessa's training needed to be kept under wraps as much as possible. I didn't want her doing anything that could hurt someone else. And the more people got involved, the more nervous she'd become.

"You wish," Reed said, his pride getting the better of him. "Give me that thing."

I handed it over and he held it to his open palm. He grinned back at Jessa, obviously trying to impress her.

"Don't faint on me," he said to her. Then he cut a deep

incision.

It didn't take long for the blood to start gushing. He reached out toward a nearby plant, but Jasmine stopped him just in time. "Just a minute. Let Jessa try."

Jessa shook her head vehemently. "No way."

She stared sheepishly at Reed, who was holding his hand, putting pressure on the wound. His face was pinched, but he nodded. "I can handle it."

I took one of her hands and placed a small green potted plant in her palm.

"Now place your other hand on Reed," Jasmine said. "You don't have to even touch his hand. Anywhere will be fine."

She carefully grabbed his arm.

Reed interjected, "Relax, I'm fine. You can do this. Just picture your own energy connecting with the plant, and then imagine it crossing to me."

She closed her eyes, and after a few seconds of nothing, asked, "Why isn't it working? I don't feel anything."

"Trust yourself," Jasmine said. "The green energy knows what to do. It knows who, and how, to heal. But you're the bridge. You are the power."

After a minute of concentration, she opened her eyes again and looked at Reed's hand. The blood was beginning to splatter on the floor. Its deep color contrasted with the glossy white surface. Reed was looking paler by the second. How deep had he cut? I was beginning to think he'd underestimated just how sharp that knife was.

"Are you okay?" I asked. I hadn't wanted to actually hurt him.

He blinked rapidly. "I think I need to sit down." Just as he bent his knees, his eyes fluttered, rolling into the back of his head. He fell to the floor, out cold.

"You have to do something!" Jessa cried, looking at

Jasmine. "Please help!"

Then she kneeled next to Reed, who had completely passed out.

I held my hand to stop Jasmine from stepping in. Jessa could do this. "Jasmine, please step outside. I'll call you in when we need you."

"What?" Jessa gasped.

Jasmine caught my eye. She seemed to understand. Her presence was a handicap to Jessa. She only paused for a moment before leaving us alone with the unconscious, bloody Reed.

"Just try one last time, Jessa," I said. "That's all I ask. Thirty more seconds and I'll bring Jasmine back in."

I knew she was upset, but she had no time to think about it. Just to act. Exactly as I'd planned. She closed her eyes, mind focused.

"Healing," Jessa whispered. "You are healing Reed. You are healing Reed with the green from this plant."

She gripped the plant in one hand and put the other hand on Reed's chest.

Sure enough, a cloud of green formed around the plant, pulsing and rising from the small leaves. It jumped up and connected to Reed. She opened her eyes and watched, dumbfounded. The gushing blood from Reed's hand stopped. The color reddened in his complexion.

Jessa glared up at me. "You are such a jerk! How could you? Jasmine was right there."

"It's my job to teach you. You wouldn't have learned anything if Jasmine did it for you. I assure you, I had it under control."

"You call *this* under control?" She stood up and held out her hands, slick with blood. "You're sick!"

I opened my mouth to argue, but my words got caught on

my tongue. I could only stare at what was dripping from her fingertips.

"What? What do you have to say for yourself?"

"Jessa, you did it."

"Okay, thanks, I got that already."

"You're not understanding. You did it. Look at your hands."

She turned them toward her and saw it too. She knew exactly what I meant. The blood that was on her hands wasn't red. It was gray. And hovering just above us, ever so slightly, was a churning mist of deep crimson energy. The red alchemy pulsed, awaiting her instruction.

"What do I do now?"

I wasn't sure what to tell her. She'd done this so fast, and I hadn't expected her to manipulate blood. This was unchartered territory. Reed coughed, waking up.

"What happened?" he asked, rubbing his head and sitting up.

"Jessa healed you. You passed out."

"Oh right, because you made me cut myself!"

"Calm down, Reed," Jessa said. "You're okay, right?"

He took a deep breath, visibly relaxing. "Dang, that knife must have been like a razor." He peered at his hand, examining the now healed wound. By then, any gray blood had returned to red. It looked like nothing had even happened. Gratitude washed over me that Jessa had been able to return the red. Had she used any of it?

"I'm sorry," Jessa said to Reed. "I'm sorry you had to go through that."

"It's okay." He obviously hadn't woken up in time to see the blood on her hands. Nor had he seen how she'd managed to access red alchemy, because he didn't say anything. He just studied his healed cut, shaking his head. He gave out a little laugh.

"You're good! I better get cleaned up. I'll be right back," Reed mused as he looked at his clothes.

As he was about to leave the room, I called after him, "Will you ask Jasmine to give us another minute?"

"Sure thing, Your Highness," he said, the door closing behind him.

"Listen, Jessa," I whispered as quietly as I could. "Don't tell anyone what just happened. I mean, you can tell them about the green, but don't tell them about the other thing."

"Why? What healed him? Green? Or..."

"Shhh," I cut her off. "Green. Don't say anything else. Reed could be listening to us right now, remember?"

"Isn't that why I'm here, though?"

She didn't have to say it. We both knew she was speaking of the red.

"Yes and no. It's why many people want you here. But not everyone. It's complicated. But please, promise me, don't let them know."

She studied her hands, but the blood was all back to normal, drying into a scaly red crust.

"If it had stayed gray," she whispered, "would it have killed him?"

"I don't think so. It wasn't that much. But I'm telling you, gray isn't good. It's the opposite of life."

"This is disgusting," she said, looking at her hands. "I need to wash them."

"You can. But first, promise me you won't say anything."

"What about Reed and Jasmine? Can I tell them?"

"No. Especially not Reed," I say. "He doesn't have your best interests at heart. I know you like him. But don't say anything to him. Or even when he's near. He can spy, remember? I think he's too out of it right now to spy on us or else this

167

conversation wouldn't be happening. I'm not sure about Jasmine yet. To be safe, just don't say anything. You need to trust me on this."

"I need to trust *you*? I don't even know you. It's been pretty obvious over the last few days that you're not looking out for me."

"What are you talking about? I'm probably the *only* one who's been looking out for you."

She opened her mouth but didn't have anything to say. That alone burned a hole in my chest. I didn't want to be hurt by this girl.

"Please, Jessa," I pleaded one more time. "Promise me you won't tell."

How could I help this girl? I meant every word. She needed to trust me.

"But it's my family, Lucas. They're keeping them from me. I don't have a choice."

"You *do* have a choice. You always have a choice."

"Maybe you're not close with your parents. But my family is everything to me. I can't put them in danger."

"Listen to me Jessa. What you don't get is that by telling anyone about what you can do, you *will* be putting them in danger."

She stared at me. "Why?"

"Because alchemy is more dangerous than you can ever imagine. And I wish I could tell you more, but I'm not even sure it's safe to talk right now. To explain myself with someone like Reed so near. You're just going to have to trust me. I've said too much already."

The door opened, pulling us into silence. Reed and Jasmine walked back into the greenhouse. Reed carried a clean wet washcloth and tossed it to Jessa. He didn't seem any wiser to the conversation he interrupted. "Thought you might want that," he said. "Now, where were we?"

He was all smiles for her, but when he turned to me, his face soured. I wasn't sure if he had been spying on us using his blue alchemy. But with Jasmine in the mix, I hoped he didn't have the chance.

"Your Highness." Reed glared. "Would you like me to cut my other hand? How about my neck? Would that suit your taste?"

Okay. Maybe pushed him a bit too far.

I shook my head. "Let's move on."

"Jessa, are you ready to keep going?" Jasmine asked, watching her. "You did a great job. I just examined the cut myself. All healed."

I waited for Jessa to blurt out the news. One word about the red and everything could come crashing down. Before we knew it, she would be using red to help Richard control others. I was sure of it. Catching her eye, I willed her to trust me. I could tell she was filled with questions. And she was dying to get some answers. But there was something else there, too. A pause. A resolution. Trust.

"Thanks." Jessa smiled. "Actually, can we get some lunch?"

The breath I'd been holding slowly released.

■

Jasmine and Reed led us outside to the courtyard, where there was a buffet set up under a tent. There were several guardians milling about with plates piled high. Of course they all stared at us, albeit less obvious this time. Reed waved to a few girls his age, raising his eyebrows. His need to flirt made me dislike him even more. But then again, who was I to judge? I used to be the same way.

Jessa shook her head at Reed's antics. "Can we hold off on

the rest of the practice for another day? That was a lot to take in back there."

"We should keep going," Reed said. "Are you sure?"

"Give the girl a break," Jasmine said. "I'd like one, too."

I nodded my approval, and Jasmine walked back inside. Looking around at the groups of young guardians around here, I didn't blame her.

Reed reached for Jessa's elbow. "Maybe you and I can go get something to eat?"

My stomach rumbled at the mention of food, but it looked like I'd be eating my lunch alone. Not unusual for me, anyway.

"Now that you mention it, I am pretty hungry." Jessa smiled at Reed.

I wondered if I should go with them. I needed to keep an eye on her. What if she said something to Reed about his blood? I stopped myself. I had to trust she'd keep quiet. For now, anyway.

I noticed Jessa was staring at something behind me. I turned to look. Sasha. I was relieved to see her. Yes, she was fun to flirt with. But beyond that, we had important work to do together.

"What?" Reed asked when Jessa failed to follow him.

"Do you think Sasha would want to eat with us?" Jessa asked.

I decided to stop them right there. I didn't like the way the three of them had been so cozy last night. Sasha and Reed were on opposite sides, even if he didn't know it.

"Actually," I said, "why don't you two go ahead? I've been wanting to have some alone time with Sasha, anyway."

I walked away before they could stop me, before I could let Jessa's startled reaction register in my heart, and went over to Sasha. I steered her away from the nearest group of people. We walked silently until I was positive we were out of earshot. But I decided it would still be best to whisper. I knew Reed wasn't listening in right now, since he was talking with Jessa. But could there be others with his ability? I didn't know.

"Jessa did it," I said.

"This isn't the safest place to talk about Jessa," Sasha replied casually.

"Haven't you ever heard of hiding in plain sight? We're supposed to be dating, correct?"

"Fine," Sasha said, glancing around her. "What happened?"

"Well, I did a little test." We both turned to watch Jessa and Reed. They had plates of food and were headed to sit under a far-off tree. Jessa laughed at something Reed said. I couldn't seem to look away.

"You were saying…" Sasha said.

"What?"

She sighed. "Oh Lucas, it's so obvious you have a crush on her. Why won't you take my advice? Get over it. She's an asset. You can't let your feelings cloud your judgment of her."

"I know that. I'm confused why she's spending so much time with a guy like Reed. Do you think she trusts him?"

"I know why. He's cute and fun. Oh, and he's nice to her. All the other guardians her age have been rude. All of them. They're friends, Lucas. Get over it already."

"But he's working for Faulk,"

"Don't worry about Faulk just yet. Jessa isn't an idiot. You were saying? Jessa did something. Did what?"

I carefully explained to her about our morning in the greenhouse. About what had happened with the knife and how when Jessa had touched Reed's blood, she accidentally used alchemy on the red.

"There's something you need to know about red," Sasha

said. "We do know what it does. Red itself is a power color. But red blood? Manipulating that controls people, Lucas. It can literally be used for mind control. No matter what happens, Jessa cannot get into Richard's hands. We may have to get her out of here."

"Why would you not tell me this! How can you be sure?"

"Look, she isn't the first to use red, okay? There have been others."

"Does my father know this?"

Her gaze held mine, unwavering. "Of course he does."

"So what do we do?"

"Do you think she'll listen to you? Keep it secret? I could warn her."

"No. Don't get involved. Just keep being her friend so she has someone else to hang with, besides Reed. We need to see how this plays out. I don't want to jump the gun and alert anyone to what's happened before we figure out what to do with her."

"Maybe. But you need to keep me informed of how this develops so I can report back to my handler."

"Your handler? What, like your boss? I need to talk to them."

"You will. In time," she said, smiling faintly.

"How long am I expected to keep this up? I need more from you guys."

"We know. And you'll get more soon. I promise."

That had to satisfy me for now.

"If you report to your handler and I report to you, does that mean you're my handler?" I asked, unable to keep myself from teasing her.

"Something like that," Sasha played back. Then she put her hand around my neck and pulled me in for a passionate kiss. I didn't know if it was for show or for real, but I didn't care.

Suddenly, I felt a whole lot better, even if it only lasted for a minute.

■

The next few weeks, we spent training time concentrating on practicing with the alchemy of green. It was one of the most valuable colors, since healing was such a powerful and useful ability.

I had to report to Richard every few days about Jessa's progress. I could tell he wanted me to push the other colors, but I was able to convince him to train her like everyone else...just in a more accelerated fashion. We'd get to the red when she was ready. That's what he believed. His impatience was becoming obvious, and I didn't know how much longer I could hold off. Eventually, we'd have to try something with the red. For now, we pretended it didn't exist. I was too afraid that she'd reveal herself in front of Reed or Jasmine, and it would all be over.

I kept waiting for Jessa to say something about her experience with Reed's blood. But she didn't. I knew she missed her family desperately. And she probably couldn't last forever with this secret. Every once in a while, I saw it in her eyes. The questions.

■

After an afternoon of practicing with plants, Jessa asked Reed to go ahead without her. That was surprising, considering the amount of time they'd been spending together lately. Everyone wondered if they were dating, myself included. But Sasha didn't think so. She'd become closer to Jessa too.

Reed raised his eyebrow at her request, but didn't ask

questions.

"Perfect," Jasmine said. "I need someone to help me categorize some plants in my office. Would you be so kind as to lend me an hour of your time?"

Reed shrugged and followed her out. That left us alone in the greenhouse and away from listening ears. The afternoon heat pressed in, making the large space feel smaller than it was.

"Can we talk?" Jessa asked.

"Not sure what there is to talk about." I picked up the potted plant and headed toward the back of the room.

The heat in here was distracting. That was why we'd been taking frequent breaks from training Jessa with green alchemy. With the heat, we had to dress lightly. She was wearing jean shorts and a tank top. Her hair was pulled back into a messy ponytail. Dark tendrils stuck to her glistening neck and forehead. She looked amazing—casual and effortlessly beautiful.

Carrying the plant, I made my way through the shrubbery to return it to its proper place. Jessa noisily followed before leaning against the edge of the nearest table, her head tilted. "Have you forgotten our conversation from a couple of weeks ago?"

So here it was. This had been a long time coming.

"Oh, that." I turned, pretending to study the plants surrounding us. "There's nothing I can tell you, Jessa, you're just going to have to trust me."

"Why do you have to act like it's nothing?" she asked, frustrated.

The truth was if I told her about her power, about red, I was afraid of how she'd handle it. I was pretty sure she would try to bolt. If she knew just how much danger she was in, how close she was to becoming Richard's pawn, what would she do? I wanted to have a solution for her. A way out. Something before I dropped this bomb on her.

"I wish I had an answer for you."

"Well, me too, because I'd like to talk to my family. You know? The people who raised me? The ones I haven't spoken with in, I don't know, three weeks? You know the deal I made with Faulk."

"I wish I could help you, but I can't. I promise I'm working on it."

"You could talk to Faulk. Or better yet, your father," she said, crossing her arms. She wasn't going to make this easy for me.

"That's not an option."

She obviously didn't understand the nature of my relationship with Richard. He was not the sort of man you could talk to about your problems. Not to mention—what did he care about Jessa's family, anyway? All that mattered was getting what he wanted. He talked, and people listened. He ordered. They obeyed. He wanted to make sure Jessa unlocked the mysteries of red. Once he found out, he would never let her go. She would become his tool, bending to his every will. Now that I knew why exactly he wanted red, I could only assume what he would do with that. The ability to control someone's mind? He would be unstoppable.

"You won't even give me a good explanation."

I held my ground. I needed to find a solution first. If I told her the truth right now, it would scare her too much.

"Fine, then you can forget about me keeping Reed's blood a secret. I'm telling Faulk. She'll believe me, you know. I did that blood thing once before."

She'd used red alchemy on blood before? When? Why hadn't she told me?

"Who else knows about that? What happened?"

175

"My baby sister, and it was an accident. She's fine. Nothing happened. I think Faulk knows. But I never outright admitted to it."

"Don't say another word to anyone about it," I pleaded.

She shook her head, jumped up, and moved to leave. I went after her. There was no way she was going anywhere. Not now. Not like this.

THIRTEEN

JESSA

He grabbed my arm and pulled me back to him. A heartbeat later, our bodies were pressed together, his eyes two heated gray slits.

"You're not telling anyone. I'll explain when I can. But I can't right now. It's not safe yet."

"Why?" I asked, my voice barely above a whisper. "You can trust me."

"Maybe I can," he said. "But you're too close to Reed. And I know I can't trust him. Please, Jessa, when I can help you, I will."

What did any of this have to do with Reed? I hadn't even been thinking of Reed. He was my friend, and we worked together. But it's not like I was telling Reed all my secrets. Yes, I was pretty sure Reed wanted something more from me romantically. But that wasn't going to happen. There wasn't a spark.

Like there is right now.

Pressed up against Lucas, anticipation welled in my chest. "Why do you care who I spend my time with?"

I never forgot whom he spent his time with. Sasha... his girlfriend. Most days, I didn't see her. But when I did, I couldn't help but like her. She was kind and friendly. She always made a point to say hello and to stop and chat. And that made it even worse, because deep down I hated that she had what I didn't.

"I care because I care about you," he said, his gaze intense.

I stepped away. I couldn't think clearly. The greenhouse humidity made me sweaty and disoriented, his closeness only added to that. "How is keeping me from my family looking out for me? Look, training has been fun and all, but I really miss them. I want those phone calls." His expression tore. Did I have to explain everything I'd been trying to tell him? I wasn't going to be an alchemist who forgot about her family. "Faulk says I can have an exception, remember? If I can learn red alchemy, then I can call them. And guess what? I can change blood. So why not tell someone? Faulk? Your father? Someone!"

Lucas practically growled, shaking his head with frustration. "And turn blood gray again? You know that's probably dangerous, right? Gray means the life is gone. How could that be okay to do to someone? No Jessa... Don't you see they're using you? Faulk? The GC? My father?"

"I thought you worked with them! Aren't you supposed to be a team or something? None of this is making any sense to me. I need you to explain it."

"I can't," he replied, running his hand through his dark, disheveled hair. "Have you not heard what I've been saying to you? I swear, sometimes you are so infuriating. Listen! Your life would be in danger if you did what they asked of you. Don't give red to them. You don't know whom you're dealing with. I do. Now, please stop asking questions and have some trust, will you?"

"All I know is that Faulk can grant me my phone calls with my family and you can't. No matter what I do, you don't give me anything I want."

Heat burned my cheeks when I realized the implication of what I'd just said. Did he read between the lines as I had? His eyes narrowed as he stepped closer, drawing the heat down even harder.

"What do you want me to give you, Jessa?"

"Nothing. I know that you have a girlfriend, even though you were seriously considering kissing me that night on the lawn. And I know that Reed is my friend, even though you are telling me to stay away from him. Why are you so jealous of him?"

"Jessa, Reed is working with Faulk. He's her golden boy and everyone knows it. And no, I am not jealous of Reed."

His eyes flamed as he took another step forward. I realized he was still holding my arm, but his grip wasn't tight anymore. It was soft. Gentle, even.

"Why do you like him, anyway?" he asked.

I had to think about that for a moment. Why *did* I like Reed? Well, I didn't have any romantic feelings for him. But I wasn't about to tell Lucas that. Something about his jealousy, even though he refused to acknowledge it, caused my chest to swell. "He's funny. And he's cute. And he is nice to me. And he's smart. Oh, and talented."

Lucas only glared even more.

"Why do you like Sasha?" I fired back.

"She's funny and cute," he replied, deadpan.

We were only about an inch apart. I ached to touch him. Instead I held still, my chin raised, as I gave him an icy stare. The normal Jessa would've stepped back or turned away. But I couldn't move. I didn't want to.

"Sasha is…Well, it's complicated with her. I wish I could

explain what we have. It's not exactly what it looks like."

When he looked at my lips, I couldn't breath.

I waited for Lucas to close the gap. To press his lips against mine so we could finally have a moment of relief. As much as I'd hated to admit it, I'd longed for this moment since I first met him. Just when I couldn't take it any longer, just when I knew the kiss was going to happen, he pulled back.

Breathing heavily, he put his forehead against mine and shook his head. I wanted to tell him to kiss me anyway, but my words got caught on my breath. The heat of the greenhouse had intensified yet again, and the air was too thick between our bodies. A bead of sweat ran down my spine. I trembled.

"We can't do this," he said, stepping back. "Sincerely, I apologize for confusing you. I don't want to play games with you. I really *do* want your trust. But this can't happen."

"Is this how you treat all the girls?" Why couldn't he just figure out who he wanted, what he wanted? An unfamiliar storm of anger gripped me. At any moment, I could say something I'd regret. This sensation of rejection hadn't been tamed the last few weeks. It had only grown into an angry wildfire.

Lucas actually had the nerve to look offended. "You don't know what you're talking about."

"Why should I believe you?"

"This is not how I treat girls. First of all, I don't date color alchemists."

I had to laugh at that one. I mean, really, was he serious?

"That's right, I guess you forgot about Sasha again."

What was he doing, trying to kiss me? And more importantly, why had I been so willing to let him? Whether he considered it monogamous dating or not, Sasha clearly thought of herself as Lucas's girlfriend. And from the looks of it, she was! I hadn't forgotten all the times I'd seen them together. She deserved better. And I deserved more.

"Honestly, it's not what you think," he insisted.

I was tired of the broken record. "Are you kidding me? I've seen you with her. Multiple times! Kissing her. I don't know what's going on between you two. But something is, so don't stand here and try to tell me it isn't."

"You're right. You don't know half of what's really going on."

A surge of courage pulsed through me and I couldn't help myself, "Then why have you almost kissed me? Twice."

"But I *haven't* kissed you. And I won't."

Somehow, that was not the response I was expecting and it certainly wasn't what I wanted. I wanted to ask why not. I wanted to demand an answer. I wanted to make him hurt, as he'd hurt me. But I didn't seem to have the courage. Not when it came to him. I turned away.

"Jessa, being with you would be dangerous."

About a million responses came to mind, but I didn't speak.

"Sure, there's chemistry here. I'll admit that. But we're not meant to be. Let's just leave it alone before someone gets hurt."

Didn't he realize someone had already gotten hurt? The more I tried to push the ache of rejection down, the more painful it was. I wouldn't let him see that. If there was one thing I had learned while being at the palace, it was that I couldn't let anyone see me as weak. Everyone here was strong. Especially Lucas. I knew the truth now. I needed to be strong.

Trying to hold onto the last remnants of my pride, I turned back and reached out my hand in surrender. That small gesture nearly killed me. "Friends?"

His expression was unreadable as he tentatively shook my hand. I hoped I was coming across cool and collected. Lies. All lies.

"Please, Jessa, trust me. We'll talk about it when I can give you more answers. Answers about everything, okay? Be patient with me." He really did look sorry now.

Why should I care about his 'sorry'?

He let go of my hand and raised his own in mock surrender. "I'll keep you at a distance from now on. Just... don't say a word about the red. As soon as I have news to share, you'll be the first to know."

What does he mean?

I realized he was talking about the color alchemy argument we'd been having earlier. Given the abrupt change in conversation, he was already moving on. I wish I could be so cold.

How could he just forget another almost kiss—brush it aside like it had meant nothing? And when had I developed such a huge crush on Prince Lucas? I was living my worst nightmare. I had become an annoying, lovesick teenager. No, it was worse, because I was one of many who dreamed of this prince.

You need to grow up.

Before I could respond to him, before I could get another chance to dig for the answers around red, he was gone. He disappeared behind the lush plants without another word. This time, I didn't follow. I waited, the minutes creeping by. I needed to get a handle on myself but I couldn't take the humidity of the greenhouse anymore, either. I gave up and practically sprinted out the door.

Not making eye contact with a single person the whole way out of the GC wing, I ran up two flights of stairs before collapsing on my cool bed, determined not to cry.

Lucas may not have wanted anything to do with me, but Reed certainly had a different opinion of my company. After I showered and changed, Reed knocked on my door and asked if I wanted to study with him. We'd been studying together several times over the last few weeks. I let him in.

Reed was nice to me when most people treated me like an outcast. He introduced me to his friends, dragged me to a few guardian dinners, and generally cared about my feelings. It was really too bad I wasn't attracted to him the way I was to Lucas. Reed would make an excellent boyfriend. Well, if I could put aside the fact that he spied on me that first night. I still wasn't sure how I felt about that. Had he done it again?

Even though I'd be one of them soon, I was not technically a member of the GC. Reed had insisted we study in GC territory but had started coming around my room when I kept telling him I didn't like it over there.

The angry stares bothered me the most. From children, teens, and adults alike—it didn't matter. They all seemed to hate me. Something about my presence upset their balance. I hoped the novelty would wear off soon, so I could learn to enjoy myself in GC headquarters. So far, no such luck.

Other than going there for training, I'd spent a lot of time studying in my bedroom. The historical texts were most interesting. They held a much more detailed account of our past than what I'd been taught in the public school system. In fact, a few things were completely different. I suspected Lucas was sending me more than a few classified documents.

Reed and I sat on the bed, studying. The late afternoon sun warmed the airy room. I leaned over my slatebook, intrigued to find another discrepancy in this text, information that was very different from what I had been taught back home. This had been happening more and more lately. "Reed?" I asked.

He sat up, rubbing his head. His slatebook pinged, the sound of a game. I smirked. Studying, huh?

He shut it off, giving me his attention. "What's wrong, Jessa?"

"It's just that there have been little things in these texts that don't add up. A lot of what I was taught as a citizen is completely different from what they're teaching you here in the GC training."

He frowned. "Well, you're no longer an ordinary citizen. You get to know things that others don't. It's all for the good of the kingdom. Don't stress yourself out over it."

"Something about that doesn't sit well with me. Only a few weeks ago I *was* an ordinary citizen."

He sighed. "Okay, I get your point. And what exactly is bothering you?"

"This says that New Colony was established in 2030, which was ninety years ago. But we've always been taught that the New Colony is younger than that. As far as I always knew, this country was reestablished sixty years ago, in 2060. Right? Because after the War, there was a twenty-year period of unrest in America, which is why New Colony was even created in the first place. Our society decided we valued protection more than democracy. We broke off from West America."

"Well, it's true. New Colony was created because people were fed up with starvation, war, homelessness, and all the other things that democracy had created. So what's the problem?"

"The problem is that these new texts are telling me that for its first thirty years, New Colony wasn't doing much to help anyone. I'm beginning to think that someone decided to change the history books to make our kingdom seem more

184

effective. What happened during those thirty years that they don't want to claim? It's dishonest to do that to people, to lie like that."

"It's just a little fib. It's not hurting anybody. I'm sure it's all meant to protect the people, anyway. Keep things stable. You know history isn't something we deal too much with in school anyway. Focusing on the future, on progress, is what's most important."

It was true. That's what I'd always been taught. To move forward rather than to get stuck in the misdeeds of the past. "But that means that for thirty years, New Colony wasn't doing anything to help anyone. Then, in 2060, when they got things in order, they decided to claim that New Colony was established much later? Why did our grandparents let them lie like that? It's trivial to assume we're not smart enough to handle the truth. If they're willing to lie about something as simple as dates, then what else aren't they telling us?"

"It's New Colony we're talking about. Everything the kingdom does is to protect the citizens. I'm sure there's a good reason those dates were changed."

"I think it's because they don't want people to know that there was ever a time this place wasn't perfect."

And really, what was so wrong with not being perfect? Our people were happy. They'd understand. Right? But maybe not everyone was happy. Maybe not every citizen actually *was* protected. I thought about Eliza. After the accident, she had asked to be transferred to another part of the palace. Her mother was sick. Her father was dead. And she'd been working since she was thirteen. How was that okay?

"See, you figured it out." Reed relaxed into the bed. He picked up his slatebook and started to play his game again. He was satisfied with that kind of explanation?

"I guess just knowing that my own government is lying to

me doesn't make me feel very protected."

"Jessa." Reed laughed. "You need to relax. There's going to be more stuff like this when you become a guardian. Trust the system. New Colony has taken care of you so far, hasn't it?"

Has it? If so, then why I am here against my will? Why is the king threatening me, and why is the prince keeping secrets?

Reed put his game away again and grabbed my hands, looking at me with his most earnest smile. I'd seen it before. "Everything is going to be okay. Remember, we're lucky to be here. No other country takes care of color alchemists. In fact, no other country even takes care of their people like we do. We're lucky."

I wondered about that. It's what we were told. Again and again, we were shown footage of the rest of the world. Sometime over the last century, everyone but us had practically returned to the Dark Ages. People were starving, crops wouldn't grow, and water was contaminated. It was a dangerous world for most. And that's why we were so lucky to live where we did. To have what we had. We had our New Colony. We had the royals. And we had alchemy.

Maybe Reed had a point.

Once again, I noticed his boyish good looks. It was no wonder that the GC girl, Brooke, and her friends hated me. I was pretty sure Reed was a highly sought-after guy around here. His buttery blond hair and chocolate-brown eyes would attract any girl.

So why don't I like him back?

Something about what he'd said still bothered me. That this system had taken care of me. But that wasn't exactly true. I was here against my will, wasn't I? And yes, I'd been trying to make the best of it, but that still didn't mean I wanted to be here. I *had* to be here. I'd spent the last few weeks suppressing thoughts of ballet and home, but I could feel it eating away at me.

I turned away from Reed, not wanting him to see me cry. But his strong hand turned me to face him as he wiped at my hot tears. *Are you kidding me right now, Jessa? More tears?*

"Sometimes I forget how new you are to all of this. I'm sorry I've been so brash about it."

"I'm not mad at you, Reed," I said, meaning it. "You're one of the only good things about being here." And it was true. He was my friend. Even if he had some backward views about New Colony, that didn't mean he was a bad guy.

There was a look in his eyes that I recognized. Immediately, I realized he was going to kiss me. Sure, he would be a fun guy to date. But I didn't have those feelings. Given everything I'd been through with Lucas, I knew I couldn't do that to Reed. So I looked away, pretending not to notice his intentions.

"Can we talk about something else?" I asked, scooting away from him.

He sighed and nodded. "So what do you want to talk about?"

"Where are you from? I mean, before coming to the palace."

He frowned. "Why does it matter?"

"Well, I don't know. I'm curious. What are your parents like? Do you have siblings?"

"Well, if you must know, that's not the type of thing we're encouraged to talk about here. So I honestly don't think about it much anymore."

"You don't have to tell me if you don't want to."

"It's okay. I don't remember where I'm from. I remember having an older brother. I think his name was Charlie, but I'm not sure. I don't remember my parents' names or faces. Except, my mother was blond, like me. And that's about it."

187

"Do you miss them?"

"I've been here since I was five years old, Jessa. You have to understand, that's not me anymore. Those people? They're not even the ones who raised me. I'm happy to be a guardian. I have a lot of respect for the teachers and mentors who taught me to do what I can. I like my life."

It made sense, but I still felt sad for him. It was disturbing. Families were torn apart so the GC could function the way the officials wanted them to.

"So, what is it you can do with alchemy? Any special talents?" I asked, changing the subject.

He grinned. "All sorts of things. I am especially good with listening. Spying, I guess. I have an affinity for blue, the communication center. And luckily, blue is valuable to us. Not many alchemists can do what I do. Listening is one of the main things I use it for. Here, I'll show you."

He pulled a blue stone from his pocket and held it gently in his palm. I'd noticed recently that a lot of alchemists carried colored stones with them. Now I knew why; it gave them easy access to organic color.

After a few moments, the color started to lift from the rock, leaving the tiniest speck of gray. The blue exploded out. It swirled and shifted around us in a waterfall of light.

And then Reed did something I hadn't seen before. He actually used his other hand to carefully guide the color into a shape. It looked like a cone. Then he pointed it toward the window on the far wall.

"How did you…"

"Everything in time. Put your ear right up to the blue. Hurry, I can't hold this for too long. It's not the easiest alchemy. But it's got to be one of my favorites."

I slowly leaned my ear against the blue cone of floating light, nervous. I felt the color touch my ear; hot and fluid, but dry. Was it going to work on my ear? I didn't want to ruin Reed's plan, so I closed my eyes and concentrated on my hearing. I didn't notice anything at first, but then I started to get something.

Birds chirped, a little girl giggled, and high-heeled shoes clacked across pavement. Then it got louder. The whooshing sound of a car zoomed by. It was so loud now. Like I was standing on a busy street corner myself.

I pulled back, the reminder of normal life stinging. "That's amazing."

Reed nodded, and suddenly what was left of the color flew back into the stone. It was blue like before, but the gray spot was still there. He slipped it back into his pocket.

"All color can be manipulated in different ways to create power. We can use it for just about anything. We're constantly developing new techniques. You'll learn this more and more throughout your training. And once you're GC, you'll get to start helping people."

The idea sent a shiver of excitement through me. Could this be something I wanted? The thought that I could embrace this life startled me. But helping people was definitely a welcomed thought. At the same time, I was doubtful I could pay the price. This place hardened people. I'd yet to see anything that proved to me that the GC actually bettered anyone. Well, except for when Jasmine healed people.

I remembered again that Reed was the one who had helped Faulk listen in on my conversation with Lucas my first night here. But so much had changed between us since then.

And yet, I finally understood something important about Reed. Something I needed to remember. He *lived* to be a guardian. He was as loyal an alchemist as they came. I knew that was why Faulk had assigned him to me. If push came to shove, he'd choose his job, his duty, before our friendship.

"Are you here with me because you want to be here? Or are you here because Faulk wants you to spy on me?"

He shook his head. "We're friends. I want to be here. I really like you."

"But you work for her, don't you?"

"Yes, I do, but that doesn't mean I run and tell her everything you do or say. I thought you knew me better than that."

But there was something about the whole situation that didn't sit well. Sure, he liked me. I knew that he even wanted to date me. But was liking me enough for him to protect me from her?

I peered into him, searching for a genuine emotion, something I could hold onto. He reached out and held my hand. His brown eyes stared into mine, pleading.

I can trust you. I don't know how or why, but I do.

"I'm sorry. I didn't mean to accuse you of anything. You're such a good friend. I trust you, Reed."

"You're right. You can trust me with anything." He paused. "Is there anything you want to tell me?"

As a matter of fact, there *was* something I wanted to tell him. I reached back into my thoughts, trying to remember what it was. I knew it was important. I knew it would help. My mind felt hazy and clouded. I nodded, pulling the tangle of memories to the surface.

Red. That was it. I wanted to tell him about the red. About the blood.

"What is it?"

I opened my mouth, ready...

Lucas's voice flashed through my mind. *Don't tell Reed. Don't tell anyone.*

But why?

It's dangerous.

I shook my mind, trying to clear the confusion. Something was wrong. I needed to figure this out before I lost my line of thought…

Wait, this isn't right. Why are my thoughts so convoluted?

I realized that Reed must be using his alchemy on me. He was trying to get me to speak. Using what? The blue? "Blue is the color of communication," he'd said. Could he communicate his ideas and will to me? Was he doing that now? He must have the ability to become incredibly persuasive when he wants to be. *What a jerk!*

I noticed then that Reed's other hand was in his pocket. I wanted to punch him, to yell and scream and kick him out of my room. Fortunately, my better judgment took over and I decided it was safer to play along. I would pretend he was actually in control.

"I don't know," I said slowly, hoping my voice sounded as airy as it had only moments before. "I don't have any secrets. I just wanted to tell you that I trust you."

"You can tell me what it is. What's your secret?"

"But there's nothing to tell. What's wrong, Reed?"

He cleared his throat, eyeing me. I smiled peacefully, hoping he couldn't sense the wild anger that burned just under the surface. How dare he treat me like this? Had he been manipulating my emotions this whole time?

"I'm sorry. I believe you. I have to go. I'm late for a class. I'll see you later, Jessa." He jumped off the bed and left the room abruptly.

Did he know I'd figured out what he was doing? There was no way to tell. He had to have figured out something was up to take off so fast. Either way, I was in trouble. Lucas was right. I couldn't trust anyone. Even my closest friend here was using me. If I was ever going to see my family again, I would have to find a way out of here myself. But after that experience, I really didn't want to tell anyone about the red. Not if they could use the blue center to do stuff like that... mess with my thoughts and emotions, and even spy on people. It made me shudder to think what they wanted with red...which was the color that signified ultimate power.

I knew then and there that I wouldn't give in. I wouldn't go to Faulk and tell her about the blood. I wouldn't trust Reed. I would do what Lucas asked until I could figure out a way to get out of this place.

FOURTEEN

LUCAS

My confrontation in the greenhouse with Jessa left me in a tangle of mixed emotions. If I became romantically involved with her, I'd lose myself. She brought out the kind of emotions in me that I wanted to keep buried deep. I couldn't allow it. I did the right thing by stopping that kiss, as hard as it was. I could only hope I didn't get pulled in by her again. There was just something about her that made me feel strong and weak all at the same time.

I found myself avoiding her for the next couple days. A few hours after our heated exchange in the greenhouse, I sent a message to her slatebook. I gave her instructions to spend the weekend reading, with a large attachment of historical texts. When she was finished with that, we'd get back to work with Jasmine and Reed. I knew I'd have to move on from green alchemy soon, and that worried me because I still wanted to stay far away from red. Maybe we could work with orange. That would lighten everyone's moods, at least.

I spent my days running or reading. One late afternoon,

when I was at the library, a light knock on the door pulled me out of my most recent Jessa daydream. It was the one I had been having over and over. The one where I kissed her in the greenhouse instead of pulling away.

I jumped out of the desk chair and brushed myself off. *Get a hold of yourself, Lucas.*

I opened the door and found Sasha peering up at me.

"Prince," she said, motioning to the guards standing watch at the door, "can we go somewhere private?"

I looked around, confused. Wasn't the empty library private enough? She moved over to a desk, grabbed a paper and pen, and scribbled: *I don't know who could be listening nearby. Let's go outside.*

I should have seen that coming. Reed always seemed to be lurking nearby these days. I thought back to all I could have possibly said inside these walls that was incriminating. Except for my conversations with Jessa and Sasha, I'd kept everything locked in my head or hidden in my private study. I should be okay.

"Sure, let's get out of here."

■

As soon as we were out of the palace, we walked into a thicket of trees to conceal ourselves. Sasha pulled a nearby blue flower from its roots. The color quickly left it and she maneuvered it into a shield of sorts around us.

"There, now we can talk."

"How did you learn to do that?" I asked.

"I can't seem to master listening in on people, but I have been working hard on creating privacy for years. Lucky for us, I think I got it down."

"And you think people are trying to listen to us?"

"Not entirely. All I know is what my handler told me. Apparently, they got this information off Richard's slatebook directly. They've been looking for more and more blue alchemists. Listening in on conversations? That has to be one of the reason's why."

"Who's your handler, Sasha?"

"You already know that's not up to me to say."

I wanted to push the issue more. I had to protect myself. But I knew Sasha was protecting herself, too.

"Okay, but tell them to make contact soon, or I'm done with this."

She grimaced and nodded. "An assignment is coming for you. Soon. Right now the important thing is that we have your back."

"I sure hope so."

Her smile faded. "Lucas, this is nothing. Things are going to get a lot more intense. Richard started another round of testing."

Another round? In the past he had pulled so much color from the land, that he had killed it. Stripped it down to nothing but gray. But that wasn't the worst part. The worst part was when his alchemists started turning their powers on people. They pulled color from their bodies or pushed mass amounts on them. Most often, it ended in death. I knew it was happening, but I still wasn't sure *why* Richard was doing it. Only a handful of alchemists were involved, *so far*.

"I have a lot at stake here. If I am caught working with you, I don't know what my father will do. We both know what he's capable of. I'll help you, but please don't put me at risk unless you're willing to bring me in on your plans," I said.

"What have we asked you to do that was so risky?"

As if this entire conversation couldn't have us both killed.

I laughed. "Are you serious? Have you forgotten how we met?"

Recognition lit her eyes and she smirked. It wasn't all that long ago that we'd met each other in that dark closet.

"Oh, right. Thank you for that. It's been a world of help to us."

The person who'd informed me about the Resistance had agreed they would help me stop my father. My only condition was that everything must happen nonviolently, to which they had agreed. So far, I still believed them. I'd heard of nothing that would spark my father's suspicion or temper. Which was good news for them, considering that he was the kind of leader who ruthlessly squashed opposition.

"We need to tell Jessa what's really going on."

"We're not sure she's ready."

"She can be trusted." Admittedly, I didn't know if it was the truth, but everything inside me wanted to tell her all my secrets. I was still worried how she would react to the news about red. But if I could tell her who Sasha really was to me, maybe she wouldn't hate me so much. Maybe she'd join our side.

"She can help us," I added.

"Are you sure this isn't about your crush on her?"

"I don't have feelings for her like that." The lie fell flat. "Okay, fine. I don't know what's going to happen there. But I do know we're friends. The point is, she's powerful. It's time we get her on our side."

"Everyone knows she's powerful. The Resistance already knows that. That doesn't mean she could handle the truth yet."

"But what about the red? She used red alchemy again, Sasha. No one's been able to do that before. I can only keep her quiet for so long. What if she gets swayed by Faulk or

196

Reed or someone else?"

"Jessa is not the only one who's ever accessed red."

"Well, I figured as much when you told me what red can do. I'm assuming one of your people figured out how to do it. Or is there something else?"

"One of ours used to. But I came to warn you. We think someone is using red on your mother."

"How can you be sure?"

She bit her lip. "We're *not* sure. But it fits, right? With what you told me."

"You still don't know who it could be?"

She shook her head.

"So you came to tell me that someone is using mind control on my mother, but you have no idea who. And that my father is starting more rounds of testing that will essentially kill innocent people? Great. Anything else?"

Sasha put her hand on mine. "I know it's a lot to take in, Lucas. I'm sorry."

"I feel like I don't even know him. That I never really did."

She sighed. "Well, if it makes you feel any better, I never knew my father, either. Not really."

"How come I don't remember you?" I had thought about it several times, but I couldn't seem to place her anywhere in my childhood, or in the alchemists I encountered.

"I was always really shy. But, anyway, I was moved to another facility when I was still a child. This is the first I've been back here in a very long time."

Another facility for training? I frowned. She must have already been a member of the GC, initiated as a child. That was practically unheard of. Most didn't qualify until their teenage years.

"You're very strong," I said, meaning it.

"So are you."

"I'm sorry you didn't get to have a childhood." We started walking back to the palace, the blue sound-shielding magic now dropped.

"Don't be sorry. It's not your fault. And anyway, I barely remember my birth family. It's all in the past now."

"Like I said, you've become strong." I admired her attitude. But still, I felt sorry for her. There was something underneath her demeanor today, a hidden pain that was just now coming to the surface. It actually made her prettier. More human and less mysterious.

"You want to know what was hard for me?" she asked, stopping. "It was where I was placed as a child. I was sent up north, Lucas. I saw it for myself, what they're doing out there. I participated."

I couldn't understand how my father managed to keep something so big hidden from the people. More alchemy? Just the very fact that it had been kept quiet, that there weren't massive protests and rebellions, was perplexing. That must have had something to do with red. How else could he control that?

"It was you who used the red, wasn't it?" It wasn't an accusation. If she had been up there as a child, there must have been a solid reason.

A single tear rolled down her cheek, a silent answer to my question.

"Lucky for me, that…talent…is gone now. It disappeared when I got older. I think I repressed it somehow. Please, don't say anything. Trust me, I learned my lesson. I can't use red anymore, and I need to make sure that nobody else ever does."

■

Dinner with my parents was mandatory. It was also incredibly unbearable. Tonight was another one for the books.

For the first ten minutes, my mother and I waited at the table for Richard. She sat silently, picking away at her measly plate of food and rubbing her head. Then Richard joined us and spent the next twenty minutes discussing strategies with his advisors. They stood in the back of the room while he ate a huge plate of roasted lamb, sweet potatoes, and freshly baked bread.

What bothered me was that I was expected to be here, to sit and listen and only speak when spoken to. I was eighteen years old, but they still treated me like an insolent child. It was called "being supportive," or at least that was what my mother had begun to say in recent years. Richard was happy to have me add something to the discussions *only* when asked.

Tonight, the topic of discussion was about lending more resources to the southern region of New Colony. Spring storms had been exceptionally bad this year and had damaged most of the local crops.

"Whom do we have stationed out there?" he asked. "Anyone good?"

"Sir, the only healing alchemists there aren't capable of handling that many crops," Royal Officer Thomas said, scrolling through a slatebook as he looked up the information. "We'll have to rush someone down there right away."

"Should we send Jasmine?" I interjected. "She's the best healer we've got. I've seen her work during our trainings with Jessa. She's impeccable. She could heal those crops. I'd be happy to go with her." I felt excited at the idea of being able to do something useful. I knew it was one of the poorer areas of the kingdom, and they'd need our support.

"That's not a possibility," Richard said, taking a large bite of food and slowly chewing. "We need her here."

Thomas paused. I was sure he was going to agree with me. Maybe he could convince Richard. Thomas had been with us for years, and there was a chance he could get through to my father. Those people needed Jasmine's help. After a moment, Thomas kept scrolling through a list, rattling off other names as possibilities. No one could do what Jasmine could do. We all knew that.

Am I the only one who will stand up to Richard?

"Why is she needed here?" I asked, but he just ignored me. I already knew the answer. He kept Jasmine around as a precaution. She was our own personal insurance policy. Not only had she healed many people—she'd healed the worst of the worst. She had the capacity to fix injuries that there was no coming back from. He didn't want her away, just in case he needed her for himself. He could argue that he kept her around for Natasha, but I was convinced that my mother was hardly a priority.

"Hundreds of people will be without jobs in that area. Thousands will be affected by the food shortage. You know that's not how New Colony operates. We always take care of our people. I'm sure we can spare Jasmine for a few days. She's the only one with enough talent to be able to fix this quickly."

"That's enough," my father bellowed, putting down his fork and wiping his face with his linen napkin. "Don't argue with me, Lucas. It isn't your place." He got up from the table, kissed my mother on her cheek, and left in a flash. The advisors and royal officers scurried out behind him. The room fell silent.

"Why is he like that?" I asked my mother.

"You and your father are so different, Lucas. Don't try to

understand him, because you never will. Just support him. That's all we ask."

I laughed. She expected me to sit back and allow his choices to let an entire geographical region of his country go hungry? No way.

"I should support him even when he's wrong?"

"You'll have your turn. He's been giving you a lot of responsibility lately. Be grateful. Don't ruin your chance to make him proud."

"Are you angry at him or me?"

"I'm not angry," she said, her pale face turning blotchy. She rubbed her temples and closed her eyes. Had someone recently gotten to her mind again?

"The old you would *never* have stood for this."

"Please, Lucas. I'm doing the best I can. I'll talk to him, okay? I'll see what I can do."

I nodded, knowing it was all I was going to get. I didn't know where to go from here. I thought about questioning her headaches, but thought better of it. She never seemed to have an answer. So I changed the subject to one I knew she relished; my love life. "You know I've been dating that alchemist Sasha for a few weeks now, right?" I said, plopping a piece of bread into my mouth.

She eyed me warily. "Oh, Lucas, I hope it's not serious. She's hardly the stuff of royalty, being an alchemist and all. Though she is lovely."

There was nothing mean-spirited about the way she said it. In her mind, she was merely stating the facts. I laughed. Apparently, her candor hadn't gone away. "All right, then. What *is* the stuff of royalty?"

She flashed me a genuine smile.

"You surprise me, Lucas. I hardly thought we'd be having this conversation already. Eighteen is old enough, I suppose, but far younger than I thought for you. You've always been so independent."

"What do you mean…having what conversation?" I asked, teasing.

"The one where you are already thinking about your future queen."

I burst out with laughter. "Don't worry, Mother. I'm not planning on getting married anytime soon. Can't a guy date around here?"

"Well, you brought up the alchemist girlfriend. Not me."

"What's so wrong about alchemists marrying royals?"

"The color guardians are not meant for leadership. They're unpredictable and dangerous. Not to mention, what they do is unnatural. We can't give them any more power than they already have."

"*Unnatural*?" I asked. I'd always thought the opposite. Had my mother always felt this way? I had never known her to be cold. Something about her tone bothered me. She sounded like a puppet, mimicking the ideas of my father. Or was it someone else?

"Anyone with that much power needs to be controlled, darling. We can't have them running the country. They're not royals. They couldn't be trusted to do both jobs. I'm sure you agree." She returned to her meal.

I'd been around plenty of alchemists throughout my life. Sure, they could be dangerous. But they weren't the ones abusing power. How could she not see what I saw? It was Richard, her husband, who needed to be kept in check.

We finished our dinner in the usual silence.

"Excuse me," I said, getting up from the dinner table. I needed to find Sasha and convince her to get Jessa on our side immediately. And if she wasn't going to agree, then I would have to do what I thought was best without her support. I strode from the dining room, cool and collected, ignoring the hollow knot in my stomach.

■

Sasha was in one of the guardian training rooms. A small crowd of young recruits were busy practicing with some plants.

"Hello, Boyfriend," Sasha said when she saw me, mockingly batting her eyelashes and fanning her face. A gaggle of preteen girls erupted in laughter at her antics.

The whole training room was crowded, but mainly with young kids. Still, I needed to talk to her privately. The palace had been busy all day, and the gardens were especially teeming with people. They were preparing for some political brunch that would be taking place the next morning. I was sure I'd be expected to attend it, whatever it was.

"We need to talk privately." I pulled her into a hug and whispered in her ear. "The gardens are out of commission right now. Where can we go?"

"You tell me. This is your house, isn't it?"

That gave me an idea. I'd always made it a point to take my girlfriends to other areas of the palace or even out into the city. But I had never taken someone to our private living quarters.

I knew my father. Despite his ruthless tactics, he was proud to a fault. Very few people were allowed to go into our wing of the palace. He liked his privacy. There was no way he'd allow any spies in his own home. It was the one place that was nearly always empty. Because that was what our area of the palace was: our home.

I took Sasha's hand, knowing if we were going back there, for all intents and purposes, it had to look like we were up to something more predictable than plotting against my father.

We headed out of the training room, several watchful eyes following us. A few older girls glared at her and turned to whisper to each other. Sasha didn't care about that. In fact, it was probably better for our cover.

"Where are we going?" Sasha played right along and squeezed my hand. Then she weaved her fingers into mine and giggled, kissing my cheek.

I laughed and raised my voice, "Somewhere we can be alone."

We continued through the GC areas and out into the main corridor of the palace. It took us ten minutes to walk from that side of the palace to the other. All along the way, people stared at our unabashed public display of affection. I was used to nosy stares. I didn't let it bother me.

I could admit to having a reputation with women in the past, but my relationships had always been fleeting. I'd never found any one girl to be interesting enough to actually want to be with her for more than a few dates. And anyway, everyone knew that despite being the most eligible bachelor in New Colony, there were very few women who would ever be permitted to seriously date me. I was "Prince Lucas," and not even I could change that.

I suspected that my parents put up with my antics because they assumed, in the end, that they'd be the one to choose my queen. And even though I didn't want to be forced to marry for Richard's political gain, a big part of me was sure that one day, he'd find a way to make it happen.

When we reached the set of large wrought-iron doors, flanked on either side by palace guards, I caught a glance at Sasha. She was pale, and her hands were shaking. For her, this was probably like walking into enemy territory.

"There aren't listening ears in here," I whispered.

She straightened up and walked through heavy doors and into my home.

There was no modern design here. And it wasn't classically southern like most of the original palace architecture. Our area was still grand, but different. My mother had decorated it with a much cozier feel.

"Wow, so this is home, then?" Sasha was busy eyeing all the closed doors.

"Is he here?"

"No, he's rarely here. He spends his time working in other offices."

"What about your mother?"

"Natasha is already in bed." I pointed to the closed door at the end of a long hallway. "She won't come out before morning."

"No one knows we're here?"

"He might spy on my mother and me. But there are some places that even he wouldn't invade. Not here. Not his own house."

I took her hand and led her directly to his private study.

The door was locked, as usual. But it was an old lock and an old door. And there were no palace guards allowed in here. Or alchemists.

"You'll have to open that. Is that going to be a problem?" I knew there were multiple ways alchemy could open a locked door.

"I'm not getting caught breaking in there."

What she didn't know was that although Richard probably kept a few things in this office, there were no documents or anything else centered around national security. I would know. I'd broken in at least a dozen times over the years, looking for information.

I pondered Sasha's presence in the palace. Her small,

curvy build and long blond hair were enough to give anyone the illusion that she was just another carefree, beautiful girl. But I knew differently. Why would she be afraid of breaking a lock?

She must've read my expression. "I don't want to risk the mission. Maybe you won't get in trouble for getting caught in there, but I will."

She was right. "Well, since my study hasn't been swept for bugs, that only leaves us one other option for privacy. We'll have to go talk in my bedroom."

She followed me down the hallway and into my most private space.

FIFTEEN

JESSA

I was avoiding everyone, especially staying clear of Lucas and Reed. The best way to manage that was to hide out in my boring room. I couldn't stop thinking about the night before when I'd attempted, unsuccessfully, to fall asleep. A thought kept surfacing in that dramatic "this is really important and you won't sleep all night until you fix this" kind of way.

You're acting suspicious.

And it was the truth. Ever since Reed had tried to manipulate my emotions with blue alchemy, I'd been avoiding him. Why shouldn't I? He pretended to be my friend, spent weeks hanging out with me, all in order to use alchemy on me, against my will, to see if I would reveal my secrets. I was sure now that he was reporting everything back to Faulk. I knew I should have told Lucas and apologized for not having believed him in the first place, but I couldn't bring myself to go looking for him. Not after our second almost-kiss and the feelings of rejection that had left a bitter aftertaste.

So I decided to get over myself and go find Reed. Maybe

if I acted normally, he wouldn't worry about me. Or maybe I should just confront him?

"Hey, Reed!" I called out, running to meet him in one of the GC hallways. "What's going on?"

"Hi, Jessa." His voice faltered. "I was just going to spar for a little bit. Do you want to watch?"

He nodded toward the gymnasium, just behind a large sheet of thick glass. There were black mats lining the floor. Most had a pair of guardians on them, fighting. Maybe it was kickboxing, wrestling, or, as Reed had called it, sparring, but all I saw was fighting. Combat.

This was so foreign to me.

"Sure, sounds fun." I smiled, forcing myself to follow his muscled form into the gym.

As we walked in, I immediately noticed there was another area in the space that I hadn't seen through the glass, filled with shiny exercise equipment. Almost every machine had a person utilizing it. Treadmills and weight-lifting machines were lined in neat rows.

The entire space was loud and buzzing with adrenaline.

Sure, it made sense that the royals would want the alchemists to be strong and healthy. But this was something else. These people were beyond athletic—they were machines.

My jaw must have been hanging open as I watched the pairs of people, because Reed reached out and actually pushed my mouth shut, laughing to himself. "Okay, so you can kick butt. Note taken."

"It's part of guardian training. Royal officers, too." He pointed to some of the people in white clothing. "And all the recruits. You'll be in here soon enough."

So they were *all* lethal. I wondered if guardians ever fought with color, but I was too afraid to ask. I think I had a pretty good idea of the answer already.

"You ready?" a girl purred from behind us. I turned and recognized Brooke, the one who'd been rude to me at my introduction party. She smirked when she saw me. "Do you want to play, too?"

"I don't think Jessa came to fight."

"Too bad." She rolled her eyes at me.

I stepped back as Reed pulled her out onto the closest mat. They stood apart for a moment before she dived for him, and they ended up wrestling. Something about the whole exchange didn't feel right. They were definitely fighting. He knocked her head against the floor hard, and she retaliated with a kick to his jaw. But despite the pain, it seemed like they were enjoying themselves way too much. The way they moved was almost sexual, but in a way that made my skin crawl. And when Brooke looked up at me and winked before wrapping her legs around his torso, I had to turn away.

I didn't know what to think. But something about watching them, about this huge gymnasium and the GC headquarters in general, felt wrong. I didn't want to be there anymore, so I left, hoping the short conversation with Reed was enough to keep him satisfied for a while. Maybe just coming down here would throw his suspicions to the back of his mind for now.

As I made my way back toward the sanctuary of my bedroom, I noticed a familiar face and stopped short. "Eliza!"

She slowly turned, before stepping back.

"Miss Loxley, how are you?"

"I'm fine. Eliza, how are you? I've wanted to talk to you ever since the accident. I need you to know how sorry I am."

She just stared at me for a moment and nodded before looking away. She took another step back, and I noticed that her hands were shaking. Guilt plunged through me. "Really,

I am sorry. Are you feeling better?"

"I'm fine, miss. Just busy working."

She'd been transferred somewhere else, I guessed, and was no longer working with alchemists. I assumed I had somehow gotten her into trouble, but I realized now that maybe she'd asked to be moved. And that was my fault. "How's your mother doing?"

"Jessa, I really don't want to talk to you about my mother. I already told you I could be in trouble for that. And to be honest, I really don't want anything to do with you."

Of course she hated me. I'd almost killed her.

"Oh, okay," I frowned. "I'll leave you alone, then."

She nodded and scurried off. Another maid joined her as they walked down the hallway, whispering to each other. I didn't recognize the other woman, who turned back to me with a snarky glare.

And then, just like that, they rounded a corner and disappeared.

I continued down the hall, bothered by everything. Why did I have to be here? This wasn't the life I wanted. I was on track to living my dreams before the alchemy surfaced. Wasn't there a way to shut it all off? Lucas had assured me there wasn't, and from what I could tell, no one else was developing anything like that. Maybe I could find a way to do it, but as it stood, I still felt clueless every day I spent in training. I was such a newbie!

And as much as I pretended it didn't bother me, it really hurt to be treated like an outcast. The other alchemists hated me. I wasn't yet in with them, no GC initiation plans to speak of. Not that I even knew what that meant. But I was invading their training rooms daily. Lucas and Jasmine gave me special treatment, Richard had made it clear I was "chosen" and Reed was Faulk's little spy. I clearly didn't belong.

Maybe it wouldn't be so hard if I could just have contact with my family.

Just then, I spotted Faulk stalking around the corner with her royal officer, Thomas. I was pretty sure he was second in command. Could I convince them to let me have a call home? I still hadn't said a word to Faulk about the blood situation, and I wasn't going to. Not yet, anyway. As much as he infuriated me, I felt like Lucas was telling me the truth. I needed to keep my mouth shut.

Just as I was about to catch up to them, I stopped short at the mention of a familiar name: *Lacey*. They had turned the corner now and couldn't see me. But I could hear their every word.

"You've had eyes on the Loxley house?" Faulk asked.

"Yes, constantly. I don't know how it happened."

There was a long pause.

"They were acting normal enough. Going to work, sending the girl to school. Anytime we questioned them, they answered everything," Thomas said.

"But this wasn't the first time. I should have known better than to let them continue on like that. Like they aren't criminals, hiding alchemists from us. It was only a matter of time."

"So you think Lacey is an alchemist then?"

Another long pause.

If they think Lacey is an alchemist, they'll take her. She'll become part of this twisted system. And my parents? They'll be destroyed.

"What do you want us to do?" Thomas asked.

Please don't bring her in.

"Don't you think we're a little late to the party, Thomas?" Faulk spat.

The next thing I knew, they rounded the corner, practically

running me over. There was no use in hiding I'd overheard them. "What's going on? Is everything okay with Lacey?"

"Lacey isn't your concern right now," Faulk said.

"She's my little sister. I have every right to be concerned."

"Did you already forget about our little deal? When you produce red alchemy, then you'll have contact with your family."

Thomas stepped back, peering at Faulk as if confused. What did he know that I didn't?

"So," Faulk continued, "do you have red or not?"

I wanted to tell her the truth. I wanted my family and speaking up would do that. But, until I knew what red did, I couldn't risk it. I shook my head.

"That's what I thought. Don't worry about your family. Worry about your job as an alchemist."

She brushed past me, heading for her office. Thomas shuffled after her, only once peering back at me. He shrugged and mouthed, "Sorry." I could tell he felt bad for me, but not bad enough to actually do anything about it. He may be the nicest royal officer around here, but he was still under Faulk's command.

Why did she have to be so horrible? The royal officers would get more done if they didn't treat the guardians like such criminals. Yes, guardians got to do some cool magic. Yes, they got to live in the palace. But at what cost? Was I the only one who saw the flaws with the system?

I couldn't take it anymore. I hurried back to my room to be alone. It was my only sanctuary. What would it feel like when I had officially moved into the GC wing? I didn't want to think about how hard that would be.

After Reed showed me blue alchemy, how he had used it to create a listening device, I'd been trying to do the same thing in private. I had stolen a blue stone from one of the classrooms a few days ago. But so far, I'd had no luck getting blue to do much of anything. I didn't know what I was planning. But I hoped to figure out some way to get in touch with my family. I still wanted to find a way to go home, but for now, communication would be better than nothing.

I originally believed blue to be a harmless color. But the alchemy Reed used it for wasn't innocent, prying into my emotions like that. At least he hadn't tried anything more—that I knew of.

I sat on my bed, holding the stone. Again, I wondered if I could access the blue to speak with my parents. Was that possible? After my run in with Faulk, now more than ever, I needed to talk to them. I looked back at the stone. I didn't want to think too hard. *Just start small.*

I allowed myself to relax and focus on the stone.

Who do you think you are? You can't do this.

Yes, the calm voice within me responded. *Yes, you can.*

And just like that, I did it.

The color exploded around me. Blue swirled through the room in ribbons of brilliant light. Tentatively, I reached out, hoping I could mold it the way Reed had shown me. But when I touched it, it spun away from me, like ink in water.

I tried again. Still, it seeped away from me in chaotic swirls. I didn't understand. Why wouldn't the blue do what I wanted? So far I could access green, orange, and even red. What was so hard about blue?

You will be able to figure it out if you practice.

If there was anything I'd learned from all those years of dancing, it was that practice and hard work paid off.

But for how long? It took you years to master ballet.

I reached again, and the color darted away in a flash. I couldn't even get close. A prickle of frustration bubbled into my chest. *Why am I even here?* My true place wasn't with these people. They only wanted to use me. I was meant to be at home with my family. I was meant to be a ballerina. The anger raged inside as I threw the stone across the room. It hit the wall with a ping and dropped to the floor. Suddenly, the room was normal again.

Maybe I shouldn't be so upset, but I couldn't help it. Jasmine had told me that not every alchemist could manipulate every color. That must be why red wasn't something others could tap into. It seemed so strange to me that Reed could control blue, and I could control red. Maybe we just had different talents.

Fatigue washed over me. I lay down on the bed, realizing that the attempted alchemy had taken an enormous amount of energy. All I could think about was sleep. I started to drift away, my eyes getting heavier by the second. A thought tried to push its way through…something about the red blood and about how I had felt the times I had turned it gray. Was that important? But just before I could formulate a clear thought, sleep swiftly took me away.

■

Their faces are ghosts. I know they are there, but I can't see them beyond the darkness. The hot lights blind me. Floating purple orbs fill the horizon. I blink rapidly, trying to clear my vision. The oxygen moves quickly in and out of my lungs, like a smooth stone skipping violently across water.

It is quiet, and the rush of blood and adrenaline swishes through my ears. A drop of sweat runs down my back, tickling my spine. Instinctively, I straighten a bit more as I take my position. The music chimes to life, and with it, I begin to dance.

I fly effortlessly across the smooth stage, creating a beautiful story with my body while the delicate melody meets me. Each movement is soft yet precise. Calculated. Studied. Natural. From the tips of my loose fingers to the strength of my pointed toes, I am in complete control.

The dance is the best of my career, validating my position as a prima ballerina. And with every effortless step, I fill with pride. The music builds to a crescendo and I leap high, my legs extended and powerful. Falling into a crouch, I complete the performance as I fall to the floor. I pant with exhilaration.

There is a pause before the audience erupts with applause. I can't help but smile widely. Catching my breath, I stand and curtsy, looking out into the crowd. I want to see their faces. I want to know them. Somewhere in the distance, over the roar of applause, someone is chanting my name: "Jessa! Jessa!"

I search for them, a prick of familiarity burning at my memory. The voice is young.

Lacey appears on the stage. My little sister is wearing a simple white dress. Her dark blond hair curls sweetly around her small face. As she steps forward, the crowd continues applauding, oblivious.

I try to run to her, but my knees buckle, and I slip. Falling at her feet, I look up. I try to speak, but no words come out. All I want to do is hug her. To get to her, somehow. But my body won't move.

Lacey smiles. A drop of crimson falls from the corner of her mouth. She holds out her hands, and I watch, horrified, as rivers of blood flow from her palms. The moment stills as drops hit the floor, thick and heavy.

I reach out, urging my body forward. I will myself to get up. To help her. But it's as if I am moving through quicksand. It's like she is behind a wall of glass. The audience continues their cheering, louder now. Maddening. Don't they see her?

Lacey falls to the floor, and the blood continues to pour from her mouth. Her eyes flutter and roll into the back of her head *as her complexion pales. Can't I fix this? Can't I heal her? I'm screaming in my head, desperate to hear myself over the noise.*

She starts choking on her own blood then. Straining to get air that just won't come. Dying under the heaviness. Someone needs to help her. I need to help her.

Something shifts in the audience. They are laughing. A chorus of cackling hysterics drowns my senses.

Lacey abruptly sits up. Her thin torso is perfectly straight. "Help me!"

■

"No!" The scream erupted as I flew out of bed.

Where's Lacey? She needs my help.

My heart pounded in my chest. My throat prickled. I shook my head, trying to clear the terror as I realized it was only a nightmare.

I stumbled out around the room to find a water bottle. I walked over to the window and looked at the dark sky outside, chugging the room-temperature water. Then I checked the red numbers on the bedside alarm clock. They blinked glaringly: 02:18. 02:18. 02:18. 02:19.

The alchemy I'd tried before falling asleep pushed through my mind. It seemed like something had happened, but I wasn't sure why I couldn't touch the blue. The amount of energy I'd used knocked me out for part of the night. Why?

I yawned and lay back in the large bed. But my eyes didn't want to close, so instead I stared at the dark ceiling, trying to make out the features of the room. I registered the door to the bathroom and the door to the hallway, where undoubtedly, there were two palace guards. Even if they'd heard me screaming, they hadn't bothered to check on me.

I closed my eyes, but the image of Lacey in the bloody

216

white dress appeared. The fear of the dream rushed back through my body.

This was about the day Lacey had fallen from the swing. It hadn't been as dramatic as my nightmare, but the fall had definitely been impactful. Blood had streamed from her palms and mouth after she landed in the gravel. I must have used red alchemy on her blood when I tried to help her. But that didn't heal her. She'd passed out and ended up in the hospital. So what had I done? Had I used the red for something else without realizing it?

It was maddening to feel like the answer was right in front of me, but I just couldn't wrap my mind around it. Not yet, anyway. What had Lacey said in the dream? *Help me.* Did she really want me to help her? And how could I do that if I was stuck here? The very fact that I had neither heard from nor seen my family in weeks was killing me! I doubted I could trust Faulk. The conversation between Thomas and her made me nervous. Plus, if she was truly trustworthy, Reed wouldn't have manipulated me. I was sure he'd been trying to get me to talk about the red. I'd been ignoring what I knew deep in my gut. I couldn't deny it any longer. Lacey was in trouble. That dream was an omen—I was absolutely sure of it. I knew with every fiber in my being that I couldn't stay here any longer. Especially after hearing Faulk and Thomas earlier today. I had to find Lacey.

I knew what I needed to do.

I stood up and walked to the tall window again. I assumed it was locked from the outside, just like everything else in this room. But what if it wasn't?

I wrapped the tips of my fingers under the rim of the windowsill and lifted. The window slid open easily, and a warm summer wind danced through the room, brushing my tangled hair out of my face. I peered out at the dark night. It waited for me. The lights of the capital city loomed just beyond the palace garden wall, beckoning. Reaching out to me.

I stood peering down from the third floor. Below me in the darkness, the edge of the palace intersected with the hard manicured lawn. Something had been slowly formulating in my mind for weeks now. Something so completely crazy, so reckless, that I'd tucked it away in the back of my mind. *But what if it works?* Before I could talk myself out of it, I lifted myself onto the window frame and jumped.

SIXTEEN

LUCAS

My bedroom was one of the few places I had to myself. Sasha slowly walked around it, taking in everything that was mine. She peered at a row of black and white photographs on one wall before turning back to me. The photos held various stages of my growth. Pictures of my childhood and more recent ones too. Behind her, the darkness waded through the large window. "You're sure it's safe in here?"

"Privacy is everything to my father. And to me. No one is listening."

"I hope you're right. What did you want to talk about?"

I sat on the edge of the bed. Sasha tilted her head and bit her bottom lip, staring at me.

"We need to talk about Jessa."

"Have you really told us everything you know about her?" Sasha asked. "Something is…missing."

Francesca Loxley, I thought, but just shrugged instead.

By "us," I knew she meant the Resistance, but it wasn't like I'd met more than two of its members. The gardener woman had been the one to convince me to join them. But she vanished after Sasha showed up, and I never got so much as a name. What about the rest of them? I wanted to meet someone higher up in the organization.

"You're right, something is missing. It's about time you take me to meet some of your leaders. I can't go down this path with you much longer. You already know that."

"Okay. I'll talk to them. I know you're right. But hey, at least you know we're serious about nonviolence. We haven't hurt anyone yet, have we?"

"But once I'm firmly on your side, how do I know you won't assassinate Richard? Then I'll become king, and you could essentially try to control me."

There it was.

Sasha stared at me for a moment, and then she laughed. "Lucas, I'm sorry to burst your bubble, but it's not like that. First of all, we don't want a king. Period. Not even you. We want democracy back. Second, you would probably become a talking head, but things would continue as they always have. It's the whole organization of the GC that needs change. And worse—the people would turn against us, in retaliation for their beloved king. Richard has enemies, but not enough. No one knows what he's really doing, do they? We're not going to kill your father."

"Okay, fine," I said. "What do you need to know about Jessa?"

"What else do you know about her?" she asked. "Is there anything we should know? Anything she's hiding? Or anything your father is hiding?"

"I know that she's ready for the truth. That's what I know."

Yes, there was more. Maybe Jessa had an older sister who was once a member of the GC. Maybe her parents knew more about color alchemy than we'd suspected. But that was information I wanted to keep to myself for now. I trusted Jessa. I didn't think she knew about any of those things. And I'd already let the Resistance in on the information about her red. That should be the only thing that mattered, anyway.

"All right, well, I've been told we need to get Jessa on our side. So I guess someone agrees with you," Sasha said.

"So what's the plan? How are you going to get her to listen to you?"

"Have you made contact with the Loxley family?"

The realization of my mistake came at me, sharp and sudden. After my last conversation with Jessa a few days ago, I had meant to reach out to her family. I'd wanted to make sure they were okay. Maybe I couldn't give Jessa everything she wanted, but that was something I should have done. She deserved to know about their situation. But I forgot. When she'd come to me about it, I'd pushed her away and had been avoiding her ever since.

How could I have been so careless?

"Did something happen to them?" I asked.

I tried not to picture them in prison, or worse, but the images burned into my mind anyway. Jessa loved her family above all else. How would she handle something like this?

"They're safe."

"The Resistance has them?"

"Yes. We extracted them a couple days ago. New Colony officials have no clue of their whereabouts. Believe me, Faulk isn't happy. It won't be long before Jessa gets questioned again."

"What are you going to do with them?"

"We want to work with the young one, Lacey. To see if she has any alchemy abilities, too. It's very likely that Jessa's powers run in her family. But the parents aren't cooperating. They don't want any of our alchemists near the little girl.

They're confused, to say the least."

They asked for the parents' permission?

That would never happen here. People were forced to give their kids up to the GC. They were not asked. That fact alone relaxed me. Maybe the Loxley family was in good hands, after all.

"So you want Jessa to talk to them?" I asked, putting it all together. This must be why they decided to let her in. If the Loxleys weren't open to the idea of Lacey being tested for color alchemy, then maybe Jessa could talk them into it.

"Exactly," Sasha said.

It wasn't such a bad idea. But it was risky. I couldn't even begin to imagine the logistics of getting Jessa in contact with her family without Faulk noticing. Not to mention, now that the Loxley family was MIA, I was certain Faulk was keeping an even closer eye on Jessa. Of course, no one had said a word to me or Jessa about any of this. Faulk must have decided to pretend the Loxleys were still under her control.

"How are you going to pull this off?"

She sat down next to me and frowned. "We need your help. Your father has been communicating in emails that he wants to take Jessa out of the palace for field training. He wants to see what she's capable of."

"Where?" I asked, afraid that I already knew.

"Not north, though I'm sure that's only a matter of time. He won't be patient for much longer."

I hoped we still had time.

"So how does this help us?"

"You're overseeing her training, right? You can ask to take her there. Make it seem like your idea. First thing tomorrow, go to the king. Request that I come with you. We'll be making contact with the Resistance while we're gone."

It sounded reasonable, but I knew there was more to it

than just this simple plan. It was too easy. Too convenient.

"Won't Faulk be coming? What about Reed? And Jasmine has been a part of her training too, perhaps the biggest part. She'll want to come but my father seems to want Jasmine here."

Sasha studied me, as if she suspected I was going to say something more. "I'm sure the whole gang can come along. If not, we'll just have to figure it out. Don't worry, I'll take care of that."

"We can't get caught," I said, stating the obvious.

"You think I don't know that? Don't forget my life is on the line too."

I knew she was right. I still didn't know too much about this mysterious woman. She had revealed that she could use red alchemy as a child, but it seemed that it had disappeared. But then what? Maybe when she grew out of it, the royal officers let it go. It was true that alchemists' powers could change over time. But other than that, Sasha was not exactly an open book.

She put her hand on mine, rubbing her thumb gently along my knuckles. Without meaning to, I became acutely aware of where we were. My bedroom.

What is going on between us, anyway?

"How long do you want to keep this cover of ours going? Because I think it's working."

"Why do you ask?"

"It's been fun. We know there are no real expectations between us, so there's none of the pressure that goes along with actually dating someone."

I knew what she meant. Most girls seemed like they all had the same goal in mind. The same eye-on-the-prize mentality. What would start out as fun would soon turn into hints of marriage. Talks about "our future." So I'd learned to always end things before it ever got further than a few dates. But still, some girls went in with that attitude from the very beginning. And how was that fair to me? I wanted to see what my possibilities were. I wanted to be a normal eighteen-year-old. Everyone assumed I was looking for a princess. I really wasn't.

She understands. There's nothing between us.

"I agree, it has been fun," I replied.

It didn't hurt that Sasha was gorgeous and sophisticated. And she was easy to talk to. That was what I liked about her the most. She had inadvertently become my first true female friend since I'd matured.

"So we agree?" she said. "That's all you want? To have fun?"

When she put it that way, I knew it wasn't all I wanted in a relationship. But it was all I wanted *from her*. I was happy to have her as an ally and a friend. That was all.

My mind shot to Jessa and that electric spark that was building between us. I thought of her sweetness and her innocence, her fire and her endearing uncertainty. Her smile... And the way she'd trusted me when I couldn't tell her what she needed to hear—that felt good. All those things had added up to something more powerful than the show Sasha and I had been putting on over the last month.

"Actually, I want more." With Jessa, I wanted more.

"Me too."

Sasha's mouth crashed against mine, hands encircled my neck. She grabbed my hair and pulled me against her. In another breath, she was sitting on my lap. My thoughts instantly went murky. At that point, I was kissing her back. I ran my hands down the curve of her back. My body tensed as my fingers gripped the warmth of her skin. She sat back for a moment and smiled sheepishly. A curtain of blond hair brushed my face.

And then I remembered what I was going to say to her before we'd started this. I cared about Jessa too much to continue with Sasha. Jessa brought something out in me I couldn't explain. She made me want to be a better man. Actually, she made me want to be a man, to grow up, to be mature for once in my life. I knew that if I continued to kiss Sasha, I'd lose Jessa.

That can't happen.

I gently pushed Sasha off of me. Her cheeks flushed.

"I'm sorry," I said, not wanting to look at her. If I saw that seductive gleam in her eye again, I might lose my cool. She was undeniably beautiful. And the old me would have gladly jumped at the chance. But I'd changed over this last month, without even realizing what was happening. I'd grown up.

"What's wrong?" Sasha said combing her fingers through her thick hair. "If you don't want more, if you just want to have fun, I'm pretty sure we can manage that, too."

"It's not that."

"Well, then if you want to make this relationship something real, you already know how I feel about that too. No hiding it now."

Sasha inched closer and wrapped her arms around my neck, glowing with determination. "I want what you want."

I was pretty sure if she knew what I wanted, or rather, *who* I wanted, she wouldn't be smiling anymore.

"We can't have a relationship. Not even a fake one. And definitely not a real one. Whatever is going on here needs to stop. I'm sorry."

"Why?"

Should I tell her?

"Is this about Jessa?" She guessed.

I shrugged, not ready to admit it to her out loud. I had

barely admitted my feelings to myself. I didn't know how to put them into words.

Sasha stepped back and did the last thing I expected. She laughed.

"What's so funny?"

"You're so transparent. Do you know that?"

I didn't know how to answer. Was I that obvious? She'd caught us almost kissing that night in the garden. How could I forget?

"You're not mad?" I asked.

She shook her head and shrugged. "Maybe a little disappointed, but I'll live. I've got plenty of options." She said it with such confidence that I wondered if she was deflecting. I didn't want to question that. I didn't want to hurt her.

"So, what are you going to do about Jessa?" She asked.

"I don't know. Maybe nothing."

There was nothing I *could* do. Jessa was still so young. She was only sixteen and hadn't lost that glow of innocence yet. And I was overseeing her training. If we got close, I knew I would lose my judgment. And if Faulk or my father found out, they wouldn't trust me with her training anymore. They could separate us.

Sasha shook her head. "If you say so."

"Are we okay?"

"We're fine. But let's lay off the kissing for a while, okay? It's getting late. I'm beat. Can you walk me out?"

I thought about that for a minute and wondered if I was ready to let the cover we'd created with our relationship die so early. As much as I wanted Jessa, I wasn't going to pursue her. I couldn't. And as much as I hated to admit it, I needed Sasha's help. Would she be upset if we played our game without any of my feelings getting involved? Without kissing?

"So, are we supposed to break up now?" I asked.

"Well, we could keep the façade going if you want. But I'm seriously not going around kissing a guy who has the hots for someone else. I'm not that pathetic. Sorry."

I felt a twinge of guilt. She was right. She deserved better.

"You could spend the night." My face burned at the implications of those words, especially in the context of what we'd nearly done. "I mean, not to do anything with me," I quickly added. "But to give the impression that we've gotten closer. Maybe we could just hold hands in public, and you could sleep here every once in a while to keep this going. And in here, we're safe to talk about what we need to."

"It's not a bad idea, actually. But don't try anything."

I nodded. But was Sasha really okay with this? On the one hand, she was laughing about our situation. But on the other hand, her ego was obviously bruised. I watched as she took her socks and shoes off and walked over to the bed. She lifted the heavy black comforter and climbed inside.

"Coming, honey?" she asked sarcastically.

Deciding I didn't want to make her any more uncomfortable than I already had, I grabbed one of the pillows and tossed it on the floor. "I'll sleep down here."

She just looked at me for a long moment before rolling onto her side with her back to me. I lay down on the hardwood floor with only the pillow for comfort.

That night, my thoughts spun circles in my head. I stared into the ceiling. I questioned, not for the first time, what I was doing here. Why did I have such a complicated life? Who was hurting my mother and why? It was something I thought about often. When Sasha had explained what red did, I knew that had to be what was happening to my mother. They were controlling her mind and wiping away the memories. Someone had access to red, but they must be hiding it from Richard. *Unless he knows about it.*

Could *he* be the one hurting her? His own wife? I hated to even entertain the thought, but it kept creeping back up. Sure, he was a bad guy, but he wasn't abusing his own wife, was he? I didn't think it was him. I would have seen something. And it's not like he's an alchemist. He would have to be using a guardian. There wouldn't be a good enough reason for all of that. Right?

No, someone else was behind this. Someone lurking in the corners, hiding their access to red. I needed to do a better job of watching out for my mom. I was letting her down every time I allowed myself to forget what was at stake.

But there was so much on my mind these days. Like, how was I going to stop Richard? When was the Resistance going to let me in on their secrets? How were we going to help Jessa and her family? It was all too much to handle. *But I had to handle it.* And, despite the various important things I needed to worry about, I couldn't get Jessa out of my mind. She danced through every moment. Every memory I had of her played itself out, again and again, of the girl with stormy, ocean eyes.

SEVENTEEN

JESSA

The pain seared through me, scorching me from the inside out. I was sure it was going to kill me. I'd jumped out the window, knowing it wasn't high enough to kill me. Instead the fall broke both of my legs.

I gaped at the bones that punctured through my skin, raised up like jagged knives from the surface. My thin pajama bottoms were hiked up to my thighs, exposing the gruesome state of my body. I bit down against my forearm as I screamed, muffling the agony. Everything in me wanted to call out for help, but despite the shocking pain, part of me still knew what I had to do. Part of me remembered why I had made the third-story jump in the first place.

You need to heal yourself Jessa. You must get moving,

Trying to slow my hurried breaths, I lay back against the cool grass. Tears pooled in my ears as I tried to focus. I looked up into the dark sky and found the pinprick of a star. It drifted in and out of focus, but it calmed me just enough to clear my mind. I placed my palms on the cool earth and willed myself to concentrate.

The grass curled around my fingertips as I clawed my anxious hands into it, digging for relief.

I can do this. I have to do this. Now.

I squeezed my eyes tightly shut against the darkness and trusted that the green would make its move. That these weeks of training would pay off. That I could heal myself, and all the pain would fade away. But the more I willed it, the more I knew I needed to relax. I needed to find some balance, to clear my mind, so the healing could happen. I caught a memory and focused.

■

The candles flicker playfully atop the birthday cake, ten winking opportunities for my wish to come true.

"Happy birthday to you!" Mom and Dad finish their booming rendition of "Happy Birthday," holding the "you" just long enough for me to take a deep breath and blow hard.

"What did you wish for?" Mom asks, turning on the kitchen light. The magical atmosphere of anticipation is lost with the sudden brightness. Still, I don't mind.

"Don't tell," Dad says. "Or it might not come true."

So I nod, keeping my mouth shut, but my eyes can't help but move to my mother's swollen belly. The baby's due date isn't for another week, and for months now, I've been worrying it would come on my birthday. I never said anything because I didn't want to sound selfish. But the truth is I am used to being an only child and I am nervous that the baby might hijack my special day. But considering the baby is obviously still in Mom's belly and the day is almost over, I am starting to relax.

"Laura, should we give her the present now?" my father asks over his shoulder as he rummages through one of the drawers. He pulls out a silver spatula and a knife, and winks at me. "Or

should we have cake first?"

That is a hard question to answer. Cake is usually reserved for birthdays, and Mom's recipe is the best. She carefully prepared it after coming home from work after her secretarial job, despite the protruding belly that had been getting in her way so often these days.

"Let's do the present first," I decide, wanting to keep the yellow iced cake in one pretty piece just a little while longer.

Mom sits down in the chair across from me and closes her eyes for a moment, a pained expression on her face. But as soon as she sees me looking, she smiles.

"Here you go!" Dad carries in the box wrapped in newspaper and tied with purple ribbons.

I only hesitate for a moment before ripping into the paper, pulling open the box. Inside the box rests the most beautiful pair of pink ballet pointe shoes I've ever seen.

I scream in delight. "I get to start dancing en pointe!"

They laugh and explain how they filed paperwork to receive more money for my activity. Every child in my neighborhood gets to participate in one activity. But since mine started becoming more expensive as my talent grew, we needed the kingdom's help to keep me moving forward.

"Thank you!" I jump up and hug my father. When I move to my mother to give her a hug, I see another look of pain on her face. "Are you okay?"

After a few seconds, she relaxes and opens her eyes.

"You better hurry and eat your cake, sweetie."

Dad jumps up and looks anxiously at my mother. "Is it time?"

Mom nods. "The contractions are three minutes apart now. We need to go to the hospital soon."

■

Her voice rung through my mind as the memory faded away. All at once, a burning heat prickled my body. It rushed through my broken legs and began to numb the area, inch by inch. I exhaled in relief and sat up to watch the magic happening, careful to leave my palms against the grass.

The green mist of energy was hard to see in the darkness. But even the darkest night couldn't hide the alchemy. The energy was so alive that it almost glowed. It threaded its way through my legs, filling every pore.

I watched and felt the healing flow through my body in fascination. It was so intense that it was as if I were in two places at once. The energy was coming from me, and from the life source of the grass. It was as if each individual blade held within it a whole universe, teeming with energy. It burst from the grass to aid me in my healing. Every bit of me was focused on my healing. Within a few minutes, my legs looked and felt as if they'd never been broken at all. The bones fused back together, the ligaments and tendons mended, the swollen skin smoothed, and the pain that was once razor sharp was now barely a dull ache.

I pushed myself from the ground and stood, moving with ease. I looked up at my open window and the dark bedroom beyond. Had I really just jumped from there? Anyone watching would say I was crazy! And maybe I was. But when someone had a strong enough reason to jump into the void, they would do it. I was proof. *Really Jessa, you should have thought of this earlier!*

I surveyed my surroundings. It was the dead of night, but that didn't mean I was alone. There were probably palace guards on patrol. Plus, the wall that surrounded the grounds was meant to keep people out. Could it keep me in? I'd thought jumping from a third-story window would be the hard part, but maybe I was wrong. I'd come too far to turn back now.

Slowly, I walked away from the edge of the palace to get a better look at where I was. There was an open space of about a hundred feet—I had to pass through it before getting into the cover of the gardens. The lawn was well-kept. It would probably be easy to sprint across, *if* I was fast.

I decided I didn't want to push my luck any farther by hesitating. I couldn't see anyone, so I set off. The lawn pounded beneath my feet. I was sure each footstep echoed. At any second, I'd be tackled to the ground and cold, hard handcuffs would be tightening my arms behind my back.

The corner of the hedge was so close now. It was all I could focus on. After a few more deafening strides, I ducked beneath it. Catching my breath, I looked back at the lawn. It was still dark. Still quiet. And still empty.

I took a deep breath and slowly made my way through the gardens. I stayed as close to the insides of the paths as I possibly could. I caught sight of a few guards farther out, closer to the palace. I stilled and watched them until they moved out of my sight. I needed to move carefully. As I walked the acres of gardens it would take to get to the wall, I thought about the memory I'd conjured up after the fall.

My tenth birthday had ended in Lacey's birth. At the time, we didn't know if Mom was having a girl or a boy. The whole pregnancy was a surprise, and Mom liked the idea of keeping the gender a secret. But ultimately, I was used to being an only child. The few times I asked for a little brother or sister, my parents had always agreed they wouldn't have another child. That never made sense to me, but my life was a happy one, so I didn't mind too much.

And then Lacey came, a squishy pink ball. I'd been so mad that I would have to share *my* birthday. But as soon as I held Lacey and looked into her knowing sapphire blue eyes,

I completely forgot about why I was so angry before. This baby, this tiny girl, was my sister. My mother had given birth to a girl! The wish I'd blown on those candles had come true.

I still believed that, somehow, Lacey had known all along. She had planned to come on my birthday. She knew how much we'd love each other, how fierce my commitment to her would be. It was only fitting.

Somehow, I didn't cross paths with another human being as I made my way to the garden's edge. I thought of Lacey the whole way. I knew that she needed me, that something was wrong, that my dream had been my wake-up call.

The palace wall was tall and smooth, made from gray stones. Each fit perfectly together, like a jigsaw puzzle. I looked up to the top and guessed the wall had to be at least fifteen feet tall. How was I going to get over it? There were no trees close enough to climb. There were no footholds. My fingers couldn't manage any significant grip on the edges where the stones met. I panted with frustration as I slid against the wall and sat down hard. How could I have been so stupid? I jumped from a third-story building, broke and healed my legs, and had just assumed that would be enough.

I shook my head. *I failed my family. I failed myself.* Angry thoughts coursed through my mind, dark and insistent. The pain of weeks without contact mixed with the fear of what could really be going on with my family. I couldn't hold my anger in any longer. In a rush to let it go, I slammed my fists back against the wall with as much force as I could manage.

So what if you break your hands? The pain of broken limbs can't compare with the pain of losing your family.

Again, my fists slammed into the solid wall, pounding even harder.

Something shifted.

I jumped away from the wall and studied it. There was a

dent in the stone. Cracks reached out like a spider web from the imprint of my fist. I held my hand in front of me, sure I had broken it, but it looked and felt fine.

What just happened?

This had to be the effect of color alchemy. There was no way I could have done that on my own. I was strong from my years of dancing, but I wasn't superhuman. And the dent in front of me looked like it had been made with a sledgehammer.

I studied my surroundings, wondering if I could figure out what color I had connected with. But in the darkness, it was hard to tell. What had I called on to help me? Looking down, I realized I was sitting in a rainbow spread of flowers.

I quickly thought about the energy centers. Yellow had to be around here somewhere, right? I remembered reading that yellow connected directly to the ability to heighten the physical. By now, I'd memorized the basic properties of each color. The pounding of my fists had come from the fear and anger I had about my family, and if I had yellow alchemy in me, those punches would have been stronger than ever.

I decided to figure out how to use this new revelation to my advantage. I stayed in the flowerbeds, kneeling in front of the dented wall. I placed my hand against it, conjuring up the same angry feelings as before.

The stone shifted.

This couldn't be safe. What if it fell on me? But the image of Lacey in my dream, calling out for help, flashed through my mind. I pushed against the stone as hard as I could and gritted my teeth, hoping with everything in me that my life didn't end here.

The stone broke apart, crumbling at my fingertips. I smiled when I realized it was only one of the square stones used to build the wall that had actually been affected. I hurriedly pulled at the pieces, clearing out the space. It was probably only about two feet wide and eighteen inches tall. But I knew I could squeeze through the space if I cleaned it out well enough.

The time for second-guessing was over. I had to move forward.

◼

My goal was to make it home before sunrise. We lived on the edge of the capital city—so knowing I wasn't far made it easier. The problem was that it took twenty minutes and three train stops to get to my neighborhood. And that was on the high-speed train. It would take a couple hours by bus, or most of the day to walk. What would be the least risky? I had to make a decision.

I didn't know what time it was, but since I woke up around 2 A.M., it had to be at least four. The train station would be opening at five. It would be my quickest route. I would just have to blend in with the early-morning commuters as best as I could, even though I was still wearing pajamas.

Why didn't I think to change my clothes?

I peered around the sleepy unknown neighborhood and made a beeline for the closest train station sign. I would have to take the risk. The most valuable thing I had on my side was time. I figured that no matter where I was, I was going to look suspicious. I needed to move quickly. I could change clothes when I got home, and then my family and I would be high tailing it out of the city.

And I would have to forget all about my alchemy training. There was no way I could return to the palace. Ever.

The urgency of my situation hit me, and I started to run. Even if the train station wasn't open yet, I wanted to be the first one inside that building. Every atom of my body pulsed with the need to be on that train heading away from the palace.

I arrived just as the attendant was opening the doors. She ignored me as she lifted the metal gates with a clatter that echoed down the city street. Like most people I knew, I didn't have any extra money. I couldn't buy a ticket. I would have to sneak through.

My pajama bottoms, which were a delicate heather gray, now had blood and grass stains on them. My sneakers were dirty from the gardens. And I was wearing a light blue cotton t-shirt with no jacket. Luckily, the warm nights of summer had stuck around. I hoped I didn't look too out of place.

The train station was mostly deserted at this early hour. A few morning commuters, dressed for business, began filtering in. I watched the attendant, waiting for her to get distracted. But nothing was changing. She just stared at each passenger that walked through the gates. Finally, someone approached her window. It was now or never. I hurried and jumped the barrier, crossing my fingers that she was too distracted to notice me.

I hurried down to the platform with the other passengers. We all stood in a row, waiting for the train. They all seemed to ignore me, lost in their own routines. I looked around for security guards, royal officers, or even worse, guardians— but I didn't see anyone. As far as I knew, no one had realized I was missing yet. I wasn't scheduled to eat breakfast for another two hours. By the time my new maid arrived with food at 7 A.M., I would have already left home with my parents and Lacey.

The sound of the approaching train pounded through the tunnels. I stepped inside quickly with the rest of the glassy-eyed people, and waited.

Twenty minutes. It was only twenty minutes until my stop. Could I make it? So far, I'd gotten here without being caught. This was the final test. Once I got to my stop, I knew I could exit the station quickly and then weave my way through a few backyards before getting to our house. No one would see me. I would get in, get my family, and get out. We'd find somewhere to hide. We'd find a way to be safe. I had no plan, but I was sure we'd think of something. We had to get away from the alchemists.

We made it through the first stop with no fuss. A few people got off, more got on, and the train kept moving. I tucked myself away in my seat, head ducked. The city beyond the windows flew by in a whirl. The sun still wasn't up yet. But I knew it would be making its appearance soon.

At the second stop, almost all of the passengers got off. I exhaled a breath I hadn't even realized I was holding.

The train started moving again, and I looked up to lock eyes with a young girl. She was staring at me. Panic set in when I realized I recognized her. How? Where from? Then I remembered: the face belonged to one of the girls from my old high school. I didn't know her name, and we'd never talked before. But the spark of recognition lit her eyes, as well. She was trying to place me.

I looked away and stared out the window, hoping she would forget about me. But a few seconds later, she sat down in a seat only two rows from me. At least she couldn't see my blood-stained pants from where she was sitting. I took a careful breath.

"How do I know you?" the girl asked with a friendly lilt in her voice.

"I don't know," I lied. Even though school had been out for the summer, I knew there had to be plenty of gossip about me. It wasn't every day that someone turned out to be a color alchemist. I was definitely visible now.

The girl frowned. Her espresso colored hair was tied in a knot on top of her head, and she was dressed in jeans and a white t-shirt. "What are you doing up so early?"

I didn't know how to get her to leave me alone.

"Just heading home from a friend's house."

"Me too. My parents don't let me sleep at my friends' houses. But I talked them into this one on the condition I would come home really early."

"Yup, same here." She liked to talk, I could tell that already.

"Where do you go to school?"

How was I supposed to answer that? *Oh, you know, the palace.* "I graduated."

The girl nodded.

The train started to slow, and I didn't know if I'd ever been so grateful to get off a train car before.

"This is my stop." I would wait to stand until the last possible second, giving her little time to notice my filthy pajama bottoms.

"Oh, okay, I've got one more stop. Have a good day."

"You, too."

"Hey, wait a minute. That doesn't make sense."

"What?" I stammered, sure she had remembered who I was. Maybe she even knew my name. She'd pull the emergency alarm, and I'd be swarmed by those awful royal officers in their staunch uniforms.

"If you already graduated, then why would you have to ask for your parents' permission to stay with a friend?"

"Let's just say they're overly protective."

The train stopped, and I darted off. I glanced back at the girl. She waved. I could only hope that in a few hours, maybe even a few minutes, she'd forget all about me. She'd go back to her world of high-school sleepovers and regular teenage life.

I quickly exited the station. The sun was barely beginning to rise. The sky was turning a lighter shade of night. Or was it a darker shade of morning? I smiled as I slipped through the first backyard unnoticed. I was almost home. I was almost free.

EIGHTEEN

LUCAS

I woke to heavy pounding on the door. The black of night was barely turning blue. The sun would be rising soon. Who was here so early?

Stumbling to the door, I opened it before remembering I wasn't alone. Sasha was sitting up in my bed, running her hands through her sleep-tangled hair.

Faulk stood in the doorway, the hall light casting shadows around her. My father was at her side. He was dressed in powder-blue pajamas, an unusual sight for even me to see. Faulk was clean and professional, dressed in her standard white uniform. My eyes adjusted to the light as I took them in.

"What's going on?" I asked, my voice raspy and dry.

"Do you know where she is?" Faulk spat.

"Who?" I tried not to yawn but couldn't help myself.

Faulk shook her head, frustrated. There was also a tinge of something else in her stance. Was it fear?

My father glared. "Jessa has gone missing."

The fog of my mind immediately cleared at the mention

of her name. Jessa was missing? What did he mean by "missing"?

"She could have been kidnapped. But from the looks of it, it's more likely that she ran away."

Richard glanced past me and froze. Sasha was in my bed, staring back at him with a guarded expression. I knew how this must look. But I reminded myself that we wanted people to think we were a couple. It was the only reason she'd slept over, even though nothing happened.

"Guardian!" Faulk gasped, startled to see her. "What on earth are you doing in here? You can't be in this wing. *Ever.*"

Sasha's eyes darted to me. I laughed, pulling on the rakish mask I'd used so many times in the past. "What do you *think* she's been doing in here?"

My father and General Faulk both turned beet red.

"Forget it, Lucas," Richard said. "Let the grown-ups take care of this. Your judgment has obviously gone sour."

"Why do you suddenly care what I do?"

"I never cared much for the girls you've dated, but I didn't interfere, either. I always assumed you knew what was appropriate. It appears, however, that I was grossly mistaken. A color alchemist? You've gone too far this time."

"What's wrong with color alchemists?"

"They don't belong in your bed!" His voice burned. "Our guardians work for us. They are not meant to be *with* us. You're the crown prince. It's high time you acted like it."

He reached past me, grabbed the door, and slammed it in my face.

Cool silence fell over us as I turned to gauge Sasha's reaction. Even in the near darkness, I knew there was anger in her eyes. I could feel it radiating off her in waves.

"I'm sorry. He's always like this around me. I forget that other people rarely see that side of him."

"You're his own son and he doesn't even treat *you* right!"

"Well, so much for the whole sleeping over idea. I don't think that got us anywhere productive."

Stupid!

"We've got bigger fish to fry," she said, getting out of the bed. She fumbled with the light switch on the wall and blasted us into brightness. "Get dressed. We need to get to Jessa. We have to find her before they do."

Jessa had not only crossed the line—she had gone far beyond it. Accidental alchemy was one thing. Even hurting her maid hadn't landed her in prison. But purposely running away from the palace? Fleeing my father and her promises to him? That was something else entirely.

I pulled on a sweatshirt and running shoes from my closet. I hurried to get dressed so I could stop this disaster from getting any worse.

"Where do you think she could be?" Sasha asked as she finished lacing her own shoes.

She didn't even have to ask. We both knew where Jessa would go. Without a doubt, Jessa was looking for her family. I'd never met a person who cared so much about her flesh and blood the way she did. She hadn't been permitted any communication with them for over four weeks. Faulk had assured her they were safe and moving on with their lives. That wasn't good enough for her. And to Jessa's credit, it had turned out Faulk had been lying.

"But they're not home anymore," I said, realizing just how dire this situation was. No wonder Faulk was so angry. She'd lost the *whole* family.

Jessa was going home to an empty house. Sasha had already told me that the Resistance had extricated the Loxley family. They were somewhere in hiding. I wondered how Richard had reacted when he'd found out about this. And why hadn't anyone told *me*?

"It'll be a trap," Sasha said. "The place has to be swarming with Faulk's people by now. Jessa is going to walk right into their hands."

"So what's your plan?"

"Obviously, we have to beat her home and intercept her. Are you ready?"

"And then what are we going to do once we get her? Just bring her back?"

"No." Sasha paused. "We need to get her in communication with her parents so she can convince them to let us see if Lacey is an alchemist."

"And how do you plan to do that?"

"I need to get the go-ahead. But I'm pretty sure the only way is to take her into hiding, as well."

Take her into hiding? Just when I realized how much I cared for Jessa, I was going to lose her. And probably forever.

Can I do that to myself? Can I let her go in order to keep her safe?

I didn't have to think twice about my answer.

"Let's go."

■

Getting out of the royal wing should have been easy. I was sure Richard and Faulk had left immediately. But I hadn't stopped to think about my mother.

Sasha followed close behind as we walked down the hallway and into the large living room. The padlocked door had guards stationed outside, but I knew they wouldn't bother us.

"And who is this?"

I jumped at the sound of my mother's voice. "Good

morning, Mother," I said, stepping closer.

She was sitting quietly on a sofa in the darkened room. A cup of tea balanced delicately in her hand and a throw blanket covered her legs.

"Your Highness." Sasha stood next to me and bowed. "I'm Sasha."

"Hello, Sasha. I'm Natasha."

"I was just walking Sasha back to her room."

"In the guardian wing?"

"Yes."

There was a long pause before my mother nodded.

"Would you mind waiting outside, dear?" she asked Sasha. "I'll only keep him a moment."

Sasha nodded, bowed again, and immediately bolted for the door. I hoped she would wait for me. Maybe she could use this time to formulate a plan for how we were supposed to rescue Jessa. How were we supposed to do that without getting caught by my father? If anyone could figure it out, it would be Sasha.

"Come sit by me." There was a softness in her voice that I hadn't heard in a while. "Do you remember much of your childhood?"

I sat down next to her, despite my urge to hurry. She was small and frail, and the thin blanket wrapped around her legs seemed to drown her body.

"Some," I said. The truth was that the very best memories from my childhood included my mother. While my father had always been so strict, Natasha had been kind. She used to take me everywhere with her. We'd play what she called "games of the wild imagination." She was never afraid to crawl through the grass with me or climb trees. I would always cherish those memories of my mother, but it was painful to dredge them up.

"You were such a bright child. Always full of energy."

"Are you okay, Mother?"

"I'm sorry, Lucas."

"About what?" I asked. What had gotten into her?

"I've been so absent lately. Always nursing my headaches. I haven't been here for you. Not like I used to. Not like you deserve."

"It's okay."

"I'm going to do better. I promise."

I didn't know whether or not to believe her, but the little boy inside me jumped at the thought. The very idea of it brought a hope I hadn't felt in a while.

"Me, too. Listen, about Sasha…"

"I'll handle your father." My mother smiled. "If you really love her, we'll find a way to make him understand."

What? Is she coming back to me?

"Thank you, Mother. But actually, I don't love Sasha. We're only going to be friends from now on."

Natasha laughed. "You young men are so fickle."

Unexpectedly, I wanted to tell her about Jessa. I wanted to spill my guts and go into detail about our exchanges with each other. But of course, I would never do something so juvenile. Too much had happened. And I needed to be careful. "I've got to go, Mother."

It took everything in me to stand up. I hadn't experienced this lively version of her in years, but I didn't have time to stick around to enjoy it.

"Wait. I need to tell you something."

Her voice had turned frantic and she reached out for my hand.

"What is it?"

"Something is wrong. I've been living in a fog, Lucas. I'm not myself."

"It's going to be okay."

"No. Something is *wrong*, Lucas. I don't know what is happening. But my thoughts...they're not right."

"What do you mean?"

She shook her head and placed her hand on her forehead. "They won't let me say. They tell me not to say, and I can't."

"Who won't? What are you talking about?"

She bit her lip and looked up at me. Her eyes went from clear and alarmed to cloudy once again.

Who's been hurting her?

"I need to lie down," she said, laying her head against the arm of the large couch. She rubbed her eyes. "I've got a headache."

One second ago, she insisted that she needed to tell me something, and the next, she was complaining about her headache. The same headache that had been plaguing her for years. It was as if she'd forgotten our conversation in the blink of an eye. This had to be the result of color alchemy. It was even clearer to me that someone was controlling her mind. Of course there was another red alchemist somewhere in the palace. But who? What was I going to do about them? As soon as I got Jessa to safety, I would come back here and help my mother.

"Please, Lucas, leave me to rest," she whispered.

Something sinister was happening, and I had to stop it. I left the dark room and hoped it wasn't too late.

■

Sasha was waiting for me just outside the doorway. As soon as I exited the royal apartment, she motioned for me to follow her. She took my hand and spoke loudly so the guards could hear. "Will you walk me back to my room, babe?"

"You got it."

No one followed as we strode quickly toward the front exit of the palace, where the cars were kept. This early, there weren't more than a few guards milling around. And of course, they didn't say a word to me. I could do whatever I wanted while inside the palace. At least, as far as they were concerned.

"Let's get you out of here before someone stops you. Your father made it pretty clear he wants you off Jessa's case."

I considered that for a moment. The truth was, I couldn't go anywhere unnoticed. I never had. We walked out onto the front-entrance steps, just as the sun was rising. I turned to the closest guard and spoke with complete confidence. "We need a car. Can you order us one? Immediately, please."

He looked at me, a little dazed at first, before nodding and repeating my words to someone at the other end of his slatebook.

Sasha grabbed my hand and steered me away from any listening ears. "We're just going to drive away?"

"I'll tell my father that I was trying to help. He doesn't have to know that we actually found her. I'll send you two away and return empty-handed, and claim that you ran off with her."

"Am I expected to leave with you but not come back? No way. That will send too many red flags. My cover would be blown."

"So what's your idea, then?"

She shook her head. "I'm finding another way out of here. I don't want anyone to know I was ever gone. You go ahead and I'll meet you in Jessa's neighborhood."

"How are you getting out?"

"Don't worry about me," she said as a shiny black car pulled up. A driver got out and walked around to open the passenger door. "We're wasting time. I'm going to get Jessa out of the capital. You just get to her before anyone else does."

"Do you have her parents' address?"

"I'll get it to you. Just go find her, Lucas. Go find Jessa."

She shoved me toward the vehicle before turning on her heels and jogging back inside the palace. How was she expecting to get out of here? The Resistance had more pull than I first realized. They had no excuse not to meet with me. This was the last time I was helping them without a proper meeting. But there was no time to speculate. I needed to act quickly.

I jogged over to the driver and plucked the keys from his hands. I closed the passenger door and hurried to jump behind the wheel. "Sorry, buddy. I'm going alone."

The tires peeled out as I sped down the driveway. In my rearview mirror, I watched as a pair of security guards ran out onto the steps. At home, they didn't follow me everywhere. They didn't need to because I never went anywhere, anyway. And no one came inside the palace without going through security first. These poor guards were probably going to get in trouble for this.

I knew Faulk had more than a head start on me. I had no time to spare. The black wrought-iron gates opened wide, and I steered the car out into the early morning of our capital city.

Luckily, my slatebook was with me and I could easily pull up directions to Jessa's childhood home as Sasha had already forwarded the address to me. Man, she worked fast. The time read thirty-nine minutes until arrival at my destination, which made me swear violently under my breath. I hurried to memorize the directions. It was a good thing no one was out this early, because I was about to be driving very fast. I would do everything in my power to make it to Jessa in half the time indicated by the directions if I could. I *had* to get to her before Faulk did.

The phone on my slatebook rang, and I answered it immediately when I saw Sasha's name pop up.

"I'm texting you a map of where we're meeting. Memorize the location."

"You're not meeting me at Jessa's house?"

"No, too obvious."

"How's that?" I asked, turning down a city street with screeching tires as I headed up the ramp to the freeway.

"Oh, you'll see. And Lucas, power down your phone now. Just in case its location is being tracked." She hung up.

I glanced at the directions a few times before shutting down the device and pushed my foot down hard against the gas pedal. I was in a race. A race against Faulk and my father. A race against my memory and the places I was supposed to go today. And right now, a race against the brilliant sunrise that was beginning to light the sky.

NINETEEN

JESSA

Something was wrong. The closer I got to my house, the more I began to question myself. On the surface, it appeared to be a normal quiet morning, but there was an undercurrent of unsettling activity. I couldn't explain it, but it didn't feel right. As much as I wanted to get home, I moved at a snail's pace. I tiptoed through the yards, hiding in the dark shadows as I willed the sun to stop rising.

I stopped cold when I spotted her. Just beyond the tall shrubs I was using for cover, a girl quickly walked past on the sidewalk. She was talking loudly, using the telephone function on her slatebook.

"But she left the station about twenty minutes ago."

She paused for a second before continuing. As she started to pace, she turned toward me and immediately recognition gripped me. The young girl from the train. I hadn't bothered to ask her name. We'd finished our conversation, but she hadn't gotten off at my stop. If she stayed on the train, what was she doing here?

"Yes, I did as you said. I identified her, kept going and then came back here on the next train. Believe me, I searched the station high and low. She should be home by now. You should have her."

Another pause.

"I have no doubt that I confirmed the right girl. It was Jessa."

I inhaled sharply and felt my fingers turn to ice. *No, they can't have....*

"Because I was ordered to track her, not stop her," she said, exasperated. "Anyway, she can't be far. Like I said, I saw her less than twenty minutes ago."

Another pause. I held my breath and willed myself not to blink.

"All right, well, I'll be there in a second. I'm just around the corner."

The girl shook her head and slid her slatebook into her pocket. Turning on her heels, she started in the direction of my house. I didn't dare move. I crouched in the bushes and began a silent count in my head.

Just make it to one hundred. Then run!

One. Two. Three.

What am I going to do? I can't go home now. Someone is waiting for me, and I know that can't be good news.

Twenty-one. Twenty-two. Twenty-three.

Who is that girl working for? Faulk? Why didn't she stop me on the train? I can't believe they had a girl from my high school following me.

Forty. Forty-One.

Should I be surprised, though? I always knew I couldn't trust those people. I need to make a plan.

Fifty-nine. Sixty.

I have to get out of here. Can I go back to the palace? Pretend that I never left in the first place? No. Surely, there are cameras at the train station that can identify me. And anyway, that girl saw me on the train herself.

Seventy-four. Seventy-five.

I just want to get to my family, to help them. Where are they now?

Eighty-nine. Ninety.

I'm in so much trouble.

One hundred.

I took a step toward my house.

I should've run in the opposite direction. But I couldn't help it. I had to know. If I could get a view of the back window, I could see who was inside. Maybe if I knew my family was safe, I could turn myself into Faulk and deal with whatever punishment came.

Ducking low, I dropped to my knees and began to slowly crawl through the bushes. I was only three backyards away from my house. If I was careful, I could get close enough to check things out without being spotted. This was my territory. I'd spent my childhood in these trees. I could go unseen.

Well, at least that was what I told myself.

Something jammed into my back, sharp and direct to the spine. I tried not to scream as I lashed out at whomever or whatever was behind me.

It was the girl from the train. She sneered down at me as she held my face to the dirt and elbowed me again. "There you are. We've been looking for you."

"What are you doing?" I spat, trying to reach out and knock her off me.

She dug her knee into my back and pinned me down.

"What do you think, Jessa? You shouldn't have run away from the palace like that. How stupid are you?"

Pain shot up my arm as she bent it behind my back.

253

"Who are you?"

"Royal officer in the making. Didn't see me practicing in that gym yesterday, did you? No, you were too busy drooling over that alchemist pretty-boy, Reed. Now, hold still so I don't have to hurt you. Though, at this point, I'm sure Faulk wouldn't mind."

The realization slammed through me that she had been there just yesterday when I sought out Reed. But there had been so many people that my eyes had skimmed over the majority of them. Well, royal officer in training or not, if this girl thought for a second I was going to let her push me around, she didn't know me at all.

I held still long enough for her to shift her weight and relax. I bucked backward, slamming the back of my head into her face. A crunching sound proceeded her shrill scream.

"Be quiet," I hissed, jumping up.

She gripped my leg as I tried to run. Her fingers dug deeply into my skin. "You asked for it," she said as she spat blood from her mouth. It poured from her nostrils. I was positive I'd broken her nose.

I kicked at her fiercely as she grabbed my other leg and toppled me back to the ground. I slammed into the thick trunk of a tree. My head stung and my ears hurt. Immediately, I knew I was no match for her. She was trained. I'd never been in a fight in my life. I was strong from years of ballet training, but I couldn't defend myself from her attack.

She pulled my hands behind my back, twice as hard as before. Pain seared my shoulders. I cried out, begging her to stop. She was going to break my arm!

"Don't move." She leveraged her body so she could use one hand to reach into her pocket. She pulled out her slatebook and began to dial. Calling Faulk, no doubt.

Don't give up! You're stronger than her. You're the one with the real power.

It hit me. Maybe I couldn't fight with my fists. But I was a color alchemist. I could fight with my energy. I could fight with magic.

I need help! I don't know what color you are. I don't know where you are. But if you're out there, I need you. Stop her. Please, get her off me.

I craned my neck and looked back at the girl, her grip still tight on me. She blinked rapidly and shook her head in confusion.

"Drop it," I said. "Right now."

The girl stared at me, still confused as the thin device fell from her hand. It landed with a small bounce against the dirt.

It's working!

"Crush it," I said, never breaking eye contact.

In a daze, she stood up and slammed the heel of her foot into the slatebook. It broke with an audible crack.

"Stay here and count backwards from a thousand. When you're found, you won't remember what happened."

She nodded before sitting down hard and counting.

"One thousand, nine hundred ninety-nine." Her voice was dazed and hollow.

"In your head, please. Be quiet."

I studied her as she did what I asked. *How did I do that?* I had been so calm and sure of myself, as if I knew exactly how to control her.

I got up and brushed the dirt and grit from my clothing, looking around for an exit strategy. The girl sat still as the blood continued to fall from her nose. It dripped, gray and thick, in streams of iron down her neck.

Oh. I'd performed alchemy on blood. Red blood. And the implications of that truth rocked me. Because I used the alchemy to control her. To take away her free will. Possibly even her memory.

It will be like this never happened. I remembered the words I'd said to Lacey that bloody day on the playground. That must have been why Lacey never remembered the accident. And later, with Reed. What had I told him to do when he was upset about his cut? *Calm down Reed, you're fine.* He'd listened. He'd relaxed about everything, not actually in line with the situation or his personality.

And this is exactly why they want you. You're a weapon. You're the tool they will use to control minds and wipe memories.

I couldn't let that happen.

I hurried to the house, but stopped myself when I saw two royal officers through the window. Their backs to me, I knew I couldn't go inside. *All this way and for what? Is my family still in there?* I snuck around the side of the house, peering through each of the nearest windows. Not one sign of them. Where were they?

I forced myself to give up and quickly made my way back toward the train station. The morning commuters were beginning to leave their houses. Thankfully, no one appeared to notice me lurking in the shadows. Not yet, anyway.

What was I going to do? Where was I going to go now?

Public transportation was out of the question. So was asking any of my old neighbors for help. Because, honestly, who would help a fugitive?

What am I going to do?

My only option now was to run and hide. The suburban neighborhoods sprawled for miles beyond our own, but they were all broken up by forested areas. I could use that to my advantage. If I could just find a safe place to think, then maybe I would be able to come up with a plan?

I hurried to the end of my block. The train station was just around the corner, but that wasn't my destination anymore. I peered from behind the hedge at the unruly bushes and trees on the other side of the street. From years of adventures as a child, I knew there were several acres of unoccupied land beyond. Hiding there wasn't a solution, but it was a start.

A couple of cars drove past, and I knew that in a few minutes more people would be walking to the train station. A dog started barking. The world was waking up, and if I didn't hurry, I would miss my opportunity to find a hiding spot for the day.

I took a deep breath, double-checked the area, and sprinted across the road. The screeching of tires peeled around the corner. I looked back, horrified, as a small black vehicle came barreling toward me. My nostrils filled with the putrid smell of burning rubber. I momentarily froze. That only lasted for an instant. In the next moment, I was diving into the thicket of trees.

The car screeched to a stop, and a door opened.

"Get in, Jessa," a deep voice called out.

I stopped in my tracks. I was just barely in the sanctuary of the tree line. I peered out in astonishment at the person on the other side of the rolled-down window. Prince Lucas.

"I don't have all day," he said, his voice almost playful despite the circumstances. "I'm not supposed to even be here. Hurry and get in. I'll explain on the way."

"The way?"

"I'm getting you out of here."

I had to trust him. It was either that or take my chances on my own. The distant wail of police sirens shook me into action. I opened the door and slid into the passenger seat next to Lucas.

He threw the vehicle into drive, and we shot forward with

a burst of acceleration. I yelped and grappled for the seat belt. "What's going on, Lucas?"

He didn't answer as he shot the car around a corner and toward the nearest freeway entrance. Few people drove anymore. It was easier to take the trains. The trains were free, and gasoline was expensive. Cars were for the elite.

"Could you slow down? You're going to give us away."

He growled with frustration as he slowed to the speed limit. We were headed south, away from the palace, away from my home. I watched in the rearview mirror as the downtown high-rises faded into the haze.

"I don't understand why you're here."

"What's so shocking about it?" His hands tightened on the steering wheel as he shifted into the right lane.

"Because you're Prince Lucas! For one, where are your guards? Aren't you, like, never supposed to be alone outside the palace? And for two, I didn't even know you could drive. And to top it off, why aren't you taking me back to Faulk? Aren't you mad that I ran away? Why are you helping me?"

The questions tumbled out of my mouth all at once.

"I know I have a lot to explain. But we're almost at the meeting point, and there isn't time to cover everything. But Jessa, you're going to be okay," he said, steering us toward the nearest exit. The area we drove through looked just like any other suburb, except maybe a little more rural than my own. Taller trees. Smaller houses. More space. Fewer people. The sleek black car probably stood out like a diamond in a bed of rocks.

"Where are we going?" I asked.

"Trust me," was the only answer I got. Great. He was always saying that.

After several minutes, we pulled into an empty field. There was no sign of civilization out here. Lucas turned off the car and peered around, looking for something. What could possibly be out here?

"Let's get out." He pulled the keys from the ignition. I sat there, gripping the edge of my seat, utterly dumbfounded. He wanted me to get out? *Here*? In the middle of nowhere? What was going on?

When I didn't join him so eagerly, he came to the passenger door and opened it. He kneeled, put his hand on the top of the door, and watched me. He didn't say anything. This close, I couldn't help but notice his beauty. The day-old stubble on his face. The way the muscles in his arms flexed. The intensity of his steel-gray eyes. He put one hand on my knee, and my body burned hot at his touch. "There's a lot you don't know about me, Jessa. And for that, I am truly sorry. But right now, you need to trust me."

"You always say that."

"This time, let me prove it to you. Someone is coming to pick you up, Jessa. Someone you know. They'll take you far away from here. Far away from New Colony where you'll be safe."

My heart raced. "Are you coming with me?"

He shook his head.

I looked past him and noticed the shifting of the tall grass beyond us. There was a strange rhythmic sound, like whirring air currents. As the noise increased, the wind picked up, and I realized all at once why we were here.

A black helicopter appeared above the trees and started to make its descent into the center of the open field.

"Your ride is here!" Lucas called out over the sound of the helicopter.

My gut tightened when I realized I would be leaving Lucas behind. I had no idea where I'd be taken, but I knew I had to leave. I unbuckled my seat belt and got out of the car. The wind carried my hair in a flurry around my face. I fought to push it back. Lucas joined in. Together, we pushed the tangle of dark strands away from my eyes. Once it was freed from the mess, our eyes locked. We held my hands against my face, each keeping our gazes on the other. Before another breath could pass between us, his lips were on mine.

The kiss was a flash of passion and movement. His strong arms wrapped around me tightly as we forgot ourselves in the embrace. His body pressed hard against me. I melted into him. My long hair whipped around us, stinging our skin with every blow. The deafening roar of the wind flying past and the sunrise heating my neck were nothing compared to the explosion of emotions racking my body. As our mouths explored each other, I could no longer tell where I ended and he began. I dug my fingernails into him, pulling him in even closer. A minute later, he stepped back, breathing hard. He closed his eyes for only a moment before opening them.

We stared at each other, grinning stupidly in disbelief. Then we turned and ran, hand in hand, toward the helicopter. Despite my fear of the unknown and the fact that I was about to fly away into an uncertain future, nothing could take away the joy of the perfect moment I'd just shared with Lucas.

We made it to the helicopter too quickly. The noise and wind were wild now. Lucas squeezed my hand as if confirming his feelings for me. Our hands released as he opened the door for me. He wasn't coming with me. I already knew that. And yet, Lucas was still a gentleman. I didn't want to leave him. Not now. Not after that kiss.

Stepping up into the small backseat of the helicopter, reality slapped me with what I saw. Or rather, *who* I saw. *She* was sitting in the pilot's seat, large earmuffs perched snugly over her smooth blond hair. Her blue eyes shone brightly as our gazes met. It was Sasha. The girl who was currently dating Lucas. And it was painfully clear from her stiff expression that she had just witnessed the most passionate kiss of my whole existence, at her expense.

TWENTY

LUCAS

"You're coming with us," Sasha called to me over the roar of the engine.

I shook my head. That wasn't okay. I needed to get back to the palace before anyone could accuse me of being part of this.

"We're not going to blow your cover, Lucas. Someone will hide the car, and you'll get to be the hero in the end. It's all worked out."

The hero? What was she talking about? There wasn't time to argue with her. Not with Jessa waiting. So, I decided to trust her. Sasha had never given me a reason not to. Not yet.

Jessa looked between us, her face flushed. She still didn't know the truth about Sasha and me. The fact that Sasha wasn't actually my girlfriend was finally something we could talk about openly. Guilt dug into me. Jessa probably thought I was a total jerk for knowingly kissing her in front of Sasha. But I didn't regret it. I could never regret a kiss like that.

"Stop wasting time. We need to get her out of here!" Sasha snapped.

She was right. And if they weren't going to leave without me, I wasn't about to put them at risk and keep them on the ground. Not for another second.

I jumped into the backseat next to Jessa and squeezed her hand. She pulled away and widened her eyes at Sasha. Trying to do the right thing and clue me in, I assumed. I couldn't wait to finally explain everything to her.

We quickly strapped ourselves in and put on the bulky headphones as Sasha began to lift the chopper from the grassy field.

"Where did you learn how to fly this thing?"

The headphones connected us so we could speak to each other above the roar of the helicopter.

"Oh, Lucas, I've got skills even you can't touch," Sasha said.

I laughed and took Jessa's hand again. She looked at me warily and shook her head. Her blue eyes matched the morning sky behind her. They were filled with confusion and longing. And hope.

"What's going on here?" Jessa asked.

"You go first, Lucas," Sasha said.

I thought about where to start, but I wasn't sure there was a good place. "First of all, we're not working with Faulk. And we're getting you away from her and my father."

"Where are we going?" Jessa asked.

"Someplace safe," Sasha responded before adding, "Oh, and Lucas and I aren't really dating. You can spare me the public displays of affection, though. I want to be able to fly this thing without barfing."

"You're not together?" Jessa shook her head.

We were flying fast and low over the landscape. It blurred by in a stream of color as we left the city behind us. Jessa glanced out her window and nearly flinched. She stiffened in her seat, settling in. I was sure she'd never flown before.

Regular citizens certainly didn't travel by helicopter. Even the wealthiest ones didn't have that luxury. Helicopters were a commodity controlled by my family.

"It's okay." I put my arm around her. "We're safe up here. Sasha knows what she's doing." *How does Sasha know what she's doing?*

Jessa seemed to relax as the chopper shot through the morning air. Luckily, it was perfect flying weather.

"I think you two have some explaining to do," Jessa said.

I paused, and when Sasha didn't jump in, I decided to start.

"A few years ago, I started to suspect that maybe the GC wasn't as innocent as it seemed." I considered the best way to explain this. "I would notice strange things that concerned me. People would go missing. Royal officers would be sent with the guardians on missions, and everyone would come back full of secrets. I had no proof of anything. And I don't even think most alchemists noticed the things I did. Most of them were kept out of the loop, and they still are. But something wasn't right."

"So what does that have to do with Sasha?" Jessa frowned.

"Well, a few months before you got here, my father pulled me in on something that confirmed my fears. The GC is running secret tests on innocent people. Dangerous tests."

"What kind of tests?" Jessa asked.

"I don't know exactly what they're for, except to test the boundaries of alchemy. But you know how when the color is all used up, only gray is left behind?"

She nodded.

"Well, it has to do with that. They're testing to see if people can live off of gray food, gray land, gray...everything."

"And they can't?"

"No," Sasha interjected sharply. "They cannot."

"Then someone sent me pictures. They were horrible. Children starving. People getting sick or dying. As you can imagine, I was upset when I learned the truth. My father was behind the whole thing and expected me to understand. He's been traveling to the test sites with Faulk every few months to check on the progress. I went with him on one of the trips. This has been going on for years. I didn't know what to do when I saw that people were dying. Richard's my father, you know? How was I supposed to stop him without tearing my family apart?"

"And that's when Lucas met us," Sasha's voice piped in. "The Resistance. We're part of a national network that was created in response to New Colony's inhuman tactics. I have been working with Lucas on behalf of those who also want to stop the king and people like Faulk. We're not violent. We don't kill people. But we have to do something before things get any worse."

"So why did you pretend you were dating? Why keep this a secret from me for a month?"

"I wanted to tell you. But I was following orders. The Resistance didn't know if they could trust you."

"Don't be so hard on him," Sasha added. "He tried to convince us to tell you everything. A number of times, actually. And if it makes you feel any better, everything between us was just a cover. Lucas doesn't have feelings for me. None whatsoever. He made that clear."

Was that true? When I first met Sasha, I had definitely been interested. But as soon as I'd met Jessa, that all changed. Again, I was amazed by how much this girl affected me. She'd changed me, simply by being herself. Simply by standing up for who she was and what she wanted.

"All right." Jessa's half-smile calmed me a bit. But she still didn't move back into the crook of my arm. I needed to feel her near me. We'd probably only been given a few extra hours together. I didn't want to miss a second with her.

"I believe you, Lucas. Now, where are we going? Do you know where my family is?"

"Don't worry. We've got them in hiding."

Jessa let out an audible sigh of relief. I hated the reminder of my own failure to take care of Jessa's family. I could only be grateful for Sasha's good news, for the safety of the Loxley family.

I peered out at the landscape again and realized where we headed, the shadow lands. This wasn't safe. This was the last place we should take Jessa. Ever. She needed to get away from the GC. Not head into their territory!

"Sasha, what is going on?" I asked, keeping my voice calm. I didn't want to alarm Jessa. "We need to get somewhere safe. This is not what I had in mind."

"This isn't just about Jessa's safety. It's also about making sure she understands what's at stake. She needs to be firmly on our side."

I willed myself not to punch the seat in front of me. "Are you crazy? Of course she's on our side!" *So much for calm.* "This is the last place she should go. Or any of us, for that matter! It will be crawling with GC royal officers."

"What's going on? Where are we going?" Jessa asked.

"Turn around," I said to Sasha. "Fly us somewhere else."

"No."

If I had to rip off my seat belt, shove her out of the pilot's seat, and fly this helicopter myself, I would.

"Jessa, look outside. Look carefully." Sasha pointed to the vast expanse of earth below. The changes in our field of vision were gradual at first. But then they came all at once. "This is what is left after these tests have finished." Sasha's voice was low, laced with the sour tinge of regret. We stared out from behind the shiny glass, our faces reflecting back expressions of disbelief.

The rolling hills, farmhouses, and the forest beyond were a sickening shade of gray. It was almost as if the land had been painted with a fine layer of ash. Only this wasn't ash. It wasn't anything.

"Where is all the color?" Jessa whispered.

She leaned in closer. The sweet scent of summer rain mixed with lavender brushed past me as her hair fell in a dark wave around her face. I breathed her in, wanting nothing more than to hold her hand, or better yet, to kiss her. I remembered how she'd pulled away from me earlier, and I decided that now wasn't the time to be distracted.

"It's all gone," Sasha said.

We stared at the vast landscape below us. The remnants of life and energy were only a memory now. We didn't have to guess how this happened. We were all too smart for that. We knew it was the result of color alchemy. *Serious* alchemy.

"You want to know what happened to the people?" Sasha asked what I was thinking. "They're dead. The life was sucked right out of them, as well."

"Why would an alchemist do this?" Jessa asked.

Sasha caught my eyes in the rearview mirror. As our gazes locked, I remembered her confession. She'd been taken as a child to work out here. She'd been a part of all of this. But color alchemy was usually strongest in younger guardians, and when her power had started to fade, she'd probably been moved on to other assignments.

Children. They made children participate in this.

"I'd known about the experiments. But I didn't know it was this big. This is so much land. How has this been hidden?" I asked.

Did my father's reach really extend this far? What he'd

shown me on my one trip had only been a fraction of this. Could he really hide something so obvious, so massive, and so egregious as miles and miles of land, all in ruins? Why hadn't anyone said anything? Why hadn't the people rebelled?

Sasha was stiff, watching us carefully.

"The GC. Faulk. Your father, Richard. That's how. Any civilians who figured it out were either killed, imprisoned, or worse—they became part of the trial."

"What are these trials even for?" Jessa asked.

"Like Lucas said, it's all about testing the boundaries of color alchemy. To keep New Colony on top. To stop West America from starting a war. To gain more power. You were smart to keep your red ability a secret. Despite what you were told, there are others who've done it before. But poorly. That's why Richard is looking for someone who can sustain the red ability, hone it in a targeted way. So far, all it's done is cause widespread pain. And now? Well, they want to be very strategic with how they use it." She looked wistfully out at the landscape.

I noticed Sasha didn't include herself in the group of "others" who had been called upon to use red color alchemy. But, in her past, she'd been part of these ghastly tests.

"Thank you for trusting me on that one," I added, looking at Jessa. "I wanted to tell you about the red, but I didn't know how."

"What happens to the people?" she asked. "The ones whose blood gets manipulated by the alchemy?"

"At best, they become extremely forgetful. Most end up with some kind of brain damage. And the worst cases die from brain aneurysms. But there's definitely more to it, and I think you already know what that is," Sasha said. "We need to stop more innocent people from getting hurt."

268

Jessa just stared straight ahead.

"Tell us, Jessa. What happened? What is it that's made Richard pursue you so aggressively?"

A small part of me hoped it was all a mistake. That maybe there was still some good left in my father. Maybe *why* he was doing this was something else entirely than what Sasha believed.

"I know why." Jessa looked at me as if it was painful to confirm the truth. "I never told you what happened before you picked me up," she said. "Someone found me. A younger girl from my old high school. She was looking for me. She was working for Faulk. She's a royal officer in training, she said. She attacked me, and when I tried to defend myself, I broke her nose."

I smiled inwardly at the thought of Jessa knocking some royal officer girl's lights out.

"I used red alchemy on her blood. I turned a lot of it gray. I was just trying to get away. And it worked."

Sasha interjected, "The red helped you, didn't it?"

"Yes…because I controlled her mind. I told her to stop screaming, and she did. I told her to sit down and count backwards from a thousand, and she did. She did *exactly* what I said."

The weight of the news was more damaging than I could have guessed. I mean, I already knew about red blood. Sasha had told me everything weeks earlier. But still, the conformation shook me.

"I'm sorry, Lucas." Jessa reached out to me, but I couldn't even move to hold her hand. "But I'm pretty sure your father wants to brainwash people. To control them…by using me."

So it's true. My father's a bad person. What happens to me now?

I really didn't know.

"This is the news we've been expecting," Sasha said. "Thank you, Jessa."

"Thank you for what?" she replied, her voice rising. "I probably left that girl brain-damaged. And I did it to my own sister. I did it to Lacey back in January. She fell and got really hurt. I messed with her blood, and while I was doing it, I told her it would be like the whole accident had never happened. And guess what? She forgot everything! I could have killed her. I could have given her an aneurysm! And then she lived for six months with a small amount of that horrible gray dead blood flowing through her veins. What kind of damage have I unknowingly caused her? My whole reason for being in the GC, the one thing that is most unique about me, is the ability to hurt other people. To control them." She laughed in frustration. "The irony is, I hate being controlled. I hate that people like Faulk and Richard only want to use me. But I've been training only so I can help them control others! What do I do now?"

"You hide," I said.

"I'm not sure it's that simple," Sasha said.

"Sure it is," I scoffed.

"We've got company." Sasha's hands gripped tightly on the controls.

She dropped the helicopter low over the terrain as the jet appeared from above. It was coming in at an alarming rate, moving in fast. My heart slammed into my chest when I glimpsed our royal family emblem on its side. The three red stars were a stark contrast to the shiny white jet.

"It's my father," I said, knowing what those stars meant.

Order. Progress. Justice.

"Then you better hold on tight," Sasha said as she veered the chopper in a 180-degree turn.

Jessa slammed into me, her slender frame flush against

my own, and I grabbed her hand. I squeezed it tight and caught her eyes. I was pleading with my every emotion that she could see how sorry I was. I shouldn't have trusted the Resistance to take her somewhere safe. I'd been so careless with Jessa, over and over. And now, this was it. These were the only moments we had left together. We'd definitely be caught. I didn't know what would happen to me. But if they discovered I was a traitor, it would be drastic. And Sasha would be executed. Would they do that to Jessa? No, she was too valuable to them. Her fate would be worse.

"What's going to happen to us? Are they going to shoot us down?" Jessa asked, panicked.

"Not if they suspect you're in here," Sasha replied.

We zipped through the air, and Sasha moved us as close to the gray earth as she possibly could. The line of decaying trees up ahead was becoming dangerously close.

"What's your plan here?" I asked.

"We're going to land in there and take cover. We have to hide."

"We can't go in there. It's all dead. We'll starve to death. Or get lost. We won't make it out."

"Do you have a better idea?" Sasha called over her shoulder as we approached the ashen forest. If we didn't crash in the landing, we'd be lost in this wasteland. Or get caught by the royal officers. I didn't know which fate was worse.

I knew what I had to do. Without a doubt in my mind, I knew I had to let it all go. All the secrets, the half-truths, and the lies.

It was time for me to save our lives.

TWENTY-ONE

JESSA

I'd sometimes wondered how I was going to die. Death by helicopter crash had never crossed my imagination. But there was no way out. We were going down. Even I knew that at the speed we were moving and the thickness of the trees up ahead, there was nothing Sasha could do to save us.

Was my life supposed to be flashing before my eyes? That wasn't happening. It was more of a sudden realization, in slow motion, that this was the end. An unwinding of stillness as everything around me took perfect form. The rough feel of Lucas's hand clutching mine. The comforting smell of the warm leather seat beneath me. The thumping movement of the chopper blades, spinning too fast to follow. The desolate gray land created such a stark contrast against the bright morning sun, the wide blue sky, and the large puffs of feathery white clouds that sat low.

"Go up!" Lucas yelled. "Right now, go up, Sasha."

Sasha didn't acknowledge him. She was still focused on attempting a successful crash landing in the forest cover. I didn't think it was possible.

Lucas ripped off his seat belt. He dove over the seat in front of us. He practically sat on Sasha as he shoved her away. They grappled for the joystick, and he pushed it down. The chopper rose.

"What are you doing?" Sasha hissed, grabbing the controls.

"Sit down," he yelled, shoving her back.

She didn't listen.

I watched in shock over their struggle.

Out of the corner of my eye, I saw a flash. The three red stars visibly announced our imminent capture.

"Someone will see you!" I yelled at Lucas, realizing he was now in clear view, sitting up front like that.

"No, they won't. We're almost there."

He pulled back with the entire weight of his body and we jolted upwards, much faster than before. In another breath, we were catapulted through a mass of white clouds. Dense and thick around the chopper, they provided momentary cover.

"Hover here," he said to Sasha, as he let her back into the pilot's seat.

"No!" Sasha scoffed.

"Just do it. And stay buckled!"

He put his hands up against the door. It slid open. I screamed, reaching for him. He didn't respond, just kept his eyes held shut and stretched his hand out into the white atmosphere. Utter concentration lined his strong features. His dark hair fell in waves, covering his face. As his whole body stilled, it was as if everything stopped, suspended in space.

Sasha gasped, realizing something I was seemingly missing.

"What's happening?" I asked.

Lucas shuddered, then looked up at her.

"Go," he said, slamming closed the door. "I got a lot, but I won't be able to hold this for long."

She nodded and threw us forward. We flew quickly out of the clouds, into the open blue again. I looked around for the plane and all at once, there was nothing. We were invisible!

"They can't *see* us?" I screamed. *Is this real?* "What's happening?"

It was like flying, but not. We were sitting. There was no wind. But the earth was barreling below and the inertia made me want to scream again. I heard the clasp of Lucas unbuckling his harness and felt him fall into my lap. "It's okay. We're completely safe. But this is quite exhausting. I need you to keep me awake," he said.

Keep him awake? Why? What was wrong with him?

"Just do it," Sasha called back. I couldn't see her, or anything besides the world flying by! But somehow she managed to maneuver the helicopter. "I'm serious, Jessa," Sasha yelled. "He can't fall asleep. He needs to hold this. He's our only chance right now. Do something!"

What in the world were they talking about?

I felt his warm hand on the back of my neck. His thumb rested in the small indent just below my hairline. An unexpected shiver ran up and down my spine. I lost my breath.

Forgetting all politeness, I leaned down and felt for his lips. The kiss was a slow burning answer to a question. With every movement, our bodies came closer to each other. Eventually, he sat up and pulled me onto his lap, our mouths never parting. I kept my eyes closed, and for that moment, I allowed myself to forget about everything. Not even the fear of death could pull me away from that perfect kiss.

I'd been pretending for weeks that I hadn't been affected by Lucas's presence. I tried to tell myself that I didn't long for him to be part of my life. But my true feelings were clearer to me now, more than ever. It was undeniable, especially in the heady caress of his touch, in the exhilarating sense of falling that was coursing through my body.

We continued kissing like that for a while before I slowly pulled away. His steady gray eyes were churning with passion—both intense and vulnerable.

"Are you sufficiently awake enough to hold this?" Sasha's voice chimed.

I looked around and saw that the terrain was no longer the lifeless gray we'd seen just before. It was pocketed with mountains, and we were flying high. There wasn't any gray in sight at all. There were just mountains and grasslands. And there wasn't another jet, another soul, in sight. Thank goodness…

It wasn't quite as terrifying as before, flying invisible.

"What happened?" It was magic, of course. But who, *and how?*

"Lucas can answer that," Sasha said.

"You're a color alchemist?" I whispered.

I didn't have to ask to know it was the truth, but I did anyway. The words were low on my breath, as anger threatened to break through. I wanted more than anything to see the look on his face. And the fact that I couldn't made me even angrier!

"So all this time you've been lying to everyone? To me?"

"I had to."

No, he didn't. "Who else knows about this?"

"Well, now, just you two. It's my best-kept secret," he said. "And now I assume the Resistance will know."

Sasha sighed. "I will have to report this, Lucas—I don't have a choice."

I didn't care about any of that right now. All I wanted

was the truth, as painful as it might be. I shifted my weight away from Lucas, sitting back in my own seat and carefully adjusting the seat belt as I considered how to approach this. On the outside, I might have looked calm, but inside, I was seething.

"How did you keep your abilities a secret?"

"I know how to hide, and sometimes I can shut it off."

"One of the first things I *ever* asked you was how to turn this magic off. You said it was impossible. You lied." All that had happened to me, everything I'd been through could have been different if I'd known how to turn the alchemy off. "Why didn't you teach me?"

"Because no one else knows. Teaching you would have risked exposing myself. If I could go back and undo that choice, I would."

I shook with the hurt that he had chosen not to help me. He couldn't see my pain but I was sure he could hear it in my voice.

"It's too late to change it now. They already know what I can do. They already know that I can access red. They're just waiting."

"I'm so sorry, Jessa." Lucas put his hand on my knee. I quickly pulled it from his grasp.

All I'd wanted since I'd first met Lucas was to forget about the GC and go home. To live a normal life. To be a ballet dancer. And to actually be a part of my own family. Apparently, he was the only person who could have helped me create that. He could have taught me hide it, but instead, he'd chosen his own agenda.

"You're just like your father." I spoke each word sharply.

Silence. Thick suffocating silence.

"Where are we going?" he finally asked Sasha.

"How long can you hold this invisibility?"

"An hour," he said. "But this is a lot for me. Maybe not even that."

Sasha whistled. "You are one powerful alchemist—I'll give you that."

A memory from my studies surfaced as I realized what Lucas had done to get us out of there. He'd done the seemingly impossible.

"You can access white?" I asked him. "I thought that color didn't count. That's what I read…"

He didn't say anything for a while.

"White is a shielding color. A protector."

The alchemy of white was like red, one of the untouched colors. There was so much about it that was still unknown. As far as I knew, Lucas was the only one who could access it. If he'd known it could be used to cloak our helicopter that meant he must have practiced with white before. Sasha was right. He was incredibly powerful.

He was also a liar.

We sat in silence for at least another half-hour as Sasha brought us closer to our destination. With every passing minute, I wondered if Lucas was growing more and more exhausted. I could hear his labored breathing. Who could hold alchemy for so long? I'd never be able to do something like this with any color, let alone anything so insane as invisibility.

"You can relax now. Go ahead and drop it," Sasha said.

Lucas let out a groan. Slowly everything appeared again, as if coming out of a fog and into sharp focus. He laid his head against the window. I looked around for any indication of what had happened to us, but I couldn't see anything but the inside of the helicopter just as it was before.

Why would a prince hide something like this?

Within seconds, Lucas was lost to a heavy sleep. Guilt

seeped into my every cell. He had saved us. And I'd insulted him. I'd called him *his father.*

"You're not the only one who'd like to shut it off," Sasha said.

I studied her for a moment. This girl was incredibly well trained, talented, and, of course, beautiful. I'd never considered the possibility that Sasha could be unhappy with her situation. What had she been through? There must have been something that caused her to start working with the Resistance, whomever they were.

"I'm sorry," I said. I'd become so self-centered lately that I'd forgotten to be a friend to Sasha. She'd always been kind to me, despite everything with Lucas. I knew now they were just friends, working on an assignment together. Yet there was a part of me that wondered, despite it all, if Sasha cared for Lucas. How could any girl get that close to him and not have feelings?

"It's not your fault," she said. "He didn't tell me, either. It would have been too late for me, anyway. I'm in too deep—no turning back now."

"But maybe I could have gotten out of all this?"

"Maybe. Probably not."

"He did." I looked at Lucas, who was still asleep.

"Yes, he *did.* But he's in this now."

After a moment, she adjusted some controls and pushed up on the joystick. We began to descend into a mountain range below us.

"Where are we?" I asked.

This area looked unfamiliar. We were moving so fast, I hadn't realized our speed as I'd kept my eyes closed for most of the invisible time. It freaked me out too much! I was sure this was a military-grade helicopter. This Resistance group, whoever they were, had strong connections.

"Canada," she said, "or at least what's left of it. There isn't much of a functioning government here anymore. We've got a hidden camp set up. Personally, I'm tired of being undercover. It'll be nice to have a break."

I considered this place. Is my new home near? Would I like it?

"You've always been undercover?"

I realized the amount of stress Sasha must go through daily. Just sneaking away from the palace had taken all my courage. I couldn't imagine what kinds of risks she must have taken to do the right thing.

"I got away from the GC when I was a kid. And then I found my way here. The Resistance trained me for years and recently helped me come back."

"Come back?" I shook my head. "How is that possible?"

Her face paled and her eyes glazed over, as if she were lost in her own thoughts. Tangled in the web of her life.

"It's complicated. Let's just say someone at the GC made an alias for me. There are enough kids who get shipped out young. It wasn't unbelievable when I showed up at the palace for more training."

I wanted to keep questioning her, but I decided to let it go for now. The thick green blanket of pine trees was getting much closer. I searched for signs of civilization. Strangely, I couldn't find anything. No houses or buildings, and definitely no people. The forest was wild and rugged. Thick underbrush coated the ground. The area certainly didn't resemble a rebellion stronghold. Not how I imagined one, anyway. We hovered above a clearing as she slowly dropped us into place. But there was nothing here.

"Sasha, what's going on?" I asked.

She turned off the engine, and the thrum of the machine began to relax. The blades, which had once moved at lightning speed, slowed to a dull whir.

Sasha turned in her seat, studying Lucas. He was still passed out. "He's going to want you to stay here."

"Well, that's the plan, isn't it?" I asked. I just hoped "here" was somewhere decent, not a tree fort. Because really, where were the people?

She frowned. "I'm sorry, but no."

"What do you mean?"

"We need your help, Jessa. You're the only one who can stop the royal family from hurting more people."

"No, I can't. I don't even know how that's possible."

"What do you think they want you for?"

"To control people. So I can't let them have me."

"Don't you get it? They're going to find a way to do it, anyway. They'll find another red alchemist eventually. Or find someone else who can separate primary colors like you did at the ballet. Do you realize that since that day whole teams are now dedicated to replicating that magic? One way or another, someone will get to the red."

"But there isn't another person. That's why they want me."

She laughed. "There was someone before you and there will be more after you. You are not the only one who will ever have red."

I paused. "The gray land. What happened there?"

"We call them the shadow lands. They're the result of intense alchemy. Someone using color for evil purposes. It was punishment to the people who lived out there. And it won't stop. The royals do it to their enemies. They'll do it to their own citizens if they must. There's plenty of ways color alchemy can hurt people. Worst part? It's all in the name of a stronger Protectorate."

"So how am I expected to stop it? Why me?"

"Because, Jessa, you have control over the blood. You've

shown ability with red that few people ever have. You have a chance of giving them what they want. You have to go back. You have to learn everything you can, and then use it against them. Fight!"

"How?"

"Isn't it obvious? You need to use your abilities to control them. Control Richard. Control Faulk. Get into their minds. Figure out their secrets. Slowly change their thoughts. *Help us stop them.*"

I sat with that idea for a moment. Could I do it? Everything inside was screaming that I couldn't. It was too much responsibility for one girl. I barely knew what I was doing. How could I take on something so important? And yet...

"What's going to happen to Lucas?" I asked, looking at his sleeping body. The dark curls had fallen into his eyes. He breathed a long sigh and shifted his weight.

"I said he was going to be the hero, didn't I? That's because he's going to be the one to take you back in. He'll turn you into his father himself. That will help Lucas get back into good graces with Richard. We'll stop by and see your family first though. You can make sure they're safe. But then we need you to go back."

I was so relieved to know my family was near. And her reasoning, it made sense. If I pretended that he'd found me and forced me to go back against my will, then we could make up a believable story. "Can I have some time to think about it?"

"We don't have much time. If you stay here, you risk not being able to go back at all. We have to make this believable in order for Lucas to stay out of trouble. We need to get you on your way back before he wakes up, because he's not going to like the idea."

"Why?"

"He loves you, Jessa," she said. "He doesn't want you involved in something so dangerous."

She was probably right that he wouldn't be too happy about taking me back to the palace. He wanted me to keep my powers away from Richard.

But love? Does he really love me?

"So we're just dropping you off?" I asked. "That's why we came here?"

"It's not the only reason. Would you like to say hello to your family?"

I nearly jumped out of my seat. "Wait, they're *here*?"

"Yes, Jessa, they are. I want to work with Lacey. Just to see if she has abilities, too. To help her train so that she won't have problems in the future. So she can protect herself. We need you to convince your parents to let us find out if she has the same powers as you. As it stands, they're refusing."

I nodded. I understood now that this world we were living in wasn't the one my parents knew. To them, life was simple. Follow the rules and everything would be okay. But I knew it didn't always work out like that. It would be torture to see my family only to turn around and leave. But what was the alternative? Someone had to stop the king. Once I was successful, I would return to them. Only then could we be a family again.

"I'll do it. I'll help you."

TWENTY-TWO

LUCAS

I woke to the distant sound of muffled voices. My eyelids felt like they were about ten pounds each as I struggled to open them. Light poured in. I blinked it away. When I shifted my weight, my neck screamed in protest. A hard knot had formed against my spine. I tried to clear my head and think, but it was bogged down with exhaustion. Why was I so tired?

I was still in the backseat of the helicopter. I breathed in the current stillness. The silence was a welcomed friend.

"You're up early," a playful voice said. Sasha was sitting on the seat next to me, no longer up front. She ran her fingers through her long sunny hair and smiled.

I coughed, rubbing my throat. "How long was I out?"

"A few hours."

I looked around for Jessa. Where were we? Just beyond the clearing of pine trees, I saw a small group of people. They were standing close, hugging and talking. I couldn't make out what they were saying from in here, but I recognized Jessa instantly.

"That's her family," Sasha said.

So they were here. The Resistance had really gotten them out.

From here, all I could read was their body language. It was obvious that they were excited to see each other. Their movements carried a love that I almost didn't recognize. There weren't families like these in the palace.

Sasha looked away, her features turning dark.

"What's wrong?"

Seeing Jessa this happy only made me happy, too. But it seemed to elicit a different reaction from Sasha. There was something strange about her posture. It wasn't like her to be upset over someone else's good news.

"They're happy to see her," Sasha said. "Good for her."

"But?" I urged her to continue. What was she keeping from me?

"But they'd sooner abandon her if they could." She shook her head. "Isn't it obvious? They are afraid of alchemy. Too bad all of their kids were probably born with the ability."

"I don't think you know them well enough to say that." But, I could understand it a little if it was true. I had caught on early that my parents didn't care for the alchemists. When my abilities developed at the ripe old age of nine, I knew they wouldn't accept me. I figured out early on how to keep them hidden, and I moved on with my life.

There was something about Sasha's last statement that stayed with me and played with a memory at the back of my mind. Suddenly, I remembered the lost alchemist from my research. The girl who'd disappeared at the age of eight. What was her name? Francesca Loxley. I still wondered if there was a connection between her and this family. I hadn't found anything more. I almost asked Sasha if she knew anything, because I was beginning to suspect that maybe she did.

"Do you think Lacey is an alchemist, too?"

"Yes. The Resistance is pretty sure of it. Jessa should be talking to her parents about it now. We want to help Lacey. Train her."

I wondered how they would react to the news. I hoped that instead of trying to fight it, they could see that helping Lacey was the better choice.

"No one's going to let her join the GC though, right? No undercover spy-girl business for little Lacey?"

"A GC life is not the plan. She's too impressionable."

I reached for the door. "I think it's time I met some of your leaders."

Sasha shook her head. "We're locked in."

"What?" I pulled on the door handle. It wouldn't budge. "Let me out, Sasha. Don't be ridiculous."

"They still don't know if they can trust you, Lucas. I'm just following orders. We have something planned for when you return home."

I laughed. Complete outrage was the first emotion to bubble up inside me.

"Are you kidding me? Would I be here if you couldn't trust me?"

"Well, there's nothing here," Sasha said. "The Resistance camp is miles away. And it's well hidden. We'll be hiking in. You're going home."

Looking around, I realized that although I could point out the thick forest, I still had no idea where we really were. And I'd been asleep for most of the ride here. We could have gone north. Or we could have gone west, but that was even more dangerous. Maybe a combination of the two. I had no way of knowing. I had lost my bearings. "Then have them come to us. And anyway, I need to know what your plan is. How are you planning to get me back fast enough without blowing my cover? This whole day has been ridiculous. I'm just supposed to go home and pretend I haven't been missing? I don't think so."

"Don't worry, Lucas. We know how valuable you are. It's handled."

Oh, great. Like that was supposed to make me feel better. I was losing confidence in this Resistance group by the minute. Who exactly had I partnered up with? I'd been so eager to feel like I was doing something right, to feel like I could help my country, that I hadn't really stopped to consider maybe I'd made a mistake. But now probably wasn't the best time to voice that out loud.

"And I'm just supposed to take your word for it?"

"What other choice do you have?"

Well, she had me there. She knew it. And she knew I knew it. For now. But there were choices. There were always choices.

"No offense, Sasha, but I'm struggling with this. I give you information, and I'm just expected to be patient and wait it out. But you said it yourself, didn't you? I'm a valuable asset. In fact, I think I'm probably your *most* valuable asset. I'm the prince, for crying out loud. What more do you want from me?"

"You *are* a valuable asset. But you see that over there?" She pointed to Jessa. She was on her knees, hugging Lacey and saying something to her parents. I caught the words "for the best" and saw them nodding.

"That's what we call our most valuable asset now. I didn't realize how easily Jessa would come around to our way of thinking. But all it took was one open conversation for her to understand how much we need her now."

"What are you talking about?"

"What you did back there with the white was remarkable,

Lucas. Thank you for that. Who would have guessed white could do something so useful? I'm impressed! But I thought that amount of alchemy would have knocked you out for another few hours, at least. I hadn't expected you to wake up so early." Was she turning on me? Why was she talking like this?

"And your point is?"

"You have to take Jessa back to the palace."

"Absolutely not."

"We need her."

"We're not having this conversation. We didn't just risk our lives only to take her back there. It's not safe. They're going to hurt her. What they're doing is unthinkable. It's so much worse than what I could have ever imagined. To have the ability to control people's minds? To make them do whatever they want? That kind of power will probably kill Jessa by the time she's finished."

"This isn't about one person. If I could do it myself, I would. But I can't be there anymore. I've already received word that my cover was compromised. I'm needed here now anyway. You're the only one with a fighting chance of getting Jessa back in that palace. They know you took off, but they *don't* know you're with us."

"And what do I do when I go back?"

"You're going to show them that you're on their side. You'll say that she never left the capital city. You found her and brought her home. The end."

"And what about the jet. They saw us, remember?"

"These windows are tinted, Lucas. There is no way they could have known for sure who was in here. Or what we were doing. Sure, they're looking for Jessa, but they wouldn't expect to find *you* in a helicopter. Plus, we already moved your car. It's safe. They're looking for you back home."

Could it be so easy? But I still didn't want to take Jessa back. Saying goodbye to her would tear me apart. I'd known that going into today. As soon as we'd found out Jessa had gone missing, our plans had drastically changed. Our plan had quickly transformed from getting Jessa to her parents to finding a safe place for her to hide…and now Sasha was telling me that wasn't the case anymore.

Maybe it never was the plan. Maybe Sasha just told you what you needed to hear to get you to bring Jessa here in the first place.

The thought had me questioning my alliance with the Resistance more than ever. Once I got home, I was cutting them out. I was done. There had to be another way than dealing with these people. I would go home and Jessa would stay here. Here…where it was safe. Where she could live a comfortable life with her family. Where she could still be trained to control her abilities, without fear of being used by people like General Faulk and my father.

"Has she made up her mind?" I asked, looking back out the window.

As if sensing me, Jessa peered back at the helicopter. Even though the windows were tinted, I knew she could see me. She stared at us for a minute, smiled faintly, and turned back to give her family another round of hugs.

"Yes, she's sure. You won't be able to change her mind."

"And who's flying us back, then? Now that you're staying here, we're going to need a pilot."

"My friends are going to fly you back to a safe place, and then you'll be picking up your car and taking Jessa back. You can trust them to get you there safely."

I was pretty sure I couldn't trust anyone in the Resistance. I would play along long enough to get home. This little false mission of theirs was the last straw. "And then what?"

"No one will know you flew off. You'll create a cover story. Take her back to the palace."

"You've said that already. I mean, what happens to Jessa?"

She stared at me for a moment. "When you get back, make sure that Jessa gets initiated into the GC. We need her working on the inside. She's more valuable to us there than she is anywhere else."

That wasn't okay with me! The last thing I wanted was to put Jessa in harm's way. But it seemed that my opinion didn't matter. I felt so out of control. Not only were they leading me around without telling me their true plans, but now they knew about my alchemy. And that was something that could easily be used against me. *Why did I put myself in this situation?*

"So if you're staying, who will be my Resistance contact?" I asked.

"Jessa will be your contact. I'm pretty sure my superiors don't think you'll turn her in for treason. They know all about your romance."

So that was it, then? They would use my feelings for Jessa against me. Because they knew, just as much as I did, that I would help her no matter what.

"Are you trying to make me regret ever having met you?" I snapped.

"Oh, don't pretend like you ever really cared for me. You should be happy that now you and Jessa have another reason to spend time together."

Could I have misunderstood Sasha's feelings? Or maybe I was just a game she had played and failed. She'd been a good sport about our faked romance. But then last night we'd gotten closer than ever. I wasn't proud of it. At least I stopped it before it went too far.

"Is this about last night? You're mad because I didn't hook

up with you?"

"Ha! Don't flatter yourself."

My reply was interrupted by pounding on the metal door behind me.

"That's your new pilot," Sasha said, reaching for the door. "Oh, and I lied. We were never completely locked in here. My door was unlocked. You're kind of naïve, Lucas."

Whoa! Why does she suddenly hate me?

She wrenched open her *apparently* unlocked door and jumped out into the clearing below. She hugged a very large, very tall, burly middle-aged man. He was wearing oil-stained brown jeans and a plaid button-up with rolled-up sleeves. His tanned skin, work gloves, and disheveled hair gave me the impression that he was probably a handyman of sorts.

"It's so good to see you," he said, "My, you're all grown up now, aren't you?"

"It's good to see you too, Hank." Sasha's earlier sour mood had gone.

The man gave her another smile, shaking his head before peering into the helicopter. He looked me up and down.

"Well, son," he said, "looks like I'm the sorry sap who agreed to see you home. You're not going to turn on me, are you? Some of the others think I'm a fool, flying a *royal*. You're not going to make a fool out of me, are you?"

"No. I'm pretty sure I'm the fool."

"Well, okay then." He turned to Sasha, "Let's get the girl loaded up. They told you Tristan is coming along too? He insisted on keeping an eye on things."

"Sounds like him," she laughed.

"We're already behind schedule," someone said, coming up to the helicopter. He was young too, probably in his twenties. He hugged Sasha and she smiled up at him, adoring. "Of course you insisted on going," Sasha said to him. "I'll see you when you get back, all right? We have a lot of catching up to do."

The guy hugged her again before sliding into the seat next to Hank. I noticed he made sure I saw the gun in his hand. Whatever. "I'm here to make sure you don't give Hank any trouble, so don't even think about it."

I only glared at the kid, then looked out of the window.

Sasha walked through the tall grass and tapped Jessa on the shoulder. Jessa pulled away from yet another hug with her father, and the two girls nodded. They exchanged a few inaudible words before they came walking back to the helicopter together. Jessa climbed in next to me, careful not to meet my gaze. Her cheeks were ashen, her eyes hollow.

"Don't do this, Jessa. Don't go back with me." I had to try and talk her out of this.

"I've made up my mind. There's no changing it."

"Are you sure?" I asked, unable to help myself.

She looked at me. Or rather, she looked through me. Through me to her small group of family members, circled in the distance. The longing on her face was replaced with an expression of fixed resolve when she focused her attention back on me. Did she blame me for my father's actions? Would she ever forgive me for choosing not to teach her what I knew about hiding color alchemy?

"Do you hate me? Are you doing this to punish me or something?"

She didn't answer. She just turned to Hank, who was busy switching on the controls up front. "I'm ready to leave."

He turned a knob. The heavy thrum of the engine came to life, an unseen answer to her request.

"What happened back there?" I asked. "Is your family okay?" I didn't know if she was talking to me, but I had to try.

"Well, let's just say they don't understand me anymore. But they love me. And I guess that's all that matters."

"So why not stay?"

"Because I love them, too."

■

"Are you sure about this?" I asked Jessa one last time.

We stood at the edge of the dim parking lot, hidden by the shadows of the setting sun. How was it possible for so much to happen—in the way of action and emotion, as well as revelation—in one day?

My car waited for me, silent and ready. I didn't know what would happen when I left this morning, but I never expected to be doing this. This was the last thing I wanted for Jessa.

"Don't ask me that again." Jessa folded her arms, bent her head down low, and ran for the vehicle.

I followed, quickly catching up to her as we sprinted across the empty parking lot. My car was the only one here, half hidden by an overgrown weeping willow whose roots had probably began tearing through the tarmac years ago.

Hank and the wannabe badass Tristan had dropped us off about a mile away and gave us directions before heading back north. This time, we'd flown so high that I couldn't really be sure where Sasha had taken us in the first place. There hadn't been any recognizable landmarks that I could identify. All I knew for sure was that north, in the mountains somewhere, a Resistance camp waited.

Once we loaded ourselves into the car, we went over our story a few times as we drove back to the palace. Within the hour, we pulled up to the gates. I hesitated, squeezing the steering wheel tight. My hands wanted to turn us around and get Jessa out of there.

Jessa studied me. "It's too late for that, Lucas."

She was right. Any more hesitation would raise too much suspicion in Faulk and Richard. I pushed on the gas and headed up the long, smooth drive. As soon as we pulled up to the front of the palace, we were surrounded by dozens of royal officers and guardians, their guns pointed.

"Stay calm," I whispered, before opening the door and casually stepping out of the car. "You can put your guns down," I called out, shaking my head. "Where's my father? This is no way to treat your prince."

A few hesitated and lowered their weapons, but most stayed put.

The massive door to the front entrance opened, and my father, mother, and General Faulk stepped out. "You heard the boy." My father's voice boomed. "Lower your weapons immediately!"

The men all stepped back as the three approached the car.

Faulk's eyes were bloodshot and angrier than I'd ever seen them. "Where have you been all day?"

Her tone, although tough, actually ignited a chain reaction of calm through every cell in my body. Suddenly, I knew that although I may be under great suspicion, no one had actually seen me doing anything illegal.

"Tracking this one down," I said, pointing to the car. "For you, Father," I added, with a smirk. "Maybe we can finally agree now that I'm not as useless as you may think?"

They stared at me for a second and then looked to the car. My mother leaned closer to the window, eyes squinting, before stumbling back. "It's her!"

Mom landed on the ground, and I ran to her as the rest of them—my father, Faulk, the guardians, and royal officers—swarmed the car.

Mom brushed herself off and looked up. Her eyes tried to focus on me, but it was difficult. She was grasping for something in her mind, but it was slipping away. A misty confusion filled her face, and she blinked rapidly. Had someone used more mind control on her today? Something was wrong. That *had* to be it!

"Are you all right, Mother?" I asked, lifting her up.

"I don't think so."

Her knees buckled, and she dropped into my arms.

TWENTY-THREE

JESSA

"I've already told you," I said, leaning back against the cool metal chair. "I don't know where Sasha went."

Faulk stared at me, silent. She was waiting for me to say something, anything, that she could use against me. And though she didn't say it, she was waiting for me to incriminate Lucas, as well.

As soon as we'd pulled up the palace drive, Lucas had gotten out of the car and left me in the passenger's seat. It hadn't taken them long to figure out I was in there. They swarmed the vehicle, pulled me out, and threw me to the ground. They handcuffed me tightly and hauled me off. Of course, after everything I'd been through, it wasn't like any of their actions came as a surprise. These people didn't care about me. They didn't care about my freedom. As far as they were concerned, I didn't have any.

"Repeat your story," Faulk said for what felt like the hundredth time.

I looked around the concrete gray room. I knew there was no added color to be found in here, except for that of the people who came in and out. But I couldn't seem to stop myself from looking for something safe enough for alchemy, because I was beginning to think I'd made a huge mistake. "I already told you. Do you really need to hear it again?"

Faulk cocked her head. "Yes, I really do."

"I ran away. I jumped out of my window in the middle of the night. I broke my legs, and yes, I even screamed. But your royal officers never came looking for me, did they? You really need to increase security around here. So anyway, I healed myself with the grass. Green is one of the only alchemies I can do. That's the reason why I jumped from that high in the first place."

"What happened next?"

"I ran to the wall. It's big. I didn't know what I was thinking. I pretty much gave up. I got really upset and hit it. And I guess I used alchemy on something there too, because one of the large stones crumbled. So I pulled it from the wall and crawled through the hole. You've confirmed all this by now, haven't you? You obviously found the open window. Was the grass turned gray just below? And I'm sure you already sealed up the hole in the wall."

She stared at me for a long moment. "Keep going."

"I rode the high speed train to my old neighborhood. You already know that. Some girl from my old high school was there and tried to make small talk. I thought that was strange, but when I got off the train and she stayed on, I let it go. But you and I both know what happened next. She attacked me in one of my neighbor's yards. That girl can pack a punch, I'll give her that. I thought she was going to break my arm."

"So what did you do in retaliation?"

"It was self-defense. And I had no idea what I was doing, actually. She was going to turn me in, and I freaked out. I think I broke her nose. Then I ran."

"And where did you go?" Faulk was ready for me to slip up. But I wouldn't.

"I hid. I spent most of the morning in one of the nearby forests. But I knew that I couldn't hide there for long. So I snuck into a neighbor's tool shed and waited it out."

"And what were you going to do? Who were you going to meet?"

"No one. I never got that far. I had no plan. I just wanted to see my family, I swear. But I knew I couldn't go to the house, not after what happened with that girl. I finally decided I needed to come back to the palace, but I also knew I'd be in trouble. You know, that girl told me she's a royal officer in training."

"She was. But it's funny Jessa. She doesn't remember the fight," Faulk said. Not for the first time, I wondered what had happened to her.

"You got me. I used alchemy on her. It made her forget. After that, I got scared, and I ran. I hid and tried to think of a plan. But honestly, I didn't have one. So when I got hungry, I just started walking back to the palace. I kept myself hidden, because I didn't want to hurt anyone else. Just in case a civilian saw me and got involved. I know it's lame, but it's the truth."

"But Lucas found you? How did that happen?"

"Blind luck, I guess. He told me that his father was angry with him for losing me. And so he spent the day driving around the city, looking for me. Just when he was going to give up and go home, he saw me darting across a street. He pulled up and told me to get in. By then I'd all but given up anyway, so I did. And here I am."

"And here you are." Faulk said. "You never saw Sasha?"

I shook my head. "No, what does she have to do with any of this?"

Of course, there was no answer.

Faulk got up and left the room without a word, the heavy door banging shut behind her.

The room was a box. No window. One door. There was a mirrored glass wall that I was sure was actually a two-way mirror. For all I knew, there were royal officers just on the other side, studying me. Looking for mistakes. But they wouldn't find any. I wouldn't mess this up.

After a few more minutes, Faulk came back into the room. She wasn't alone. King Richard sat down across from me.

"Your Highness." I attempted what probably looked like a pathetic bow, considering I was handcuffed to the chair.

"Hello, Jessa."

"We're curious about a few things." Richard narrowed his eyes on me. "Why is it that one of our best guardians would also go missing on the same day as you, and yet you two never crossed paths?"

"How should I know? Maybe Sasha took the distraction as an opportunity to run. It might come as a surprise to you, but you don't always treat your guardians right."

We both watched as I tried to raise my hands from where they were cuffed to the chair. They barely moved. *Case in point, dear King Richard.*

"But, Jessa, you're not a guardian, are you?"

It was not a question.

"But I want to be," I said, quickly catching his attention.

This was the part that had to be convincing. Otherwise, I would be stuck in a room like this forever. And everything I risked to come back here would be for nothing.

"You think I'd let you join my Color Guard. I don't need you to be a part of anything so important to get what I want from you."

My heart dropped into my stomach, fear threatening to

take over.

"General Faulk told me that if I could figure out red alchemy, I would be able to have weekly phone calls with my family. And I promise I tried, but I couldn't do it. I got desperate to see my family and I made a mistake."

"Oh, yes, you certainly did," Richard said. "There are rules for alchemists, Jessa. Rules that are there for a reason."

Rules meant to control us! I nodded. "And you're right. Because I ended up using alchemy while I was out there, Your Highness. And you probably already know by now that I changed that girl's blood, turned it gray. Don't you see? Just when I had given up, something got triggered within me, and I did it. I did what you wanted."

"So?" We both knew he had all the power right now.

"Well, when Lucas found me, he explained that you probably had my family on lockdown because I ran away. Personally, I didn't get close enough to my house to see much of anything. But I did see that they weren't there."

I began to cry, allowing the tears to fall as heavy as I could manage. "Lucas said that breaking the rules would only get me into more trouble. But if I was really good, if I worked hard for you and did what you needed me to do, then you'd let me see them again. Please, that's all I want. Don't punish them for my mistakes. Let them be free and let me join the GC so I can prove myself to you."

By the time I finished my speech, hatred boiled inside. But I worked harder than ever to maintain the outer appearance. I was the prodigal child, coming home for forgiveness. Maybe his pride would be enough to keep me safe.

I knew he didn't really have my family. The Resistance had gotten them out already. But he would never have to know that I knew the truth.

"I don't buy it," Faulk said, stepping forward. "From day

one, she put on a show and lied to everyone. Who's to say she's not doing that now?"

Richard stood and looked down at me for several moments before turning his back. Just before the door closed, he turned to Faulk. "Immediately begin training her for the GC initiation," he said. "I want her."

■

I wasn't returned to my bedroom. Nor did I end up in a prison cell. Instead, I was taken straight to GC headquarters and was left to wait there alone in one of the training rooms. I was still dressed head to toe in the stale gray jumpsuit. The space was similar to the others, with glass walls and modern furnishings.

Nobody said anything about who would be joining me, or if there was something I was supposed to be doing here. So I just waited and watched as people walked down the hallway, glaring at me.

Great, these are going to be my peers. They hate me more than ever.

Reed materialized on the other side of the glass, talking to someone. About me, I was sure. I recognized Brooke, the girl from the ball and the gymnasium, the one who obviously had it in for me.

I couldn't hear what they were saying, but it didn't look like it could be anything good. I shrugged. The girl stormed away in a huff, but Reed gave me a tight half-smile before walking away.

I couldn't help but remember how he'd tried to use blue alchemy on me. How he tried to mold my feelings to reveal my secrets. Should I confront him? If I acted like nothing happened, would it be easier to become a part of this operation?

Jasmine walked into view and waved at me from behind the glass. The two guards at the door nodded at her and left us as she walked into the room. She wore her usual wardrobe. "Why don't you dress like the rest of them?"

She paused, looking down at her blue cotton dress. "I made a deal with the king. I'm his best healer. I do not ask to be reassigned. I do whatever he asks of me. But I get to be myself. And part of that means I dress how I want to dress. I have free range of the grounds here, too. Makes life a little easier."

"You do *whatever* he wants?"

"Yes. Is that a problem?"

"Nope," I said, faking a smile.

I could only imagine what talents Jasmine had that the king found so valuable. But I knew I would also do whatever he wanted with my own talents, at least for a time. I smiled at Jasmine, sorry I'd said anything at all. If I was going to pull this off and take Richard down from the inside, I couldn't raise any suspicion. At one time, I thought she understood me, but after what she'd just confessed, I wasn't so sure.

She studied the room, as if she was looking for something. But there wasn't anyone else in here. In fact, it was quite bland. She opened her palm, where a small blue flower lay crushed in her hand.

"How's Hank doing?" she asked.

My heart stopped. Hank was the kind older man who'd flown us back in the helicopter. How did Jasmine know about Hank?

"No one can hear us," she said, gently rubbing her thumb against the flower, the blue color staining her skin. "Don't worry. It's safe."

"You're part of the Resistance? Are you here to help me?"

301

"Yes. I was Sasha's handler," she said. "And now I'm yours. We have important work ahead of us."

A group of laughing teenagers burst into the hallway beyond the heavy glass, and I nearly jumped out of my skin. We watched as they continued down the hall, and it became quiet again. Even though Jasmine was using some kind of blue alchemy to mask the sound, it still felt risky to be having this conversation.

"Jasmine, I'm terrified. What am I supposed to do now?"

"Fit in," she said, not bothering to keep her voice down, evidently confident in her alchemy. "Train with the guardians. Be a team player. Then join them. Get initiated. Do whatever you need to do to gain the king's trust."

"Anything else?" I laughed. She made it sound so easy, but I knew it couldn't be that simple. And what did initiation even mean?

"Yes. Get over your squabble with Lucas."

"Why should I? He lied to me."

"Because we need you to be successful where Sasha failed."

"What do you mean?" I asked, beginning to question again what Sasha had really been here to do. Who was she, really?

"We need him to be absolutely committed to us," she said. "And we're convinced the best way to do that is to get him one hundred percent committed to you."

"How am I supposed to pull that off?"

"Easy. Make him fall in love with you."

I thought about that for a moment. Could I do that to Lucas?

"You must keep it all very hush-hush. After Richard found Lucas and Sasha in bed together, he was incredibly angry. That won't help us. So instead of being public, you need to keep your relationship a secret. I'm sure that a forbidden love angle will make it even better for him anyway."

My brain could only focus on the one thing she'd said: *After Richard found Lucas and Sasha in bed together.* My chest burned. Lucas had said that his relationship with Sasha had only been for show. Apparently, he'd lied about that too, and now I was expected to pretend it didn't matter? How could I?

I bit my lip and nodded, allowing my thoughts to return to my family. They were most important. I would do anything for them, even if it meant being close to someone as deceiving as Lucas. And the truth was, I still cared for him. Deep down, I still wanted to be with him. This wouldn't be too hard.

"I'll do it," I said, interrupting Jasmine. "I don't need convincing. I'm in."

She reached out her arms and pulled me into a hug. It caught me so off guard that I just stood there, frozen. She smelled like sandalwood and lemon. I allowed myself to melt into her embrace for a moment before she let go.

"You can trust me," she said, her eyes focused intently on mine. "We're doing the right thing here. We'll stop Faulk and Richard. We'll help Lucas make the changes needed. We'll stop the killings. We'll use alchemy for good."

I believed her. I wasn't alone anymore.

"There won't be royal officers or guards around you anymore. You're officially in training, which means you'll have freedom to move around the palace. Just don't try to sneak away anymore. Stick to the GC wing. We'll start tomorrow. But today, you need to go to Lucas. He needs you."

"What do you mean by that?"

"Just go."

I stood there, confused.

"I mean it, Jessa. You need to go now, and hurry. He's in the royal wing. I suggest you run."

I lost all my previous apprehension. She wasn't going to lead me astray. The Resistance needed me to hurry, and so, I ran.

■

Flying out of the room and down the hallway, I made my way through the palace. And Jasmine was right—no one stopped me. I got several strange looks, but there wasn't a single cry of alarm. I guess that meant I was finally on the inside.

Within minutes, I was approaching the large wrought-iron door that marked the private residence of the royal family. It was surrounded by palace guards. It was late, and I was sure I needed an invitation.

I hesitated, but the door opened and Lucas walked out. He beamed at me. Here was the boy I wanted, the boy I maybe even loved. And yet, he had betrayed me. He'd kept his secrets for too long.

"You came just in time. She's doing much better. Come see!"

What was he talking about? Before I could ask, he grabbed my hand and pulled me back through the door with him.

The room was large and beautiful, as one would expect. And in the middle of it all, Queen Natasha stood with her arms open wide. "I remember you! You're Jessa!" She rushed to me, her white silk robe fanning out behind her. Pulling me into a hug, she then spun me around and giggled. "You're so pretty!"

I just smiled, unsure of how to behave. Here was the queen of New Colony, a woman I'd barely seen in passing but who had always been untouchable. And she was spinning me around and acting like a whimsical schoolgirl. What was going on?

"It's an honor to meet you." I curtsied.

Lucas smiled and put his arm around his mother. "Why don't you sit down and rest? You've been ill."

"All right, dear," she said, flashing him a smile. "If you say so."

And then she ran and actually jumped onto the couch, landing in a pile of pillows. She leaned back and grinned up at Lucas, laughing hard. Her auburn hair fanned out around her, framing her pale face.

"She's been ill?" I asked, not quite believing it.

"You didn't see?" He knelt on the floor, holding her hand and staring at her with admiration. "She passed out earlier. When I got out of the car, she fainted right into my arms. The result of another headache, I'm sure. But then Jasmine came. She helped. You feel better now, Mother?"

"Yes, I feel better than I have in years."

I watched Lucas and his mother. Their bond was tangible. Despite her strange behavior, I was happy for Lucas. He deserved this small happiness.

Natasha sat up then and rubbed her forehead. Her face tightened.

"Are you okay? Is your headache coming back?" Lucas asked.

"Who is that?" the queen said, pointing at me.

Lucas's gaze traveled between us.

"That's Jessa. Remember, you just talked to her a moment ago? She's my friend."

"No, I didn't." Natasha stood up, wobbly on her feet. She put her hands on her knees and began breathing deeply. "Son, I need to lie down. Please ask your friend to leave and walk me back to my bedroom."

Lucas's mouth parted, as if he didn't know how to respond.

"It's okay," I started backing up toward the door. I didn't want to be here, anyway. Why had Jasmine sent me here? To see *this*?

Lucas nodded back at me and then focused on his mother, helping her across the room. Just as I was about to turn around and exit, the queen let out a pained scream.

She grabbed her head, her hair flying in wild fire streaks around her as she tumbled to the hardwood floor. Lucas was at her side in an instant, and I rushed to help.

"It's all gone!" she screeched. "It's all gone!"

"What's all gone?" Lucas asked.

She started convulsing, arching her back and banging her head against the wood floor. Lucas struggled to hold her down, to try to do something, anything to help her. And then the beloved Natasha, Lucas's mother, the queen of the New Colony, went completely limp. The color immediately drained from her face.

Lucas carefully slapped her cheeks. "Mother!" he cried, shaking her gently. But she didn't move. He looked around, panicked.

We spotted the potted plant at the same time, and I jumped up and practically dove for it, stumbling over my feet. I grabbed it and pulled the heavy pot to the two of them as quickly as I could. As soon as it was within reaching distance, Lucas put one hand on it and the other on his mother. I followed suit and did the same.

I concentrated as hard as I could, focusing all the energy within me on healing her. I knew Lucas was doing the same. We sat like that for several long moments, willing something to happen as we pulled the color from the plant in waves. The green was swirling around her, almost frantic. But it wasn't doing anything. She wasn't changing. It just moved for what felt like forever. Eventually, the color began to calm, and then all it once, it flew back into the many leaves of the plant.

I sat there, stunned, looking at the lifeless woman before me.

"No!" Lucas gasped, pulling her head into his lap. "No, no, no…"

I didn't know what to do. I just sat there like a statue and watched, horrified, as Lucas rocked back and forth with his mother's body in his arms. He sobbed, and I felt tears on my face, too.

Something stopped within him as he carefully placed his mother back down on the floor.

"I don't understand! What happened to her?" He was beginning to hyperventilate.

I didn't understand, either. But when I looked down at her body, I grew cold, because suddenly, I knew. Dark gray streams of liquid were dripping heavily from her ears, pools of death that could only lead to one logical explanation. Queen Natasha had just been murdered by a color alchemist. I was sure that someone had messed with her blood. But who? I *knew* I hadn't done anything to hurt her. Sasha said there were others like me, ones who could get to the red. And yet, would Lucas believe that? Would Richard? Faulk?

Who did this?

I crawled backward, my knees sliding across the hard floor.

"No. No, I would never," I choked.

Lucas stared up at me as he lifted his mother's body into his arms. I just sat there. I couldn't bring myself to move.

A moment later, the doors swung open, and Faulk appeared in the living room. She was saying something, but I couldn't hear it. I couldn't understand anything, as if I were witnessing the whole scene from behind a murky sheet of glass.

Lucas stood up. I expected him to explain, but he moved right past me and just stood there, dazed, his mother's body in his arms. And that's when several palace guards stormed the room.

"Queen Natasha has been murdered," someone said. Faulk? I thought it was her voice.

The moment slowed further. My ears buzzed. I sat there motionless as the men swarmed the room, pushing me out of the way. Would they blame me? I found my back against the cool wall, as I stared at the world around me. I studied the plush white rug, the dark wood floors, the disturbed potted plant with its spilled soil...and Lucas. His black shoes, motionless, as he held his mother. The pool of her gun-metal blood widened between us.

TWENTY-FOUR

LUCAS

I failed. I went off on some hero's mission, leaving my mother stuck here. Alone. Vulnerable. Hadn't she tried to ask for help just this morning? She'd acted so strange, worse than ever. *I knew* something was wrong but I'd gone anyway. Too caught up with the Resistance. And even that turned out to be a bunch of lies. In the end, the Resistance had used me. They got Jessa. I got nothing. And now, my mother was dead.

This is my fault. I clutched her body, unable to let her go.

"The queen has been murdered," Faulk repeated.

Her words shook me. Looking around, I took in the wide pool of gray blood circling where I stood. The liquid gunmetal streamed out of my mother's ears, her mouth, her eye sockets. Alchemy.

"Someone's messed with her blood," I said to myself. But I looked up and saw Faulk nodding.

"How did I let this go unnoticed?" Faulk questioned. "It was my job to protect your family, Lucas. I'm sorry."

I never thought I would see the day that Faulk would

apologize to me. I took no glory in it.

One of the royal officers reached out and took the body.

"It looks like the color has been drained from her blood." Thomas stepped into the room. "Red alchemy."

My eyes flashed to Jessa's. She shook her head more. She didn't speak, equally in shock at what we'd witnessed.

"Jessa Loxley, you're under arrest." Faulk shook her head.

Immediately, palace guards and royal officers swarmed her. They pulled her into standing and shoved her wrists into handcuffs.

"No, it's not her," I said. "She just met Natasha today. I think my mother has been having problems for a long time."

The guards continued, ignoring me.

"I didn't do it, I swear," Jessa cried.

"The headaches! Faulk, her headaches have been a problem for years. It couldn't have been Jessa."

Faulk peered at me briefly before motioning for Jessa to be taken away.

"Aren't you listening to me?"

Thomas stepped closer and wrapped his arm around my shoulder. It did little to comfort me. "She's the most likely suspect, Lucas. And she was on the scene when we arrived. What are we supposed to think?"

"I at least have to question her," Faulk said. With a pitying glance, she left.

I looked around, unable to process everything. There was blood everywhere. Some of it red, but mostly gray. I grimaced. I was covered.

And my mom is dead.

Someone had laid her on the floor with a sheet pulled over her body. More people were coming into the room now. Where was my father? Did he know yet?

"Why don't you go get cleaned up?" Thomas said. He

motioned me away from the horrific scene. He walked me to my bedroom and ushered me inside.

"Take some time, all right, son? Take a shower. Find your bearings. I'll come and check on you soon."

He was right. With shaky hands, I closed my door behind him and stumbled to my bathroom.

I don't remember getting undressed. I don't remember stepping into the shower. But I must have, because some time later, I found myself sitting on the shower floor. The water beat down on my stoic body. When it turned lukewarm, I considered getting up. But I didn't move until cold water pelted me.

I got dressed. What was I supposed to do now? There was a light knock on my door, and Thomas let himself in.

"How're you holding up?"

"I don't know." It was true. I didn't.

"Your father's not doing so great either."

I wasn't ready to face him. As much as I hated Richard for the awful things he did, he was still my dad. I didn't want to see him grieving. For as many issues we had, he always seemed to have a strong bond with Mom. Losing her wouldn't be easy.

"What about Jessa?"

"There will be an investigation," Thomas said. "It could have been her."

"No, it wasn't. It was someone else. I know it."

"What do you mean?"

"This isn't new alchemy. Jessa's only been here for weeks. Whoever killed my mother has been tampering with her blood for years. So much of it was gray. That couldn't have happened quickly. Plus, why else would she have all those headaches?"

"The headaches were chronic. Unrelated."

"I don't think so. They were a side effect of red. Someone was getting inside her mind. To control her and then take her memories."

Thomas peered at me. "Why would someone do that? Why take that kind of risk?"

"I'm not sure. Information about my father, maybe? Secrets about the alchemists. It could be anything. We're royal. We know more than we let on. Controlling one of us? That's valuable."

I was pacing the room at this point. Thomas crossed to me.

"Sit down, son," he said, motioning to the bed. "You're getting worked up. We'll get to the bottom of it. Don't worry."

I did as he asked and sat on the edge of the bed. But I didn't want to calm down. I wanted to figure out this. Who murdered my mother? They wouldn't get away with it.

The old man sat down next to me, putting his arm around me again. We were never too close, but he was a family friend. He'd been with us my whole life. His comfort was the only thing I had. "Tell me again. What do you think Natasha knew?"

I shook my head. "Could be anything. Like I said, she was royal."

Suddenly, a sting ripped my bicep. I jumped. A small pinprick of blood bubbled up on my skin. *What the?* I glanced around, confused. That's when I saw it. The thin needle in Thomas's fingers. I jumped back, slamming into my headboard.

"Stay away from me!"

"Don't fight me on this, Lucas." Thomas lurched toward me. For an old man, he was strong. His body loomed over me. He reached his hand toward the trail of blood running down my arm.

"What are you doing?"

"You know too much," he said. "It's okay. I'll be more careful with you than I was with Natasha. I never meant for her to die. It's too bad. She was rather useful to me over the years."

"You! Why?"

"Don't you get it? She found out who I am." An alchemist. It made sense now. A royal officer for all these years, hiding magic. He couldn't do both. That wasn't allowed.

"Get away from me." I gritted my teeth, catching his hands as they reached for me. We were in a tug-of-war. He pushed toward my blood.

"You royals think you have all the power," he sneered. "But do you have any idea how powerful I am? I'm a royal officer *and* an alchemist. I'm not a slave to Richard. I've controlled Natasha for years."

"You're crazy! You had nothing to gain from that. And you killed her!"

We fought harder. Locked in a tight grip. But I could feel myself gaining headway. I was almost free.

"Don't be so dense. You know what they say? The woman controls the man. Natasha was always his weak spot. She could get him to do just about anything, especially in the early days. Let him believe he's in charge. I never cared. I was in control."

"You're sick." With one final push, I slid from the bed, ready to run. But he was too quick. He grabbed my arm and pulled me back. His fingers were slick against my blood. The connection was instant.

"You lose," he said. "Now it's time to forget this conversation."

I could feel the alchemy starting. It was as if bits and pieces of this whole exchange were fading away with each passing moment. I reached out, looking for something, anything to help me. My free hand gripped my pillowcase.

"You don't know who I really am. You're convinced Jessa killed your mother. In fact, you're going to lead the charge against her. Make sure she's executed. We don't need another red alchemist around here."

I nodded my head.

He let go and stood up. Bits of gray blood were smeared across my arm.

"Clean yourself up. I was never here." He didn't even look back as he left the room.

I sat motionless.

All along the answer was right in front of me. Of course I wasn't the only alchemist hiding in plain sight. All these years Thomas was my favorite royal officer. I'd thought he was kind, but he was more evil than anyone. His need for power had caused my mother's death.

I slowly let the pillowcase loose in my hand. As it unfolded I stared at the gray handprint left behind. White. It was my biggest secret.

White was a shield. It was also the alchemy that came easiest to me. I'd used it growing up to keep myself from suspicion. I could hide my alchemy because of white. It was my buffer, my protection. Earlier I'd revealed myself when I'd hidden our helicopter from radar. And again, just now, white saved me.

What Thomas didn't know was that I too was an alchemist. He thought he was controlling my mind, erasing my memories, but I was fighting back. Pulling white into my body through that pillow, I'd blocked him. I shuddered to imagine what would have happened if I'd failed.

I jumped up and bolted out of my room.

I went to the basement prison, looking for the action. Following the commotion, I found my father and Faulk surrounded by royal officers. Thomas stood front and center. The group was huddled outside a cell that I assumed was Jessa's.

"Son," Richard looked at me, his eyes bloodshot. "What are you doing down here? Go back upstairs."

"I know who killed Mom."

Thomas smiled faintly. "Jessa? Yes, we know."

I paused, staring into his dark eyes. How had I missed it before? His kindness wasn't kindness at all. It was manipulation. Arrogance.

"No. It wasn't Jessa. Thomas murdered her. He confessed."

Thomas took a step back, his eyes darting around. "That's ridiculous."

I looked from my father to Faulk. They were skeptical. "He's an alchemist. He just tried to manipulate my blood. He wanted to control me. But whatever he did, he messed up." I held up my arm. The evidence was all right there. I never had cleaned off the mess of gray.

Thomas sprang into action. He pulled open Jessa's door and ran into her cell. She was still handcuffed, still dressed in the gray prison outfit. He yanked her into his arms. Her body jarred violently in reaction. "I'll kill her. I know you need her. She'll be dead if you don't let me go."

"Thomas," Richard replied, "don't you dare."

"I mean it. I'll break her neck."

"Drop her," Faulk yelled.

"Then let me go. Let me out of this Godforsaken place."

There was no chance at that. He'd murdered the queen. What did he think he could gain from this? I watched Jessa carefully. If anything happened to her, I wouldn't survive it.

I'd already lost my mother. I couldn't lose her too.

Jessa whipped her head back. A loud crack sounded. Blood gushed down Thomas's face. He swore, throwing her to the ground. His face dripped blood. He jumped back on her just as we swarmed the room.

"Stay," Jessa yelled as her hand connected with his bloody face. Her red alchemy went into full force in an instant.

Thomas froze.

My father and Faulk stared at the pair. It was all out in the open now. Here was the proof of Jessa's magic. Red alchemy. Blood alchemy.

■

It wasn't long before Thomas was arrested and thrown into a gray prison cell. I didn't know what would happen to him, but I hoped it ended in execution. He murdered my mother. He deserved nothing less. I was relieved to have caught her killer. But even still, her death rocked me.

I hid out for a couple days, grieving in my bedroom. I couldn't eat, sleep, or talk to anyone. I didn't know where to go from here. It was just me and my father now. A man I'd spent the last couple months of my life spying on. A man I no longer respected or trusted.

Pulling myself from my hole, I made it out to the gardens. Fall was approaching and the change of seasons left me depressed. I would give anything to go back and save my mother. But it was too late. I never saw what was right in front of me. And she was dead.

I found my favorite clearing and sat on a stone bench. I concentrated on my breath. In and out. I tried to picture my future. I saw nothing.

"Hey stranger," Jessa said. She walked into the clearing

tentatively, wringing her hands. She was dressed in black alchemist gear, her brown curls loose down her back. "I saw you walking out here. I thought I would come and say hello."

I didn't know what to say.

"I'm sorry about your mother." She sat down next to me. "I just wanted you to know that I've been thinking about you. Lucas, you're not alone." Slowly she wrapped her arms around my torso in a side-hug. I breathed in her familiar scent, welcoming her touch.

"I can't believe after all that, we still ended up back here," I said.

"I know."

"I'm not going to work with the Resistance anymore," I whispered.

"I know."

"But you are?"

She nodded and looked up at me, her blue eyes glassy with tears. I hated that answer but knew there wasn't anything I could do. She'd made her choice. I'd made mine too. I leaned down and gave her a small kiss. She was the only good thing left in my life. I needed her.

We held each other as the day faded to night. There were no words between us, and a million reasons why we couldn't be together. But still, we were fighting for the chance.

EPILOGUE

SASHA

I honestly couldn't remember the last time I'd slept so deeply, without the constant worry that my whole life could come crashing down at any moment. It had been years since I'd been back here. Years since I'd felt this kind of safety.

Upon waking, I went outside. There was something about the mountains that brought me back to my center. I stared up at them and smiled, breathing in the fresh morning stillness and allowing the stress of everything I'd just endured to melt off me in waves.

"Those aren't mountains, you know," Hank's gravelly voice said from behind. "They're hills. If you want to see real mountains, you've got to go out west. The Rockies will blow your socks off."

I laughed. "I wish I could, Hank, but there's nothing that far west for me anymore. No reason to go when New Colony's capital city is near here. I'm a freedom fighter now, remember?"

I winked and put the words "freedom fighter" in air

quotations, even though we both knew I wasn't joking. None of us were joking about this.

"For the view." He sat next to me on the fallen tree stump. "You should go for the view. It would be worth it, just for that."

"So I take it they got back safely?" I asked, changing the subject.

I was referring to Lucas and Jessa getting back to the capital city under Hank's supervision. He nodded, and as the moment stretched, a knowing silence filled the air. We watched the peaceful quiet morning that could only be found in places like these. Places away from New Colony, the guardians, and everything else a part of that life.

"Are you going to make me ask?" he said.

I folded my arms. I already knew what was coming. We could pretend that I'd been returned to base camp because of a blown cover. It wasn't entirely true though. Faulk didn't know for *sure* that I had taken that helicopter. I was here for something more. No one had to spell it out for me.

"They abandoned me. And now you expect me to forgive them just like that? Just pretend like nothing happened?"

He shook his head. "You don't have to forgive them, but we need you to push your feelings aside and work with the girl. For the good of everyone."

And what about what I need? I wanted to scream. They hadn't even recognized me yesterday. Never even blinked twice.

I only nodded.

"Thank you, Frankie." He stood up. "I knew we could count on you."

"Don't call me that. I haven't gone by that name in years."

He stared at me for a moment. "So you're not going to tell them?"

"I'm not telling them anything. Why should I? They don't care about Francesca anymore. And neither do I."

I stood and brushed the sticky pine needles and grit from my jeans. I turned to Hank, one of the few people who knew me from before, who was with me from the beginning. "Please, just let me be Sasha."

His expression was pained, but he only nodded. I knew he wanted to say something more. But what else was there?

I guess, of all people, maybe Hank understood me. He was the one who had gotten me out of the GC when I was still only a small child. He'd brought me back to the people here and taught me everything I knew. Hank became a father to me when I had no one else. When my real father had forgotten about me. When my real parents had let me be taken from them without so much as putting up a fight.

They never even tried to save you. They just moved on with their lives. Raising Jessa, forgetting you, and having another baby. You were replaced. These were the words I'd repeated to myself for years.

"When do I start training her?"

Lacey. The little sister I never met until yesterday. And even just during the short hike back here from the landing spot, Lacey had reminded me so much of Jessa. I had left Jessa as a toddler and didn't get to see her grow up. But still, little things about Lacey bore striking similarities to Jessa. It had nearly killed me to keep my anger at my so-called parents in as I'd led them back to camp, but I'd somehow managed to put on a show for them. I had managed to keep my cool.

And the whole time, they had no idea who I really was.

"As soon as you're ready to start training her, we'll get started."

But that was the tricky thing about this whole situation,

wasn't it? We both knew there was no such thing as being fully ready. Not really. Not for us. There was just sucking it up and doing what needed to be done.

I peered back through the trees, into the brilliant wilderness of the forest, and drew in a slow breath.

"I'm ready now."

END OF BOOK ONE

CONTINUE READING

The story continues with book two coming Fall 2017.

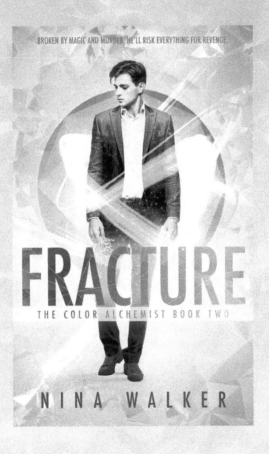

BROKEN BY MAGIC AND MURDER, HE'LL RISK EVERYTHING FOR REVENGE.

FRACTURE

THE COLOR ALCHEMIST BOOK TWO

NINA WALKER

Among Shadows is an email list exclusive. This thrilling short novel dives into Sasha and Tristan's history with the Guardians of Color.

COMING SOON

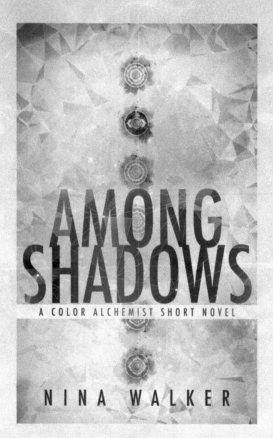

ACKNOWLEDGMENTS

I am bursting with gratitude. There are many people who are instrumental in my author career, and this book. I wish I could name everybody individually. First, let me start with you.

You, my reader, are everything. We're connected, you and I, by our love of reading and the stories that come to life in our imaginations. I wrote this book for you. Keep reading books and supporting authors. **If you enjoyed this book, please share it with your friends and take a moment to write a review.** As an independently published book, that is the fastest way Prism is going to get to more readers. We have to do this together. And do you know what I've realized? I want to do this together.

I have to thank my wonderful husband, Travis. I'm so lucky to have met you all those years ago in High School Debate. Babe, you're the Policy to my Lincoln Douglas. You're my partner in everything and this accomplishment is just as much yours as it is mine. You know that I couldn't have done this without you, right? I love you.

Thank you, Mom. You've supported me in innumerable ways, from giving me free reign over the cabin to write when I needed a quiet place, to sending me random articles and success stories in the middle of the night. You're the best!

And thank you to all of my family for believing in me. I love you people more than you know.

Thank you to all those friends out there who championed

me. To Team Sisterhood for buying me a kindle, I blame you for my KU addiction! But seriously, you're my best friends. Thank you for loving me as I am. Thanks to Team Forward Fitness, especially the TFF Diamonds and to our gracious leader Brigitte. You ladies are my soul sisters and have changed my life in ways you don't even know.

Thank you to my friends near and far. To everyone who asked me about the book, even if it was just to be polite, you made my day. Your support continues to blow me away.

A huge virtual hug goes out to my incredible developmental editors, Nirmala Nataraj and Mary Kole. This book went through quite the journey because of your talent. Hats off to Madeline Dyer for the copy edit. A huge thank you to Kate Foster for helping me tie it all together in the development of the second book. And my ARC team, wow, your support and help means the world to me. Thank you!

Molly Phipps, thank you for creating the beautiful book covers and website. You took an abstract idea and created something truly magical. I have no words to describe your talent.

And can I just mention my YA literary girl-crushes? Lauren Oliver, Maggie Stiefvater, and J.K. Rowling to name a few. Your stories are what made me want to be a writer. Please keep telling them.

And last, but actually first, thank you to my Heavenly Father and to my Savior. *Whatever you do, do it all for the glory of God.* – 1 Corinthians 10:31

ABOUT

NINA WALKER is an emerging author of young adult fiction. She lives in Utah with her husband, children, and two ornery cats. When she isn't busy writing or chasing after her kids, she's helping busy women prioritize their health in online support groups. *Prism* is her first book.

Connect with Nina:

Facebook at fb.com/ninawalkerbooks
Instagram @ninawalkerbooks

www.ninawalkerbooks.com

CPSIA information can be obtained
at www.ICGtesting.com
Printed in the USA
LVHW030914080221
678693LV00001B/60